# JACKSON FREEMAN

Irene Josewick Eckman

authorHOUSE®

AuthorHouse™
*1663 Liberty Drive*
*Bloomington, IN 47403*
*www.authorhouse.com*
*Phone: 833-262-8899*



*Published by AuthorHouse 10/22/2020*

*ISBN: 978-1-6655-0414-0 (sc)*
*ISBN: 978-1-6655-0438-6 (e)*

*Library of Congress Control Number: 2020920264*

*Print information available on the last page.*

# Contents

# Note from the Author

Heartfelt thanks to my friends who urged me to write the story I carried in my soul for many years. To my husband Laird for his patience, my daughter Carole for being my cheerleader, and Evelyn and LeRoy, who helped find statistics about the Baltimore fire. A special thanks to Dr. Kenneth Lloyd for his knowledge of disinfecting property after plague at the turn of the century and Dr. Tom Detesco, who knew I needed something other than housework to keep me happy.

Reading a book full of regional accents can grow tedious. I deliberately wrote this story without them, allowing only a few exceptions to make certain characters more colorful. Most writers think they need to author stories about people who perform death-defying and heroic deeds. Was Jackson Freeman one of them? He did not take well to the new era of the machine, but could he adapt and outsmart?

Most Negroes in 1904 did well in Baltimore but found a different world when they tried to make their fortune outside the city. This is a story of one man who beat the odds. It is a story meant to entertain. All names and characters are figments of my imagination, but the backdrop of the story is based on historical fact.

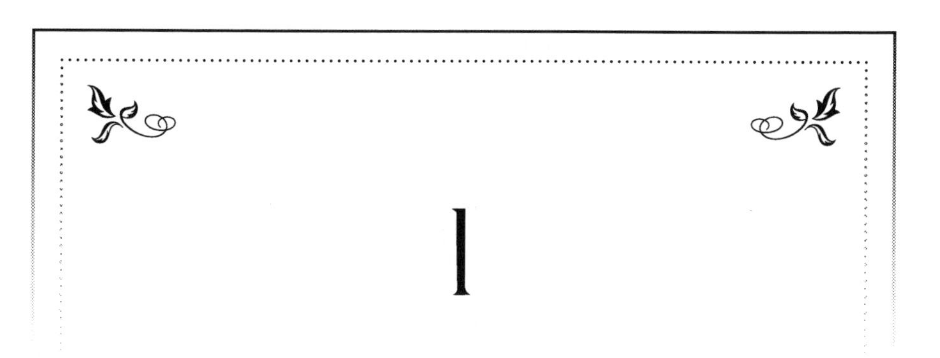

# 1

Death comes to all families. One now; another later. The hurt is absorbed by the coming together of relatives and friends who reminisce, share comfort food, and drink hard liquor. They share spontaneous laughter and tears as some deed or misdeed of the deceased is recounted. All things die. Even cities. Some go through the process of decay, their leavings eventually becoming tourist attractions. Others make spectacular exits then rise again, alive and beautiful. So it was with Baltimore.

February 7, 1904. The leaden skies this bleak, windy morning streaked a tinge of pink across the horizon. It looked as if the clouds had a lining; a lining which was prettier than the dress. The wind picked up speed, the clouds seemed to swirl to deliberately cover the pink slip and turn the skies to mauve. The grey stone church took on the eerie look of a lavender fortress. Inside, the congregation became conscious of a difference in the light. Some of the children stole side glances at the beautiful stained-glass windows. The morning turned dark and ominous.

The parson was to be commended. He cut out the Bible classes to start church service early because of the incoming storm. The choir was lustily singing the second hymn and all sinuses were cleared for the gospel song. The melodious voices of the choir shouted or waned as indicated by Jackson Freeman, who was leading them with his left hand while chording the piano with his right. The ladies of the choir liked to watch his black hands, large but graceful, caressing the air with his fingers for a quiet round sound or grabbing a fistful of nothing to make a strong musical point.

The choir and the congregation finished the hymn with a great crescendo. As Jackson lowered his arm, he noticed two things. The end of his shirt sleeve was frayed and, even though the music and the singing had stopped, there was a steady moan around the windows of the church which was almost as loud as the singing had been. Most everyone felt apprehensive, but the humming had lulled Jackson into another world. The parson's voice drifted away. Jackson's thoughts were mostly of Clarabelle, who had just three weeks ago given birth to their third child. Orphaned at 14, frightened and alone, Clarabelle was living in poverty when Jackson first set his liquid brown eyes on her as she trudged along the path to the dismal section of town where she lived near the swamp. Jackson remembered her high breasts and large buttocks moving in synchronized beauty. Her muscular long legs took her quickly past the longshoremen. She always managed to pass very closely to where Jackson was working, giving him a long side-look just before clearing his passionate gaze.

It was not long before Jackson followed her home and took her for his own. Such wonderful days! The pair had their ups and downs, but 13 years of marriage made them comfortable with each other, or so Jackson thought. Twelve years older than Clarabelle, Jackson appreciated her loveliness. She was not beautiful in the usual sense of the word. It was the cool look in her large eyes and the petulant drop of her thick lips that drove men wild. It belied the giggly personality she had playing with her children or while lying sensually in Jackson's arms, letting him tease her.

Lately she was cool toward him. He reasoned she was still getting over giving birth. She was just now able to wear her pretty dress to church again. Still, the feeling that she did not want him to make love to her persisted. Jackson's need for Clarabelle was great. "I always make her laugh and I make her happy," Jackson mused. She usually responded in a good way to his lovemaking. He was a skilled lover who knew when to be tender and when to be in authority.

The choir rose to sing Jackson's favorite hymn, "O Victime de tous Les Crimes" and Jackson's daydreams ended abruptly. Being familiar with the hymn, Jackson could conduct and still steal soft glances at his whole family sitting in their usual pews. His beautiful tenor voice could be heard above the rest of the singers. How he loved to sing!

The men in the Freeman family were all handsome. Jackson had classic, well-defined Negroid features. His small cupped ears were close to his head which housed a high, intelligent forehead and high cheekbones.

His eyes were a rich dark chocolate color mirroring his complexion. A large sensuous mouth gave his otherwise strong-featured face the impression of a weak chin. This flaw somehow, gave the frontal view of his face the incongruity of strength and vulnerability both at once. But his profile belied pure strength. This was the dominant feature that suggested Jackson Freeman was in charge of himself in any situation. He was naturally thin and wiry; his arms and legs seemed too long for his height and delicate body build. When Jackson Freeman smiled broadly, which was not often, though he had a good disposition and a gentle countenance most of the time, his smile could "light up the sky at midnight," as Mamma liked to say.

Jackson was not smiling now, however, as he noticed how tired Pappa and Mamma looked. The children, Clara and Oliver, seemed subdued. Clarabelle was irritable. He watched as she raised an arm to check the knob of thick hair at the nape of her neck, accidentally tilting her hat to an unattractive angle. Angrily, she shoved the shabby hat back into place. The baby in her arms caught her mood and began to cry. Clarabelle made no attempt to hush little Clarissa, who was now wrestling against the blanket in which she was encased. The two older children, Clara and Oliver, should have been thinking about their Catechism lessons but Jackson knew they were thinking about how boring the church service was and what they would do when they were set free of their religious duties this Sunday afternoon. Clara was not a pretty child. Her features were coarse, and she was in that gawky stage. Her knees seemed too large for her legs and she had begun to stoop when she noticed her breasts developing. A decidedly sway-back walk gave her the appearance of being shorter than she really was. Clara, at the age of only 12, had high aspirations; perhaps she would become a great teacher or be like Amanda Bowen Carroll, a smart business woman who managed a local boarding house and who folks said was the granddaughter of a free-born African chief.

Jackson licked his index finger and rapidly turned the pages of the hymnal to be ready for Julia Corothers' solo. Pressing the middle of the book with the flat of his hand made a noise. Oliver looked at his father and Jackson caught the slight movement of his head. Jackson openly admired his daughter but secretly wished he could see something, anything, to admire in his son. Like Clara, Oliver spoke French fluently. But unlike

Clara, he was reluctant to use anything that sounded as if he were educated in front of his school chums. "Street bums," that is what his grandmother called them. Well, one of those street bums had a sister who was giving him signals. Oliver was aware of how handsome he was becoming. His broadening shoulders, small waist, and rounded hips were all messages of his coming manhood. Perhaps when it finally arrived in full, he could answer some of those signals with the assurance older boys had when it came to seducing women. Noticing his father's paternal glance, Oliver feigned a smile.

Miss Corothers stood up to sing her solo. When Jackson played the introduction to her number, the wind became louder making the piano sound as if it were not in key. She gave Jackson a look. He shrugged his shoulders and she gamely began to sing. Jackson played louder so that it would not happen again. He and his brother Thomas exchanged glances and tried not to laugh.

Doctor Thomas Freeman, the oldest and the most successful of the Freeman family, sneered to himself as the pastor cried out from the pulpit, "And in Isaiah it is written, 'No man spares his brother.'" What he means is, "No White man spares his brother," he thought. Thomas hid the hate he had for White doctors from his family and friends. Pretending the daily shouldering with the White medical professional people was normal and that the White doctors treated him with great respect became a way of life. He was one of the finest doctors in the whole Baltimore area and still it meant nothing to the White medical society. He was a Colored and he had better know his place. This was the reason, and the only reason he was not allowed to practice in the hospitals. Somehow it did not rankle as much when he had a wife and two sons to go home to every night, but after his family died of an intestinal germ no one knew how to cope with, things became different. Thomas kept to his doctoring while festering inside. Hating Whites became as much a disease as the virus which took his family. He lowered his handsome pock-marked face as if to pray. The secret meetings out of town with Feona Wilson were beginning to pall on him, too. How could he have started a romance with a young girl who did not even know how to read? More to the point, however, was how to stop this ridiculous affair without Feona telling the family as she had threatened. There she sat, as close to the family pew as she could.

Thomas watched as the red feather of her cheap hat moved forward and with a matching red glove, she tapped his mother's shoulder. He heard her whisper, "Mrs. Freeman, do tell Clarabelle I can help with the baby. She do seem fussy today."

Winona, who was very much aware of all the things that went on with the people she loved, stiffened at Feona's touch.

"Thank you, Feona."

She left it at that. Nothing could take her mind off her son Jackson. She was proud of all her children, but Jackson was her joy. There he was, playing the piano and leading the choir, which he always did when the organist was ill and could not play for the service. He was so much like her husband Winfield. Not in stature. He took after his Mamma, so he was shorter than his brothers. However, he did have his father's long legs and graceful walk. He had his mother's facial structure, her noble nose and large hands. It was his father's good thoughts, good humor, and willingness to please that made him so much like Winfield. Winona looked lovingly at her husband. He looked so thin and stoop-shouldered! It seemed as if the whole family was just not feeling well. With such terrible weather, what did a person expect? It was hard to get up this morning. Hard to put a good breakfast on the table. Hard to get ready for church. Winona probably would not have come to church this morning if it were not that Clarabelle told her she would be there with the baby. She worried about Winfield out in inclement weather. She did not worry about Jackson or Thomas. They were strong.

They were as different as peas from mush but both men were to be admired for their stability and exceptional intelligence. It was her husband and their youngest son William who Winona worried about. As for William, he worried about everything including how to keep his wife India happy. Winona knew that if William was successful at his well-established catering service, India would never leave such a comfortable berth. The beautiful light-skinned woman was a good influence on William and their daughter Winifred. William was proud of his wife. She wore chic clothes and knew how to represent her husband and his catering service to good financial advantage. Winifred, a year older than her cousin Clara, was spoiled and already wore the mask of boredom she thought spelled sophistication. As for Winifred's brother Collier, who could harness this energetic boy? Everyone in the family could see that William constantly made mistakes trying to discipline his son. when Collier became unbearably silly, it was Uncle Jackson who laughed with him. It was Uncle Jackson who taught him how to play baseball. Sometimes Collier would pretend he was the talented prize-fighter, Joe Gans who was the boxing champion since 1901, and who would hold the title four more years. Playing fisticuffs with his Uncle was fun and always turned into a tumbling match. Collier would be beside himself with glee! Winona smiled at the thought.

Suddenly, Clarissa became very fretful and seemed to be extreme agitated. Clarabelle was not feeling well by this time and was as restless as her child for the service to come to an end. People seated nearby gave Clarabelle loving side-glances as she tried to console her wriggling bundle, so it was natural for Henry White to turn around and exchange a meaningful look at Clarabelle. She responded to the look, her cheeks blushing warmly. When would she see Henry again?

Henry White was everything Jackson was not. A tall, athletic figure and though his clothes were on the loud side, somehow, he carried them off well. At twenty-five, he already carried a scar on his handsome face caused by an irate husband who probably ended up much the worse for having provoked Henry to a fight. He was proud of his regular features as was his doting mother, Lucy. Clarabelle knew his faults. Womanizer, heavy drinking and although he did not seem to work much, there was always money for gambling. What she resented most was that Henry was seeing other women now that the little one was taking up so much of her time. Clarabelle could not sneak out to keep the affair going as smoothly as it had been. But for the children, she would have left her easy-going husband this very afternoon. She was so tired and getting so warm, she offered the fretful Clarissa to Winona who happily cradled the baby in her heavy arms.

The storm worsened and everyone was anxious for the church service to conclude. The chorus of "Amen" was loud, followed by much shuffling and buttoning up of coats. Jackson quickly gathered the music and thumped them into a neat pile. The Freemans made a habit of meeting on the stair landing to keep in touch with one another before going home and Jackson was slowly making his way to the aisle when he noticed Henry, followed by his mother, hurrying to catch up to Clarabelle. Jackson wondered why that was. He was aware of Henry's womanizing, but surely not with Clarabelle. So why would that thought come to him? Straightening his back and lifting his chin, he watched closely as Henry gave Clarabelle a warm greeting. "Mornin', Clarabelle," he said, his voice soft and low. "Awfully cold for a Sabbath day, ain't it?"

Clarabelle looked up lovingly, a little coquettish. "Mornin', Henry." Then melodiously, "Never too bad a day for goin' to church." The meaning was clear. Clarabelle meant to be near Henry every chance she could get.

Winona, hearing the sweet tones and seeing the self-conscious grinning that spelled trouble for Jackson, deliberately intervened with a salutation of her own. "Mornin', Lucy," her eyes narrowed, "Mornin', Henry."

Henry cocked his head and gave Winona a look of steel. He never liked the strong personality that prevailed in some Colored women and did not mind showing contempt for anybody who told him in words or gestures they did not admire him. Lucy, trying to ease the situation, became part of the group. Inching toward the door, they all felt the icy, damp weather waiting for them outside. Lucy hunched her shoulders against the occasional puff of sharp wind as the church doors opened and closed. "My, my," she said, wrapping her coat against the cold, "It surely is windy and raw today. Maybe a might too cold for the young 'un. They are so..."

"No weather keeps us from comin' to church, Lucy." Winona interrupted, a little more testily than she intended. "Why our family has been comin' here ever since Pastor Livingston was preaching and that was 1835. Just think of that, Lucy!" She was bragging now, by trying to lighten her voice. "Yes, been comin' to this church a long time." She wrapped Clarissa tenderly and patted her lovingly. "Yes, baby, and you gonna come here and go to Sunday school just like your Pappa and Mamma."

The Freemans slowly made their way to the stairway where they always met after the service was over. Clarabelle was breathing hard. Winona touched her arm. "You all right, Child?" Clarabelle waived her hand as if to say she was all right.

Winona looked over her shoulder to see if Nola was following her. She had been unusually quiet this morning and when Winona looked into her vacant eyes, she felt a chill go through her that was not caused by the open door of the vestibule. Nola was a thorn in Winona's life. Jackson found her playing in the swamp and simply brought her home with him. It had been easier when Nola was a child, but she became a burden now that she was older. Nola had drooled on her scarf. Holding the baby in one arm, Winona creased the wet away from her face. There was a devil in the girl. Winona believed it to be so.

Jackson caught up with his family in the vestibule where Thomas was waiting. Feona walked close to the vestibule entrance and greeted Thomas who quickly averted his eyes when he saw her. Feona did not let him get away that easily. She stood with him and the Freeman family. Once they were all together, they went to the stair landing as they always did. Hoping to be invited to a family dinner or at least a get-together, she was disappointed when Thomas coldly told her he would be busy all afternoon. She entertained the idea of pouting and acting hurt but thought better of it, remembering the consequences of that ruse the last time she used it. Clutching her woolen cloak around her neck and lowering her head, she plunged into the windy street hoping no one would notice the tears welling in her eyes.

William, the youngest son, held his father's arm as they went down the stairs to the landing. Winfield gave his son a look of appreciation. William made his way to Thomas. He sidled up to his brother and said, "There's some talk I don't like, Thomas." Thomas raised his head as if to ask, "What is it you don't like?" William never liked that gesture. He supposed it was a pose Thomas used as a doctor to give him a professional demeanor, but he still did not like it.

William lowered his voice. "There has been talk that Coloreds shouldn't handle food. The White legislature is thinking of passing a law to prohibit Negroes from handling food. I would lose my catering business. They are saying since we have such a prevalence for TB that we are carriers. I don't know, Tom…are we?" William kept a smile on his face while talking about his worry-some problem. He did not want to frighten India. "What in the world will I do if they pull this off? We are being shut out of every profession as it is!"

"Well, so far it is just talk," Thomas answered. He shifted himself in front of William so the family would not see the worried look on his face.

"I fight this damn Black-White thing every day of my life. Just remember one thing. We are better off in Baltimore than anywhere else. I'm sure if there is a way to stop this, I can get some of the doctors to testify that all that needs to be done is to have people examined for all diseases. Don't worry so."

"What's the matter, Son?" Winfield asked. "Trouble?"

"Nothing's wrong, Pappa," Thomas said as he patted his father gently on the back. He turned to William, "whatever happens, we'll fight it, that's all." With that, he began to chat with the rest of the family.

Jackson kissed his Mamma, shook hands with his Pappa and his brothers, took the knitted cap Collier was holding and pretended to throw it away. Collier laughed, grabbed the cap out of Jackson's hands, cradled it under his arm and ran around the family group as if he were avoiding interference as he ran toward an imaginary goal line. Everybody laughed at his tomfoolery, except Clarabelle.

"What's the matter, Clarabelle?" Jackson asked. Clarabelle was staring into space. Jackson put his arm around her and gave her a quick reassuring hug. "She shouldn't have come out on a day like this," Jackson announced to the family. Trying to lighten the situation, Jackson looked around the group to talk to somebody and settled on William's son. "Collier! How you doing?" Collier waved their special sign, a wide-open hand raised, lifted and lowered twice. Jackson looked at Thomas. Thomas raised his eyebrows to indicate he was well, then turned to William. "Remember William, don't borrow trouble."

"Trouble?" Jackson felt uneasy. Everyone looked so ill and now Thomas was talking to William about having trouble. He reached for Clairissa, who was restlessly wriggling in her grandmother's arms. His eyes met Thomas'.

"We are all under the weather, Son. I'm worried about your father." Jackson stole a quick look at Winfield. "I don't feel well, either. And just look at poor Clarabelle. We better all get home."

"You ready to go home, Clarabelle? Children, button-up your coats." Jackson was rounding up his family and everybody slowly started up the stairs, grateful the Pastor saw the necessity of getting everybody home this blustery day. There was a pause in the church vestibule. Everyone listened to the strange wail, waxing and waning with each gust of the wind. The murmur sounded as if someone or something was trying to speak to the people huddled at the double doors.

Then it happened. A muffled explosion coming from the docks. Jackson stiffened with the feeling he should do something to protect his family. Thomas stopped halfway up the steps, turned and looked at Jackson.

"What the hell was that?!"

"That was an explosion!"

Jackson's heart was beating fast.

Clarabelle came out of her lethargy, her eyes wide with fear and trepidation. She instinctively reached for Clairissa. Jackson relinquished the baby to her mother, freeing himself in case he had to act. Someone flung the doors wide open and now the sounds of the fire engines were heard. Everybody was looking toward German Street, from whence the discordant noise ominously undulated with the wind.

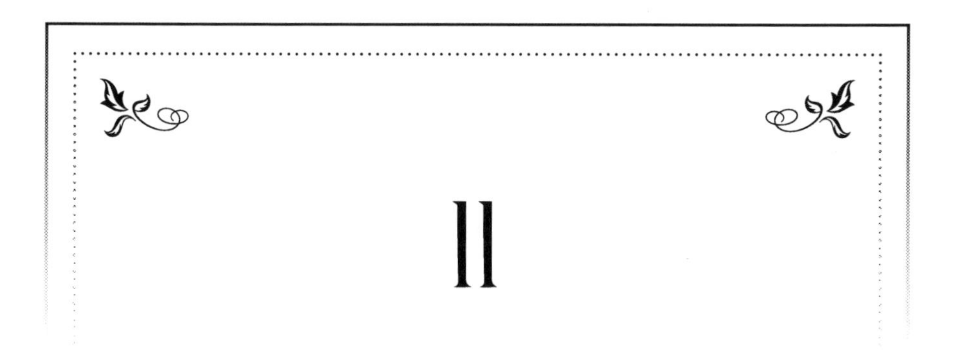

# 11

Gathered in a cemetery in Stanton, Ohio on February 7, 1904, a small group of people shuddered in the cold. Anna Schein hunched her shoulders against wind that made leaves dance around the cemetery slabs. Her face was chapped from the cold moisture that was not quite rain and not quite snow. She tried to stand straight. Everybody was looking at her from time to time during the funeral service at the gravesite. She had wrapped a large shawl around her head. Holding most of the fringed cloth up to her face helped hide the fact she was not mourning. The coffin was lowered into the neat earthen slot. Some of Willie's friends began to cry. People had liked Willie Schein. It was Willie who was strong enough to help pull tree roots to make a field suitable for farming. Willie, who was always there with the extra horse and, Willie, who offered his wife Anna to help with nursing of the sick and birthing.

Anna's mind wandered as the minister droned on. All these people had tolerated her all these years. Willie married her after her father died. He had been a field servant to the big German. It would not be respectable for Anna to live in the house without her father and Willie had to be respectable so, he asked her to marry him in name only. Anna had no place to go. She had no alternative. Willie promised to be good to her. Besides, he liked her cooking. Anna knew Willie's friends would never accept her into their society but then she had gotten used to the beautiful farm which was the best in the valley. Anna was not dumb. She made Willie make out a will. He laughed at the prospect of death, so, in order to get his way, which was particularly important to him, Willie did indeed make out a will leaving everything to Anna. Now Anna was the richest widow in the county.

From Cemetery Hill, Anna could see the church where she and Willie were married. The huddled mourners could not imagine the compromises Anna made in the troubled union. Anna kept her eyes downcast, kept her hand close to her face, and bent her head to one side in what she believed to be a look of bereavement. She was not sorry Willie would be laid to rest in the cold ground. Willie scorned any nursing from her, so she let him have his way. There was no fighting him. Better to leave him alone. She was not one bit sorry for what she did. It was finished. Funny. She did not hate him anymore. Anna almost smiled at that but caught herself in time. Maybe she could have done things differently during his illness. She could have tried to get one of his friends to make him take his medicine or at least to listen to the doctor she brought from town to see him. Maybe if she had insisted he kept to his bed he would still be alive. She had done none of those things. No. Willie was dead and that was that.

Jenny Miller gently put her arm on Anna's shoulder. She and her husband Fred were newcomers to Stanton. When Fred bought their farm about a mile from the Scheins, he and Willie became good working friends, helping each other plow and harvest. Jenny was a good deal younger than Anna and not experienced in many household duties. She relied on Anna to teach her how to keep food all winter long. Canning could be tricky if it was not done right. Yes, Jenny was young. And again, it was Willie who saw to it Anna helped Jenny to use the loom, can foods, and teach her to do all the mundane tasks women routinely do. Perhaps that is why Anna never liked Jenny. If Willie had kept out of it, Anna might have learned to like her. Perhaps not. Anna wanted to laugh and sing the latest songs, but Jenny was too rigid and strait-laced to let herself act in any way she thought was unladylike. Somehow despite their close relationship while doing work, the two women never became close friends. Anna wanted to be better than she was and resented the fact that Jenny could read well. Anna made out words on the page very slowly and Willie laughed at her writing. He said it looked like chicken scratch. There was one other big problem she was aware of, and that concerned the actual property. She knew Keith Cailern had tried for years to get Willie to sell him parcels of farmland. He would stop at nothing to take the farm from her. She must do something besides lean on Willie's lawyer, even though he was sympathetic to her needs.

Fred put his arms around Jenny, pulling her closer to him. Jenny was not yet showing her pregnancy, but Anna knew. She also knew the Millers wondered why someone as virile as Willie never had children. At the age of 47, he often went to the "House on the Hill" or the "House at the Heavenly Divide," as it was known to all the men in Stanton who patronized the gambling tables and the girls upstairs. The large, comfortable home that had once belonged to the family who founded the thriving little city of Stanton was quite rundown when Belinda Resnick took it over and made it into a "House of Ill Repute With a Good Reputation." "You will always get your money's worth," she would brag to one and all. She kept her word, too.

Anna was relieved when Willie went to the house at the top of the hill on their wedding night. But it never stopped his vulgar advances. He teased and annoyed her every chance he got. It was his way. Remembering his fat, callused hands made her shiver. Jenny patted Anna. "Oh, if you only knew what thoughts I had just now, you would not give me solace," Anna thought to herself as she closed her eyes. So many bits and pieces of life with Willie danced in her head.

"Ashes to ashes…," the Minister droned on. The skies grew darker. Each cloud frowned on the huddled group and swept over them as if they were in a hurry to leave the cemetery. The wind swirled around Anna's skirt.

Anna shifted her weight and caught sight of the grave next to Willie's. His first wife. The stone was neglected and crooked. Had he ever loved her? For that matter, had he ever loved anyone? He was never known to be capable of tenderness. As long as Anna had known him, he always had indulged his sex at the brothel. Perhaps, that is why they never had children. It was well-known that his first wife had loved him. It was also well known he treated her shabbily. What did it matter now?

Willie had filled the barn with hay, the corn crib was full, foodstuffs were in the cellar along with apples, maple syrup and potatoes. She knew his favorite hiding place in the barn. There, he kept his schnapps. She was good for a while before she had to worry about farming the land. Spring would come again. What then? "Worry about that when the time comes," she thought.

"…dust to dust."

The Minister closed his Bible and shook Anna's hand. He gave her a look of sympathy and slowly walked away. Jenny and Fred waited for Anna to make a move to leave. "Please let us get out of this weather. It is too cold for Jenny. We'll get some tea and I have a casserole waiting for everybody. That is if anyone would care to come." Everybody shook their heads making some excuse not to come to the house, which was exactly what Anna expected. Anna tried again, "Please, get Jenny home, out of this terrible weather. I'm going to stay and see him buried." Fred hesitated but the wind seemed to be getting worse so, he hustled Jenny into the surrey.

Anna watched Willie's friends disperse and soon, she was alone with the old man who already was pouring dirt in the grave. She watched the dirt slowly piling up. Finally, the old man patted the loose ground. Anna, without looking at the old man, offered him his money. He put his hand up to the brim of his battered hat, slung his shovel over his shoulder and started his walk to the church.

The weather worsened. Billowing black clouds raced across the sky. It was as if the winds were cleaning away the past. She finally took her eyes off the grave. Anna felt exhilarated.

It was over.

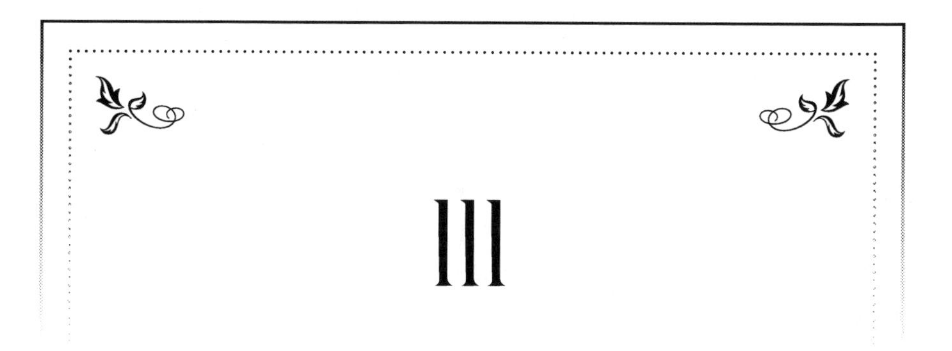

# III

The men of the congregation filed out of the double doors of the church and stood around in small knots not knowing what to do or what action to take. The worshippers from all the other churches were now rushing out of their pews to mingle with one another. They were frightened. The children, sensing great danger, clung to their parents but throughout the turmoil and the wail of the fire wagons, there was no panic.

Two more crashing sounds alerted the Freemans, still on the landing of the stairs, that something was terribly wrong. Jackson wanted to get his family home as quickly as possible so he could find out what the trouble was. "What do you think is happening?" he asked Pappa. Winfield looked confused. This bothered Jackson. "It's all right. We are all safe here." Winfield held on to Nola. She was not aware of anything that was going on, she was happy to have Winfield hold on to her arm. Jackson turned to Clarabelle, "Take the children to Mamma's house. Wait for me there," he said as he buttoned up his coat and jammed his felt hat on his head. "I'll be all right," he consoled her when he saw her ashen face. Clarabelle gave him a look of disgust which he did not understand. Jackson motioned to his brothers to follow him out into the street.

It was because of the storm; Sunday School was cut short and the service ended early, but Jackson was not prepared for the twenty-five mile an hour wind that hit him as he walked out of the church. He and his brothers joined the people milling about. Another tremendous explosion stopped the people dead in their tracks. Everyone looked at each other questioningly. The third explosion wired Jackson into high gear, "C'mon! C'mon!" he shouted as he started for the docks where he surmised the explosions were emanating. He thought, "German Street?" He would make for it. That is where he made his livelihood so he better find out what the trouble was.

Jackson made straight for the streetcar, already filled with parishioners from other churches. Eager hands helped Jackson on board. Black or White, did not make any difference in times of emergencies. As the car entered the heart of Baltimore, everyone became aware of the smoke curling heavenward melding with the clouds. Flames were twisting and writhing with the cold wind. Smoldering debris of cinders and pieces of blazing wood rained down on them. People were running in every direction. The car stopped. The heat was intense. They could get no closer to the raging fire.

Jackson was right. It was German Street. But what to do? It is times like these that strange thoughts come. Jackson looked down at his new shoes. Too late to think of anything. He ran to a group of men who were getting organized for action. He recognized Mayor Langly, who was delegating some men to lead groups of men to do specific assignments to avoid overlapping responsibilities. Langly was well liked by the Baltimoreans. He had easily won the election and he did not disappoint the people. Jackson watched him from a short distance.

Two of Jackson's dock buddies joined the group, giving Jackson courage to walk over to them. "What happened?" Jackson asked.

Tall, sleepy-eyed Sherman just shrugged. "Guess there was a cigarette butt went through the floorboards of the building and caught fire to some blankets in the room below at the John E. Hurst warehouse."

"But someone else said that reject celluloid toys in a bucket caught fire," Sherman's friend Billy chimed in, "and after the firemen put it out, it kept on smoldering. Then it caught fire again and the flames shot up the elevator shaft. The building next door caught fire, too! No watchman on Sunday, you know.

"Sherman shrugged his sparse shoulders again, "like I said, who knows?"

They approached a big fellow standing next to the man Jackson had recognized as Mayor Langly. The three men joined them hoping for instructions on how to fight the fire. As they were waiting, Jackson turned and looked at the warehouse. The flames were consuming the last timbers of the two buildings which were the first victims of the fire.

Fierce gusts of wind coming up from the bay were feeding embers to the other buildings. The roar of the flames sounded like a tornado and every now and then another shack crumbled to the ground bowing to the God Prometheus.

Jackson had lost the where-abouts of his two brothers. He just assumed they were doing other tasks. He did not know when he lost his hat but then he was perspiring in the hell he had entered, so it did not matter. Jackson did think about being careful of his shoes, however. Mostly his thoughts were about his work at the docks. That was of the utmost importance now and here he was watching the place melting, twisting, and dissolving away. Why did he let Clarabelle talk him out of buying a piece of land? Farmers were always able to eat, and he had always wanted to be free from White bosses telling him what he could or could not do. Why was it she could not understand that?

Jackson heard voices raised in anger. The mayor was mad!! Jackson moved closer to Langly to hear what was going on. "This should not have happened," the mayor said excitedly. "These buildings are fireproof. Why, the Engine Company No.15 responded within forty seconds. The firefighters turned a chemical hose on it thinking they would be back at the firehouse by lunchtime." The big man the Mayor was talking to was perspiring and now turned red with anger.

"I know, Langly, but the burning rubbish contained celluloid novelties and as the firemen played the hose on the fire, the toys burst into flames. The next thing you know, the flames shot up the elevator shaft. It took about seven minutes later, and a fire set off a terrible explosion on the upper floor, blowing out all the windows in the neighborhood."

The big man wiped his face with his handkerchief.

"That's when the whole building caught on fire from top to bottom."

He stopped to give more orders to the men who were working with the couplings on the hydrants. Seeing Jackson and his two buddies waiting to help, he called out, "You fellows can help with the hoses. We're expecting a wagon of water pretty soon now." He turned back to Mayor Langly and continued, "A hell of a wind carried the fire out of the windows of the upper floors to the next building, and on and on it went."

A group of men on the fringes of the street began to shout, "They're coming! They're coming!"

Wild-eyed horses careened around the corner almost toppling the men on the fire wagon. Stopping close to the hydrant, one of the horses slipped on the ice, skidding into the other horses. It took all the men quite some time to calm the frightened animals down before anybody could do anything about the fire. Through the confusion, Jackson heard a voice calling to the big man.

"Hey, McCrackin, we're gonna get equipment from Washington and Virginia. They're on their way now."

Jackson began to help the men who were now frantically pulling out the hoses. Spread out on the street, they looked for all the world like the intestines of the fire wagon. It seemed as if everybody was working at a disadvantage. The wind never let up, penetrating their clothes with water that turned to ice. The men were oblivious to the cold on one side of them and the heat on the other side of them. Just fight the fire.

Jackson's hands were bleeding from the frost but when all the hoses were uncurled he smiled, knowing the water would divide the fire from the rest of the town. His smile turned into a frown when everybody stopped to contemplate the hydrant. All was quiet except the crackling of the fire. McCrackin kept nervously taking his hat off and rearranging it on his head.

"What the hell are we going to do?" McCrackin looked puzzled at the unpeeled hoses. Jackson moved closer on the half-run.

"What's the matter," he boldly asked.

"The couplings won't go on because of the cold. There's ice in the threads."

"Someone get a stick and light it," he shouted.

"We've got to get this hose on."

McCrackin looked at Jackson.

"How fast can you run?"

"What do you need?"

"I want you to find the chief engineer, George Horton. Tell him these are the second bunch of hoses that don't fit the hydrants. He'll know what to do."

Jackson ran from one group to another asking for Horton, but it took quite a while before he found out the chief engineer had been struck down by an electric jolt from a fallen cable and was taken to the hospital.

Jackson ran back to McCrackin where the men were still trying to work the hoses into the hydrant.

"McCrackin!"

Jackson was out of breath.

"You'll have to depend on your own resources. Horton is in the hospital. He was struck by an electric bolt from a fallen cable."

"Oh, for Christ's sake! Ain't anything gonna go right? Is George all right?"

"Don't know," Jackson replied. "But it looks as if you are making headway with the couplings."

"Hey, yeah, we got it now!"

The big man turned to Jackson.

"What's your name?""Jackson Freeman."

"Good job, well done, Freeman."

McCrackin looked at Jackson.

"I didn't think anyone could find anybody in this mess. All right, turn the hoses on."

A small stream of water poured out of the hose. Shouts of "hooray" from the men turned to a moan of disappointment when the water coming out of the nozzle trickled a short distance. McCrackin looked at Jackson.

"Better'n nothin'," Jackson offered.

"Keep it goin', men," McCrackin yelled. The mayor disengaged himself from a knot of men to see who was approaching them. They were talking very excitedly.

"We just found out a special train is coming from Wilmington and one from Washington, New York, and Hanover with fire equipment. We're going to be all right. We'll get this damn fire out!"

As the man spoke, two more explosions rocked the earth.

"I just hope the trains will be here in time."

Billy poked Jackson on the shoulder and said, "As long as this is all we can do around here, let's go down and make sure all the horses are safe. Some of them are on the second floor, you know."

Jackson nodded and carefully let go his part of the hose. He looked at the progress of the fire. Many of the burned buildings had their upper floors demolished by the fire while the lower stories were unscathed. He pulled out his pocket watch. It was mid-afternoon. By now, every fire department in Baltimore was at the fire sending small, thin streams of water to battle the blazing buildings. Jackson was about to follow Billy when McCrackin called out to him.

"Hey, Jackson, see if you can get everything off the streets. You know, anything that burns. Ropes, leather, barrels and any bottles with combustibles."

As Jackson turned to the task McCrackin asked him to do, he looked around and began to realize the scope of the devastation going on. The windows of the Baltimore skyscrapers, reflecting the fire were silently waiting to be consumed. He stood hypnotized by the licking flames which seemed to be reaching, reaching, reaching. He knew the job relegated to him was useless. All hands were working at breakneck speed. No one noticed the wind picking up little burning torches and carrying them to other buildings.

"Hey! Get goin'!" McCrackin shouted.

Alarmed at the sweeping devastation around him, Jackson found his second breath, courage, and wings on his feet as he ran from one hopeless task to another, turning away the moment he ran into trouble breathing. Already several firemen had to leave the area because of injuries and smoke inhalation. He hurled ropes on a wheelbarrow and pushed the load into the bay. Too tired to continue at the speed he was going, he sat down. It was very dark now. The flames looked bright against the black sky. Jackson saw a silhouette of a man leading two horses. Billy was still finding some of the animals. As he sat there in the smoky night, Jackson began to wonder where his brothers were. He hoped William was taking care of the family. Perhaps Thomas was down here in this inferno helping anyone who became injured. The thought crossed his mind that his family was not feeling well. He had such an urge to go home. The fire made him feel as if he had a temperature. Enough! He had work to do. Best be at it!

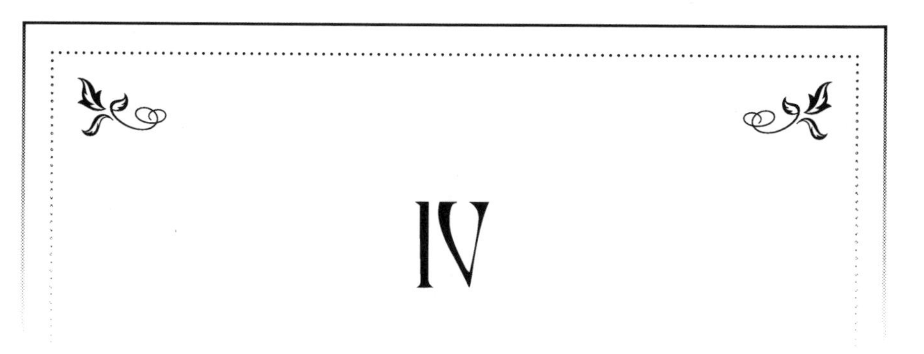

# IV

At Fells Point, Thomas Freeman was setting up a medical station away from the fire. His hands were so cold he could hardly open the bottles of medicine. Resourceful as he was, Thomas had a few bottles of aspirin he had filched from the hospital after a meeting with his white colleagues. While respectfully holding the door open for the head of the hospital with his left hand, Thomas put his right hand in back of the door, making it a matter of stretching his arm back to reach the shelf where three bottles of aspirin were waiting to be lifted up and put in his pocket.

"Well," Mamma had warned him, "If you steal it, you will need it." Better not to steal it and not need it. So, here he was using up all the aspirin for the fire fighters, the Colored as well as the White men.

The empty storeroom was looking very much like a hospital room by the time Thomas' nurse arrived with more medicine, bandages, and cotton. Sarah Wilson was bright, efficient, and well-educated. She quickly took her coat and hat off, straightened her hair a little, and was ready for whatever would come this terrible day. Everyone knew Sarah was deeply in love with Thomas. She fervently hoped for more than respect for her nursing abilities. Thomas smiled at her.

"I can always count on you. I thank you for that."

Sarah felt her cheeks get warm. She felt sure Thomas was interested in her.

Soon the room was full of men coughing, their eyes burning from the smoke and ashes. Thomas recognized Mr. Perkins among the firefighters. What was the good grocer, Mr. Perkins, doing here? He was too old to be fighting the fire, but here he was coughing and wheezing with everybody else. Thomas watched Perkins closely while dressing a wounded man's arm. Mr. Perkins was a most respected man around the Colored people. He always threw in something for the children in a small paper bag when a bill was paid. Not candy. An apple that had some good in it or a bunch of grapes, then again, it might be a melon that was good on one side. Thomas dismissed his patient, put the bandages back in the clean box before seeing to Mr. Perkins.

Suddenly, Perkins began to throw up. Thomas rushed to his side. Sarah noticed the quick action Thomas took and joined him. "I didn't think anything was wrong with him, Doctor. I thought he came to help us," she said putting her arms around Mr. Perkins' shoulder. Thomas investigated the bowl. Blood.

"Mr. Perkins, how long have you been doing this? How long have you been sick?"

Mr. Perkins put his hand to his forehead, he looked up at Thomas for help.

"Long time, Doctor." His voice was thin and raspy. "Didn't want to tell the missus. You know how frail she is. I know how busy you are, but I have never felt this bad. Can you help me?"

Thomas put a thermometer in his mouth. "Do you cough all the time?"

Perkins shook his head.

"Well, we'll see what's going on here," Thomas said cheerfully. He looked at the thermometer. Perkins saw the look of concern.

"I do cough a lot at night, Doctor Tom."

Perkins no sooner got the words out when he doubled up and used the pan again. It sounded as if he would turn inside out. Thomas waited until Perkins got his breath.

"Never been this bad," he gasped.

His eyes met Tom's.

"What is it, Doctor Tom?"

Thomas was a knowledgeable doctor and knew tuberculosis when he saw it. Mr. Perkins knew what he had.

"You can't handle food now, Mr. Perkins," Thomas quietly told him. "You know that, don't you?"

Perkins nodded that he did.

"Go home and get some rest. Close the store until you can get somebody to run it for you. I'll give you some medicine." Thomas rummaged in his bag for peppermint.

"All this will do is sweeten your mouth. I want you to take a tablespoon every time you vomit."

He helped Perkins out of his chair.

"You must keep quiet and still. I'll see you as soon as I can." Then remembering he was not Perkins' doctor, he added, "or until you can get another doctor."

Perkins gave Thomas a hard look.

"I respect your doctoring, you know that, but maybe the missus..." his voice trailed off and he lowered his head. Softly he said, "I think I can make it home now. Thank you, Doctor. And thank you, young lady."

Perkins put on his hat, buttoned up his coat and shuffled out into the cold, windy night. Thomas wanted to help the man he had admired all his life. Perkins was one of the Baltimoreans working tirelessly for the betterment of Colored people. Henry Perkins was the one who stood up at council meetings trying to uplift the living conditions in the poorer neighborhoods. It was through his efforts the large pipe was settled in the middle of the playing field the children used. It helped to drain the area and kept the mosquito population down.

The door thrust open making everybody turn their heads. "Doctor Freeman! Doctor Freeman!" The shouting came in short bursts from Ella Hanson gasping for air as she spoke. The young girl, who would never understand anything above the nine-year-old level, was hysterical. Her eyes were open wide, her hair was matted and twisted from the wind which had woven frost all over her head. When Ella saw Thomas, she screamed, "You're wanted at home."

She was so frightened she was shaking. Thomas took a step toward her, thinking to comfort her. Ella's eyes widened with fright. She curled one shoulder around her face and quickly drew away from him stopping Thomas in his tracks.

Calmly Thomas asked, "What do you want to tell me?"

Ella rolled her eyes upward. She was thinking hard.

The young girl swallowed hard, her thick lips kept opening and closing as if she were talking to herself. Then she stood up straight ready to recite her message. Ella's hands were nervously twisting at her sides. She started to speak her piece looking at the ceiling as if she were reading what she was about to say. Remembering was hard for her.

Taking a big breath, she slowly began, "Yore Mamma says you have to come home quick." Trying to think of the rest of the message, Ella pulled the sides of her loose-fitting coat down one side then the other. "She says … she says…," Ella's voice started to rise higher and she started to cry. The words were tumbling out now, "She says it's bad and your Pappa is bad and the baby is bad …and everybody's gonna catch it." She dropped on her knees, "Yore Mamma helped to clean Mister Baker's house and Missus Clarabelle wasn't feeling good enough to take care of the baby. Doctor Freeman, please help me."

She clasped her hands together and waited for the doctor to answer her prayer.

Everybody in the room was staring at Ella. Thomas gave them a smile and said, "I don't think anything is as bad as she says. She is slow, you know."

The men went back to visiting and comparing their wounds. Thomas quickly went to Ella, picked her up off her knees, put his arm around her and steered her away from the patients. He checked to see if she had a fever or any symptoms of illness. Looking her straight in the eye, Thomas spoke very deliberately to her, "You are not sick, Ella. You will be just fine. Do you understand?"

Not waiting for an answer, Thomas gave Sarah a meaningful side glance. She caught the look and walked over to him slowly to not call attention to the patients.

"Take over, Sarah, Ella will help you. Won't you, Ella?" Ella, already forgetting her outburst, nodded that she would indeed help Sarah.

"But Doctor, Ella is no help. She might do more harm than good. With her mentality, I cannot tell what she might do." Ella frowned at that and her lower lip protruded.

"Just keep her occupied. She can hold bandages or iodine for you."

He patted Ella. "Nurse Sarah will clean you up. Your hands must be cleaned and stay clean, and you must not touch anything to dirty them, do you understand?"

Ella nodded that she understood. She smiled at her good fortune.

"Sarah, I want her here in case you get someone with a bad burn. You can send Ella to her house to get her brother to fetch me. Please do the best you can until I get back."

The concerned look on Sarah's face gave him pause. "Don't worry. I'll be back as soon as I possibly can. Oh, by the way, see if you can get any information out of anybody who comes in. Ask if they know where Jackson is, and if he is all right."

Thomas hurried out the door carefully avoiding the icy threshold. Sarah felt a chill and it was not the cold air that caused it. She remembered the smallpox epidemic that took many lives just before she and Thomas started school that fateful summer. Thomas became terribly ill and smallpox kept him back a grade, making it easier for Sarah to be close to him.

Thomas hoped his car would start. It was a while and a lot of effort, but the faithful automobile started with a great sputter. Thomas went past Mr. Perkins' house. It was dark. Perkins must be sleeping. Good. He steered the car back to Mamma's house. It could not be anything too bad, he himself had vaccinated the whole family against smallpox. Ella must not have understood. Thomas felt his cheek. The scars had been part of him so long he did not notice them anymore. Of course, other people see the scars every time they look at him. Thomas had to erase that from his mind, otherwise, he would not have been able to be the success he had become.

Winona met Thomas at the door. "I heard the car. Oh, Tom, I'm so worried! I'm so hot and I don't know if I should be near the baby… and the baby is feverish, too. Clara and Oliver can hardly keep their heads up. Clarabelle is too week to stand and what's worse, Pappa can hardly get his breath. Thomas gave his mother a quick hug and ran to his father, who was sitting in his old armchair in the bedroom. Thomas tore open his medical bag to get his stethoscope.

"Pappa! Pappa! Pappa!" Thomas tried to get a response. He was too late. Winfield Freeman, the patriarch of the family, was dead. Thomas wrapped his arms around the frail old man he loved with all his heart and cried. Winona stood transfixed in the doorway unable to move. She had peeled down to her petticoat trying to keep cool, but nothing helped her fever. Suddenly she began to tremble. "Mamma, please keep away. I'll put him on the bed." Winona nodded listlessly, then she winced and doubled over. Thomas ran to get her to the chamber pot. She was already bleeding from the rectum. Now, Thomas knew what had struck the whole family. The damn intestinal germ that took his wife and children! Winona was breathing hard. She held on to Thomas who gently helped her to the floor. Although Thomas was a big man, she was too large a woman for him to carry. He helped her to Pappa's chair. Winona held out her arms to him. "The baby… see to the bab…" Thomas watched helplessly as her life slipped away. He put a blanket around her and kissed her. The baby. He went to the bassinet and picked up the baby who was sleeping so soundly he had to make sure she was alive.

Would Jackson become ill? Probably not. He worked two jobs and did not drink much water at home.

Thomas went to the other bedroom where Clarabelle was taking care of the children as best she could. He gave Clarissa to her.

"What's the matter with Pappa? Thomas! Why, why do you look at me like that?"

Thomas could not say the words.

"Oh, no!"

Clara moved restlessly. Clarabelle whispered, "Please Thomas, tell me how bad it is."

Thomas felt Clara's forehead, then he went to Oliver, always taking care not to disturb them. Quietly he said to Clarabelle, "You have to be very brave. Mamma and Pappa are gone." Clarabelle put her hands to her lips to stifle an outcry. "Now just be calm. I'll see if the doctors at the hospital can help us." He unwrapped the baby's blanket and noticed the tell-take blood stains. Quickly changing the diaper so Clarabelle could not see it, he kept reassuring her using a lighter, soothing voice. "Lay down and rest. We're going to be all right, you'll see." He touched her forehead and put a thermometer in her mouth. "Now be quiet," he cautioned her. Clarabelle did as she was told all the time trying to see something in Thomas' face that would tell her how bad things were. He showed no alarm as he read the thermometer. "How much diarrhea have you had?"

"We all have had it bad. The children are exhausted. I'm feeling a little better, thought."

"Where is Jackson? Do you know?"

"Still to the fire as far as I know, Tom."

Clarabelle began to feel tired.

"I haven't had any news of him. He doesn't even know what is happening here. My mind is going around in circles. I don't know how bad the fire is, do you know anything? What if Jackson is hurt? Oh, my God! Please help us!"

Thomas patted her hand. "Try not to get too upset. I know it is hard under the circumstances. The fire is burning up all of Baltimore, Clarabelle. Jackson is too smart to get hurt." They both smiled at that.

"There, that's better."

Thomas checked Clara and Oliver again. Their temperatures both registered one hundred and five, and they were both having trouble breathing but so far the breathing was steady. Thomas brought a pan of water closer to Clarabelle.

"Keep everybody as cool as you can and that includes yourself, Young Lady! I'll be back from the hospital as soon as I can with medication and a nurse, I hope. If I can't find one, I'm sure Sarah will be glad to help us. Thomas put the chamber pot close to the bed and went to the kitchen. He took a sample of the water the family had been drinking. He made sure the gas lit lamps were at a safe flame and came back to the bedroom. "You won't be alone. I'll see if Mrs. Rogers will come and sit with you. She will have to know about Mamma and Pappa. They have been neighbors for over thirty years. She is going to take this awfully hard. Is there anything I can do for you before I go?"

Clarabelle was almost asleep, but she managed to say, "No, thank you. Please hurry, Tom, the sooner you go, the sooner you will be back. I'm so frightened. I know the dead can't hurt you, but I'm scared of them, even though it is Mamma and Pappa." Under her breath she began to pray. "Our Father who art in Heaven…"

Thomas waited until he knew she was asleep. He took a quick look around. Everything was still. All he could hear was the steady breathing of his patients. Thomas felt he could leave and get Mrs. Rogers who lived across the street. As he opened the door, he felt Death walk in. Thomas ran out of the house.

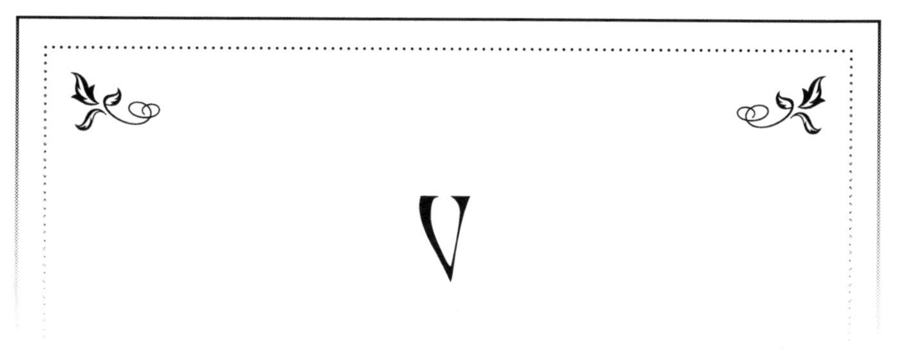

# V

Jackson tried to get enough strength to get up and rid the next block of more combustibles. He closed his tired eyes. The wind became extraordinarily strong and for a while, it swept back the heat of the fire. Jackson shivered. Suddenly a bright light seared through his eyelids. His eyes opened. Large, white flames leapt across the street setting a new block on fire. German and Hopkins Place were diagonally opposite the Hurst warehouse where the fire had begun. If this block was to be saved, it had to be now. Jackson abandoned his wheelbarrow; he ran as fast as his swollen feet could carry him -- back to the fire wagon. A few men were still holding the hoses on the fire, but they had not made much headway.

"You have held this street," Jackson exclaimed, "now you have German Street going up in flames!"

He looked around.

"Where is McCrackin?"

One of the men stepped out of the darkness.

"What do you mean? We got it figured out with the different groups of manpower we'll get this fire out in a couple more hours." The man came close to Jackson's face and sneered.

"What do Colored men know about fighting a fire? McCrackin ain't here. He's eating. There is a table of stuff the ladies set up. There's a table set up for you Negroes, too."

Jackson did not waste time with the ignorant man. He needed McCrackin so he started for the tables. As luck would have it, McCrackin was coming back from his meal. "McCrackin! We have a problem we are not going to be able to solve. Hopkins Place and German Street are on fire and the wind seems to be getting stronger. Can we get some water down there?" Just as McCrackin was about to answer, there was a loud cheer from the fire-fighters. The two men looked at each other. Billy came out of the darkness and gave Jackson a big hug. Even with all the smell of smoke, Jackson could tell he had been with the horses.

"Billy, you stink!" Jackson said. Everyone had a good laugh.

"What's all the hollerin' about, Bill?"

"Whooeee! The fire-fightin' equipment comin' from New York and Washington are here, and it's about time!"

Billy did a soft-shoe step. The news took away the tiredness and pain.

"Tell them to go down German Street," Jackson yelled at Billy who was already going to get the new fire-fighting equipment. McCrackin gave a quick look. He was in charge here. Jackson gave him one of his "Light-up-the-skies-at-midnight" smiles.

"It just came out, McCrackin."

McCrackin smiled back. He liked Jackson.

"Did you get something to eat?"

"Show me the way and point me to it."

The two men walked through the smoke to the food tables. It tasted smoky and the bread must have been there awhile, but to Jackson, it was just what he needed to give him back his strength. He drank three glasses of water, and a full glass of beer with his food. His feet must have swollen. He felt them tingling in his good shoes. Everything seemed better now that the equipment was here. Everyone was relieved.

Jackson heard an outcry. He motioned for McCrackin to be quiet. Billy was telling something to them and waving his arms for them to come to him.

"I have a bad feeling, McCrackin."

Jackson, McCrackin and some of the men around the table started to go toward Billy. Billy met them halfway.

"It's the same story, McCrackin, their couplings don't fit our couplings! What will we do now? Let the damn fire burn all of Baltimore?"

"We just have to fight harder. Right, Boys?"

The men cheered McCrackin's words, "We're ready! Just tell us what to do!"

McCrackin grouped some of the men around him.

"Your bunch go down to the harbor, draw up the water in tarps and set up a reservoir of water."

Jackson watched the men, now with a renewed burst of energy, as they tackled the tarps. It would be a long time before they would pour any water on the fire. He could see it was pointless to bring up German Street again. Slowly, without any enthusiasm, Jackson went back to the job assigned to him.

Jackson went as far as he could go without getting burned to see what was sitting on the porch of a store. He could not read what was in the barrels. Jackson was determined to find out. Taking a cardboard box he found in the alley, he wrapped it around him. It might be a buffer from the heat. This way he would be able to get close enough to read what was in the first barrel. He tried several times to get near the porch. Since that didn't work, he decided to try to roll one over to see if there was any writing to indicate what was in them. He looked around and found a rake. Probing and jabbing didn't move them... they were full, all right. But with what? Jackson needed help. Billy. He would look for Billy. As Jackson walked away, he heard the fire whip up. The store was engulfed in flames and inside the store was heard the pop, pop, pop of bottles. The fire lit the window sign. Furrley's Whiskey Shop. More explosions in the shop frightened Jackson, who was now backing away from the fire as fast as he could. Two more explosions. Jackson turned and ran as fast as his tired feet would go. He was a half a block away when the store blew apart. Breathing hard and coughing from the smoke, Jackson watched helplessly as the fire raged on. Thank God he had gotten away in time. Finally, one hundred and fifty two barrels of whiskey caught fire and the burning liquid flooded the streets, destroying three firefighting apparatuses.

The fire raged into Monday. Tugboats raced through the harbor trying to save boats anchored there. Other boats turned back to sea to avoid being consumed by the fire. Late Monday afternoon, thirty-six fire companies and a fireboat made a desperate stand at Jones Falls, but Jackson did not even try to go with them to help. Early that morning he heard a great cry of joy coming up from the edge of the water. Jackson could see two ships. Fire-fighting ships! A huge spray of ocean water was a beautiful sight. The spray, however, did not reach far enough inland. The water hardly touched the flames. The ships were unable to get near enough to quell the raging inferno.

Was Jackson the only one to see the handwriting on the wall? He was now limping on shoes that were ruined from the ashes and dirt. His arms felt like lead hanging from his shoulders and his back was hurting, probably from being so tense. Jackson leaned on his wheelbarrow. Wiping his face with his sleeve, he remembered thinking about his shabby cuffs. He smiled wryly. "Not as young as I used to be," he thought. How good it would be to take a shower. How good it would feel to lay in Clarabelle's arms and sink into blissful sleep. He had given his all. Now all he could think about was his family. That's where he wanted to be. Maybe all of Baltimore would go up in smoke. He was needed at home to take care of his own. As he looked around, he realized the fire had spread to all the downtown buildings and the little water that was coming from the fire-fighting ships and all the fire-fighting equipment would not stop the blazing, beautiful Baltimore City. Jackson's heart sank. No telling how far the fire would go. The desire to be with his family became too strong. He made up his mind. He was going home.

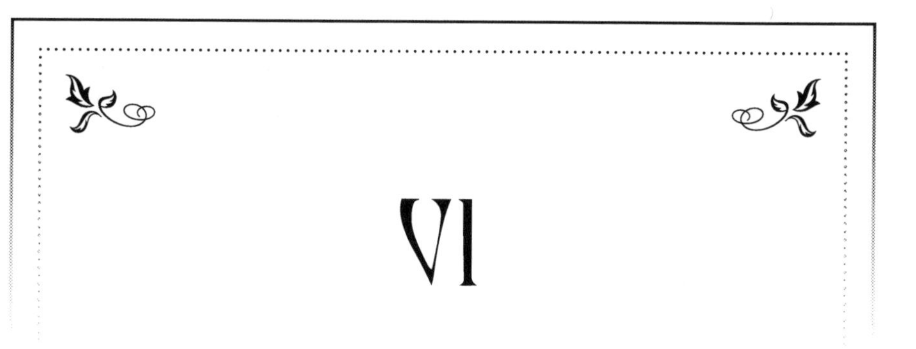

# VI

Jackson did not know the stand at Jones Falls was successful. After thirty-six hours, the firefighters were able to stop the devastating fire. He leaned against the wind feeling the chill down to his bones. Having lost his hat, he pulled up his collar over his ears. As he walked out of the ruins of Baltimore, he passed people standing in clusters anxious for news about the men who were still trying to keep the flames down. The Evening News had moved in the old building the Herald had occupied at Eutow and Baltimore Streets and would send Baltimore news to the Philadelphia Press, their "copy" forwarded by wire and special messenger. Baltimoreans would have a paper today!

Jackson buried his head deep in his shoulders, his hands jammed in his pockets against the cold.

"Got to get home. Got to get home," went through his brain like a broken record. As he came closer to home, his mother's home, he noticed people moving away from him as he approached them. Someone called out, "Ain't nobody t'home, Jackson!" and Jackson stopped to see who was speaking to him.

"Keep away, Jackson, don't want no influenza here!"

Jackson turned the corner to his house running as fast as he could. He soon had to slow down. His lungs ached; his legs felt like rubber. Influenza? Who? Mamma? No. Everyone seemed a little down but... influenza? Then why did he have this feeling he had to get home as soon as possible? Everybody should be in their own homes by now. But Jackson made for his mother's house. Maybe she was tending to the baby since Clarabelle was so tired. Or sick. Or what? As the house came into view, Jackson noticed the curtains of the other houses were moving. The neighbors were watching him. Nobody was on the street and he could hear the crunch of the cold snow as he put down one faltering step after another. Suddenly he heard a car. Thomas! No one else had a car in this neighborhood. Thomas pulled up to the curb and Jackson hopped on the running-board.

"What is wrong, Thomas?"

"You haven't heard?"

Thomas stopped and Jackson jumped off the running board, making for the house as quickly as he could.

"Jackson, come back here! Uh... you can help me with the packages."

Thomas gave Jackson a weak smile as he opened the door of the car. Thomas did not ordinarily use such a commanding voice. It did make Jackson come back to the car.

"Jackson," Thomas began, "It's a germ. They all have it, so I kept them all quarantined at the house. I don't know how this is going to turn out."

Seeing Jackson's face turn to stone, Thomas quickly added, "There are medicines I can give them, but I really don't know if they will work. The doctors at the hospital gave me the best medicines they have for this damn germ.

"There is a lot of diarrhea."

Jackson's eyebrows raised. He remembered the germ that killed Thomas' family.

"Let's not worry until we know what the hell this is. So far, everybody is holding on."

Thomas looked at Jackson and smiled, trying to show him that things were not too bad.

"You all right?"

"I'm all right, Thomas. I'll help you."

Jackson reached for some packages on the back seat of the car and picked up cotton and gauze cartons. As he turned to go to the house, the world began to whirl about him. Jackson opened the door, took one step out of the car, and fell on the sidewalk. Thomas slid from the driver's seat to the passenger side to help Jackson get up on his feet.

"Jackson, you can't go in there or have you had a lot of diarrhea, too?"

Jackson nodded in the negative.

"If you're confined, you won't be able to help me at all. Two days of no sleep, all that exertion. You'll be sick, too. You'll have to rest. Now give me the cartons, wait for me in the car. There is a throw on the back seat. Put it around you. You're all wet. When I come out of the house, you'll have a full report about the family. I'm sure they'll be all right. Clarabelle told me she was feeling better last night. That is good news, isn't it?" Jackson looked hopeful.

"If everything is all right, I'll take you to the parsonage. Then I have some burn patients to take care of. Please help me by doing as I say."

Jackson nodded meekly, got back into the car, wrapped the blanket around himself and waited.

What was it Thomas had said? Everybody had it?

"Oh, by God, the baby!"

Jackson wailed and held his head between his hands. The thought was terrible. He bent low, holding his stomach, aching with the pain that little Clairissa would be so ill. Just three weeks old!

It was quite some time before Thomas came out of the house. He climbed into the driver's seat, aware Jackson's eyes never left him. For the first time, Jackson looked at Thomas as a professional doctor. Thomas tried to avoid looking at Jackson's haunting eyes. He noticed the dark circles and helplessness Jackson felt. The weary lines in Jackson's face deepened with his misery. His hair was encrusted with ashes and soot. With no expression on his face, Jackson asked the dreaded question.

"How bad is it?"

Thomas remembered Clarabelle asking the same question. He patted Jackson's hand. Might as well tell Jackson the gravity of the situation.

He lied a little.

"Mamma and Pappa will not make it. The children have a good chance."

"Mamma and Pappa?"

Jackson brightened, "Clarabelle and the baby? They have a good chance, too?"

"I don't know. You know Clarabelle had a hard time giving birth this time and isn't really herself yet. Babies do not always have much stamina."

Thomas could not go on. Suddenly his professional dignity was gone. He put his head down on the steering wheel and wept. Jackson pulled his brother to him. They clung to one another for a moment.

"Jackson, try to dry your hair with the throw. We don't want you coming down with anything. I'll take you to the parsonage now. You'll have to stay there until ... well, you know."

Because of the icy roads, the drive took some time. Jackson did not seem aware of the conditions. He crumpled into the corner of the seat, staring straight ahead. Thomas would look over at him occasionally wanting to say something cheerful but there was nothing to say. There was no conversation between them. Silence has its place.

When they arrived at the parsonage, Thomas helped Jackson to the door, quickly ringing the bell. The sooner he got Jackson settled, the sooner he could get on with doctoring. There was a sound of scuffling, muffled voices, and then silence. Thomas was about to ring the bell again when the door opened. Reverend Harris smiled as he ushered them into the vestibule. Through the corner of his eye, Thomas saw the hall door close.

"What brings you here on such a terrible night, my Son?"

Thomas explained the situation. The Reverend took Jackson by the arm.

"No need to worry, Thomas, Jackson can rest here. We'll take good care of him as long as necessary. Can you make the stairs, Jackson?"

Jackson nodded he could.

Thomas was relieved.

"Thank you, Reverend. Now, I must get back to my duties." He hugged his brother lovingly.

"Get some rest, now. We'll get through this."

To the Reverend he said, "Pray for us. I am reluctant to go but I have so many things to do. Sarah is at the clinic all by herself then, there is the family... no need to go on. I know you understand. Bye, Jackson. Sleep. That's doctor's orders!" Jackson smiled weakly.

"I'll come get you as soon as I can. Thank you again, Reverend."

Thomas handed the Reverend a bottle of pills.

"One every four hours," and he hurried out the door into the cold evening.

Thomas took one last look at the parsonage before entering the car. He hoped Jackson would sleep through the days of his family's sickness. Thomas knew he could not do anything except lie to Jackson about being able to do something for them. The symptoms were all too clear. No amount of medicine would stop the intestinal germ that ravaged their bodies.

When he arrived at the clinic, Thomas could not park close to the door. There were wagons in front of the empty store he had furnished with medicine and furniture for the people who were fighting the fire. He became angry at having to walk to the door. His temper was his downfall. Everybody told him that. Here he was tending to firemen when he could not even put his family in a hospital. Yes! He was mad! Just who the hell did they think they were? He was frustrated, but his hands were tied.

Thomas got out of the car, pulling his coat collar closer to his throat. Tilting his head forward and dropping his chin into his scarf, he began watching his feet. His expensive black boots faded into bare black feet as he thought about the day he decided to become a doctor.

Lean and long of limb, holding his catch of fish, he was walking back to town. At fourteen years of age, he had not felt the full hatred Whites had for the Black men of the community. He was strong, lithe, and quite well-read compared to most of his friends, including the White boys of Baltimore. He was proud of himself, as were his Mamma and Pappa. The sound of his bare feet on the hard path was familiar to him. His loose shirt flapped around his thin body. He threw his head back, closed his eyes to the sun, bouncing his head first to one side, then the other in an exaggerated walk of jubilation. He was feeling the happiness of youth when suddenly, for no reason, he began to feel something was very wrong. He stopped and listened. There was moaning and crying coming from a group of children. The adults were crowding over someone. More people were rushing down the path leading to the river. Thomas ran with them to a clearing. Seeing one of his school friends, he shouted, "Bailey! Bailey! What happened?"

Bailey waited for Thomas to catch up to him. He was crying, hardly able to speak.

"Emily, Little Emmilly..."

"Emily? What about Emily?"

"She dead!"

"Dead?"

"She dead, Thomas, you deaf?"

"How did it happen?"

"She was playin' too close to the muddy bank, rolled down to the water and, poor baby, couldn't do nothin'. She cain't swim." Bailey's eyes opened wide with the horror of the scene he just painted.

"Happened to me once, but I was older and you know, Tom, I could hardly make it out of the water."

He shook his head., "A little baby... what can a baby do?"

Thomas felt his body go limp as if all the cares of the world were cast off him. A strange sensation came over him. Very deliberately he walked through the crowd and bent down, picked up the little three-year-old-Emily, who was now turning blue. Finding a log, Thomas quickly turned the child over on her stomach, rolling her over and over on the log until water spewed from her mouth at every turn. After what seemed like an interminable amount of time, the little, water-logged child began to cough, making terrible sounds as she tried to take a breath. Thomas was not sure when to stop rocking the limp baby. Only when Emily began to scream, did he stop and turned the frightened child right-side up. Gently holding her close to his chest, he tried to soothe her. She in turn coughed and then gasped for air with the little strength left in her. The knot of people who had just stood by watching the dying girl come to life moved forward, all talking at once.

"Tom! You brought her back to life. It's a miracle!" Bailey was astounded.

Then a hurricane swept a path through the crowd. Emily's mother had been summoned by a friend. She was frantic. Pushing everybody out of her way with the strength of a wild cat, she screamed.

"Emily," tearing the child out of Thomas' arms. The gasping and coughing continued as Emily fought to breathe. The child threw her head back and pulled away from her hysterical mother. Thomas took charge of the situation. He took the baby from her mother's arms and, holding her with her back toward him, he made a chair with his left arm, holding her with his right arm. This way, the fretful little girl could better move forward to spit out the phlegm and water.

Finally, Emily became quiet. Limp and tired from the mighty effort, she leaned back on Thomas's chest. Someone in the crowd, Thomas did not remember who, was holding the child's mother to keep her from preventing Thomas' tending Emily.

Now Thomas held the little girl out to her mother, who grabbed her and held her close, rocking back-and-forth with motherly love. Picking up one end of her apron, she wiped the tear-stained little face.

People who witnessed the miracle crowded around Thomas with many questions.

"How did you know what to do?"

"Where did you get such an idea?"

From the young girls he heard, "Oh, Thomas, you are wonderful."

Thomas remembered looking at each person's face. All these people, who always laughed at his family for trying to better themselves, were now praising him. Thomas stood tall and said, "I read it." He watched as they nodded their approval. Each person took a turn patting him on the back, telling him what a hero he was. Milling about, the crowd fell into small groups re-telling their own perspectives of the miracle.

Emily's mother came forward and awkwardly put her arms around Thomas. Thomas suddenly felt very tired. Tears began to well up. His throat felt kind of funny, so he kept swallowing. That helped to keep him from crying, but nothing could stop him from shaking. He gave the child's mother a weak smile which told her he understood her gratitude. Then he turned and sat on the riverbank to recover. Bailey followed his friend.

"Thomas. Are you all right?"

"Thomas." "Yes, Bailey, I'm all right."

Thomas was contemplating the swirling water, which just a few minutes ago almost murdered an innocent little girl.

"You know, Bailey, I could be a doctor."

"What you sayin'?"

"In one of the books I read, it said that to be a good doctor, you had to be unafraid to try everything until there was no hope. I know I can do that!"

Bailey gave Thomas a look of an experienced skeptic.

"Oh, sure, you have all the money in the world to live on while you learn from the White doctors."

He laughed at the idea.

"You really somethin', Tom, you know that?"

"I'll get the money."

"Family gonna help you," taunted Bailey.

"They will."

"I'll help you, Thomas."

"You?"

"I don't tell anybody about it, but I got some money saved." Bailey looked proud. He grinned, "Worked hard, got fifty dollars. You can have it, Tom. You smart. You can do it. I'll take it out in trade."

He slapped both knees with both hands at the joke he had heard many times but never really understood.

"At that moment, Thomas made a decision which would serve him well the rest of his life.

"If I'm ever going to be somebody, then I'm gonna take all the help I can get. Nobody is going to be important. Only me. Someday, I'll pay you back."

As Thomas reached the steps of the clinic, his bare feet slowly turned back into black boots. Thomas would always regret that Bailey died before he could pay back the money he owed him. Doctors cannot fix all accidents.

When Thomas opened the door, he found the place in turmoil. The men who fought the fire were now fighting coughing spells, eye irritations, and burns. Thomas put more wood in the center stove and set about starting work. Sarah noticed how dejected he looked.

"What was the problem, Doctor?"

He had to talk to someone. Dear, sweet Sarah. He wondered if he should he tell her. Thomas pulled Sarah aside.

"I'm trying to keep my head on straight, Sarah. Mamma and Pappa are dead."

Thomas held Sarah's hand as she recoiled, "But what's worse, I'm lying to the whole family telling them I can help them. Oh, God! I can't do anything for them. It's that intestinal germ. I even went so far as to tell them I would get some medicine from the hospital. Missus Rogers is with them. I am convinced that this thing is not contagious. However, I'm not taking any chances with ignorant people who might blame the virus for an illness."

"Oh, Thomas, is there anything I can do?"

"Let's get cleared away here. I told Clarabelle you might help her. Was that all right?"

"Yes. Let's hurry and get these men doctored up and perhaps we both can look in on them."

As Thomas worked feverishly to help the stricken men, he tried to think of what to do for Clarabelle and the children. When the clinic cleared out, Thomas and Sarah sat down with a cup of coffee.

"I guess you have no news about how the fire is going or you would have mentioned it by now."

Sarah shook her head.

"I don't know how to tell Jackson. You know how devoted to Mamma he was. Poor Pappa, he didn't even have a chance. He had been so frail lately. I'm so frustrated. I don't know where to turn."

Thomas crumpled in his chair.

"My God! Do you realize they are all going to die? Poor Jackson."

"Thomas. What can I say?"

"Nothing. You are here. I'm so grateful to you," Thomas hesitated.

"Uh, you know I care about you. I have been a fool. I know you heard about me and Feona. I'm ashamed of the way I treated her. I never cared for her the way I care for you. Will you forgive me and think about us?"

Thomas leaned closer to her.

"The fire, the dreadful germ eating away at Clarabelle and the children, have made me realize how little time we all have to enjoy life."

"Dear Thomas." Sarah reached for his hand. They both sat quietly looking into each other's eyes. The moment was broken when two men came in with cuts and bruises. Sarah got up to tend to them. Thomas watched her with great admiration.

When she returned to the table and her coffee, he continued. "I came to the house and found Jackson. He is extremely sick. No, I guess I should say he is exhausted. I took him to the parsonage. He will sleep for a long while."

"You found Jackson! Does he know about the situation?"

"No, he doesn't know anything yet. I don't know how I'm going to tell him. He's going to lose his whole family and I can't do anything about it."

He raised his voice, "I'm going crazy trying to think of something that would work on that damn bacteria."

"Hush, Tom, they'll hear you," Sarah cautioned. You're so tired, why don't you go in the back room and lie down for a while. If anything comes up that I can't handle, I'll come for you. Please, Tom."

"No, Sarah, I can do this. He rolled up his sleeves, washed his hands, put on a white coat, and took care of the patients as they came in. He was not only a good doctor, but he had a great sense of humor and made each patient feel better just by talking to them. Most of the men went back to fighting the fire. Thomas did his best even though he did not know if he was to be reimbursed for all his efforts. What was the difference? He never had been paid much even though he was considered one of the best doctors by all the medical hierarchy of Baltimore.

When the clinic cleared out, Thomas finally did go to the back room. Sarah smiled at him showing her approval. He tried laying down for a while, but he just couldn't relax. His mind kept working. He tried to get into a comfortable position. Finally, he gave up.

"Sarah!"

Sarah rushed into the room.

"Yes, Tom."

"Sarah, I just can't lay here. I keep thinking about Clarabelle and the children. You send Ella for her brother if you get a bad burn patient. That's what I would do anyway."

Seeing Sarah's troubled look, he quickly added, "I'll be all right. I'm going where I'm needed. I'll tend to the family."

Grabbing his topcoat, he bolted out the door. He slid into the driver's seat and buttoned his coat. As he was about to start the car, he changed his mind.

"Nothing I can do for the family. Mamma's friend, Missus Rogers took care to see that Mamma and Pappa were taken to the funeral parlor. Thomas knew she would stay with Clarabelle until the end came. India must have taken Nola to her house. And where was William? Thomas decided William must be getting food down to where the firemen were.

He was most concerned about Jackson now. How was he going to cope with losing his family? Remembering his own depression after his family were interned, he started to think how he could help Jackson get over this. Best he check-up on Jackson now. The motor sounded very loud in the cold dawn.

# VII

Jackson awoke with a start, his mind a complete blank. He could hardly move his legs, his groin ached, and his head felt like a throbbing machine. He ran his tongue over his teeth. They felt like rocks with moss growing over them. The taste in his mouth was awful. The ceiling was unfamiliar. He pulled up his left arm and rested on his elbow. With swollen eyes, he took in the strange room. He knew where he was but why was it so quiet? Where was everybody? Although he was very calm, he had a terrible feeling all was not going well with Clarabelle.

How long had he slept? Where was Thomas? Jackson cautiously pulled his legs out of the covers and stepped on a soft rug. He looked at the beautiful colors. Such a strange feeling stepping on a soft rug. The rug in his bedroom had no pad under it and the design had turned to a gray, mud color many years ago. Deliberately, he made himself stretch and move. Jackson felt his feet and knew that shoes were out of the question. He sat on the edge of the bed staring at the fascinating colors. It all came rushing back to him. The fire, the hours of hard work trying to quell the flames, the cold wind, Thomas helping him out of the car. Worst of all, the pain of not being able to be with Clara, Oliver, Clarabelle, and his sweet baby. Jackson remembered pleading with Thomas...

"Please let me at least see Clarabelle... let her know how much I love her and the children. Tell her I will pray for this to pass. I promise I won't go near them."

"No, Jackson, we have to be practical, whether we like it or not. If Clarabelle... er ...if Clarabelle ah..."

"If Clarabelle dies, damn it!" Jackson shouted at his brother. "Say it!"

"Try to be calm. Please! I'm doing the best I can. You know that."

Jackson hid his tortured face in his hands. He was softly praying. Thomas stopped the car at the parsonage.

"We're here." Jackson looked up. Ashes were still clinging to his face. His tears made a clean furrow as they came down his cheeks. With a smile, Thomas chided Jackson, "When we get in there, please take a bath. Nobody can see what you look like with all that dirt on you."

Jackson smiled weakly, "You think I can see her soon? And the children, too?"

"Sure," Thomas answered reassuringly, "as soon as you rest, eat something and for heaven's sake, shave and get clean."

Then things began to get muddled up in Jackson's mind. Something or someone was talking, but what was it all about?

Vaguely Jackson remembered being put to bed. He had tossed and turned restlessly, trying to get comfortable. There were voices in the hall. The Reverend was talking to someone. Jackson knew that voice. Henry White was pressing the Reverend to help him. Henry? What was his problem? Jackson began to make out the words.

"She always comin' on to me, Reverend. I always liked Clarabelle, but I didn't start this thing goin', she did."

The reverend's voice was pontifical, "Don't blame Clarabelle Freeman for something you were only too willing to participate in, Henry. You are both sinning in the face of the Lord and you must stop it now. When Doctor Tom called me about taking Jackson in, I did not ask what was wrong with Clarabelle. All I know is that Winona and Winfield have died, the children are sick, and Clarabelle is not able to take care of them. No one knows if this sickness is contagious or not. We are taking no chances. That's all."

"Oh, my God! Dear sweet Jesus, please help me!"

There was more murmuring, then the slam of the front door. Jackson tried to understand what he had just heard but his exhausted body finally gave up and blessed sleep took over.

Jackson tried to remember more of that night, but it just made his head swim. Clarabelle. How could she love Henry? He must be mistaken. Surely his mind was playing tricks on him.

Finding a bowl of clean water, Jackson shaved and washed his face. He cleaned the razor, but what about the beautiful bowl holding the dirty water? He would have to leave it. There was a pattering of footsteps in the hall and a soft knock at the door.

"I thought I heard you get up," a singsong voice drifted through the door.

"Is there anything you need? Fresh clothes for you on the chair, Mister Freeman."

Jackson felt silly asking.

"Would you tell me where I am?"

He looked at the robe he was wearing, "Please come in."

A brisk young lady entered, "You're at the parsonage. The reverend put you in his room. I'm Thelma Reeves. I've been looking in on you. Your brother, Doctor Thomas, is very worried about you. But don't you worry, I'll get word to your family... er... your brother, and he'll be here right away. He stops in every day, you know."

"Every day? How long have I been here?"

"Two days, Mister Freeman."

"My family, do you know how they are?" Jackson pleaded.

"Doctor Thomas had been treating them, as you know. Why don't we wait until we see him? He'll be able to give you the latest news when he comes. Oh, I'm sure everything will be better by today."

Jackson brightened, "You think so?"

Miss Reeves adjusted her glasses and in a soothing voice said, "Things have a way of looking better in the morning. Now, why don't you come downstairs and have some breakfast? By the time you are through eating, Doctor Thomas will be here, and we'll know more."

Following Miss Reeves down the stairs on his swollen feet, holding his shoes in one hand and holding the banister with the other, Jackson gingerly took the steps carefully. It helped to lean on the railing. His eyes were still burning a little and as he looked down into the living room, the walls began to ebb and flow. He descended slowly, letting Miss Reeves lead him into a lovely dining room where he gratefully sank into the chair she pulled out for him.

"I'll be right back," she said cheerfully.

Jackson stared at the lovely tablecloth. The design seemed to move. He did not have a handkerchief to wipe his eyes. Jackson looked around to see if anyone would see him. He was alone. He picked up a napkin and wiped his eyes. Leaning back in the chair, Jackson began remembering again. Clarabelle and Henry White! Why? He thought back to the first time she allowed him to make love to her after the baby was born. Even though his desire for her was more than he could stand, he was sure he had been careful with her. She certainly didn't want that first encounter, he recalled. Perhaps that would be the last time he would make love to her.

Jackson rose slowly from his chair.

"She's dead," he said out loud to himself.

Where did that thought come from? He sat down.

Again. "She's dead."

Miss Reeves swooped into the room with a tray of bacon, eggs, grits, toast, and the wonderful smell of coffee emanating from a beautiful china cup. Almost singing she said, "Here we are." She set the food in front of Jackson. Slowly he began to eat but nothing tasted good. He just knew he should eat something to keep up his strength. Besides, Miss Reeves was good enough to make such a wonderful meal.

"Thank you, ma'am," he said quietly.

Miss Reeves smiled.

"Why, you're welcome. Now, I'll go get you a glass of water. I'll be back."

Jackson smiled at her.

"That's better."

She turned and disappeared again.

Jackson picked at his food. His mouth still had the taste of smoke. Miss Reeves pushed the kitchen door open and bent forward into the room.

"Just checking up on you. How are we doing?" she asked as she brought Jackson a glass of water. Setting it down on the table, she noticed Jackson had not eaten much.

"Well now, we can do better than that."

Jackson began to resent her patronizing manner.

"Doctor Thomas said you must eat," she continued, "to get back on your feet, so to speak. Doctor's orders, you know."

"Oh, please, Miss Reeves, I'm very tired. The food is delicious. It's just that I'm going at a slow pace."

He faked a smile. She stood over him and waited. Jackson was too tired to make any more excuses. As he ate, he did begin to feel better and said so. She smiled and went back to the kitchen. Looking around, Jackson felt like such a failure. Here in this beautiful house was color, space, and dignity. He had been here before, but the house had been filled with a lot of people and besides, Jackson had never been interested in what a house looked like. This is what he did not give Clarabelle.

Where was Thomas? When would he come? Jackson was becoming nervous about not knowing what the prognosis of the family was. He could wait no longer. He pushed back his chair, pulled the napkin off his lap, neatly placed it next to the plate of half-eaten food, and stood up. He did not feel too shaky, so he reached for the coffee, which was the right temperature now. Enjoying the black elixir, he drank it down to the last drop.

Jackson squeezed his eyes shut and pushed his feet in the shoes he had put by his chair.

"Miss Reeves!" he called out. She came quickly into the room.

"More coffee, Mister Freeman?"

"No, thank you ma'am. I thank you for the breakfast, but I'll have to leave now. Would you be so kind as to show me where my coat is? Oh, and will you please tell my brother I went home?"

Miss Reeves didn't respond like the patronizing nurse she had been all morning.

"Mister Freeman! I am to take care of you until Doctor Thomas returns for you. You are to wait for him and anyway, you can't enter the house. Not now. The law doesn't allow that. If you won't eat any more, then please sit in the living room. The fire will keep you warm. I've sent for your brother and he..." The sound of the doctor's car stopped her remonstration.

Jackson limped to the front door and opened it. Thomas lifted a hand to stop Jackson, "Stay inside, Jackson." He ran through the door to escape the old weather. As he entered the house, he cautioned Jackson, "Stay inside. You are too rundown to be out there without a coat."

Jackson did shudder from the cold as Thomas shut the door. Thomas put his topcoat over Jackson's shoulders.

"You look awful. You must..."

"Stop it!"

Jackson faced his brother square on.

"Thomas, for God's sake, tell me about Clarabelle and the children, and how are Mamma and Pappa?"

Miss Reeves made a quick return to the kitchen side of the swinging doors, leaving the men to themselves.

"Jackson, take it easy! I don't think you know how ill you are. Over here," Thomas led him to the fireplace in the living room, "sit down. You're ready to collapse."

Jackson and Thomas sat in the large armchairs and faced one another. The embers were low, but Jackson felt enough warmth to shrug Thomas' coat off his shoulders.

"Jackson," Thomas began to deliver his words very carefully. "When you first came to the house, Mamma and Pappa had already died."

He watched Jackson's face turn to stone.

"I knew you were too ill to tell you the true conditions as they were. I had to bide my time."

Jackson looked crushed.

"Clarabelle and the children?"

Thomas tried to keep the conversation as professional as he could, but this was his brother. He rested his arm on one knee as he leaned forward to tell the truth about the rest of the family. He tried to speak but could not find the words. His eyes welled up with tears. He could no longer pose as the indifferent doctor talking to his patient. The man who owed so much to his older brother could stand the tragic turn this sickness had taken no longer. Thomas covered his face with both hands and sobbed. Jackson stared at Thomas.

"All dead?" he asked softly.

Thomas lifted his head. He just nodded.

"All dead," he repeated.

Jackson started to get up but felt faint. He sat back down, falling against the back of the chair. Thomas got hold of himself. He wanted to comfort Jackson but did not know how. He had cursed the fact he couldn't save his own loved ones. He had cried until Sarah became worried about him. The Freeman family rallied around him. Thomas remembered how Sarah helped him get over his grief. Now, he was watching Jackson go through the same horror. Jackson stared at the floor. He looked so placid that it frightened Thomas.

"Jackson?"

"Did they suffer?"

"No, you remember how it was with my family. They went into a coma and really, Jackson, they slept away. Mamma took care of little Clarissa as long as she could. She was a strong woman."

Thomas had to stop to get hold of himself.

"Then she just gave up. Clarabelle slept away and honestly, Jackson, I thought I could save Clara and Oliver but... but there is nothing that can stop this germ. Isn't it ironic? You and I don't know what the hell it is or even if it is contagious. We don't think it is because there hasn't been an outbreak. We're at a standstill."

Thomas noticed Jackson wasn't listening anymore. He just could not comprehend the magnitude of his situation. All life seemed to go out of him. He leaned back in his chair and tried to absorb the enormity of the news. Thomas reached out and touched Jackson's knee. "Please stay with me tonight.

Jackson came to life.

"Oh, no, Thomas. I must make arrangements for the funerals. You'll help me, won't you?"

"Jackson, they are already interred. Just like we buried my family. Remember? You and I were the only ones at the cemetery because we didn't know if the germ was contagious. Jackson! What's wrong?"

Jackson rose from the chair, his eyes opened wide with the look of a frightened stallion. Lifting his chin high, he summoned his Savior.

"Dear, sweet Jesus, where are you? Who shall I pray to now?"

Reaching around Jackson, Thomas picked up his coat. He spoke to Jackson with an authoritative voice

"Please come home with me right now."

Jackson slowly dropped his chin and since he did not know what else to do, he let Thomas lead him to the door.

"Is Baltimore still burning?" Jackson asked vaguely.

Putting on his coat, Thomas began reciting the damage. "Well, you know, looking from Lombard you can see O'Neill's on the left, you see Union on the right. Then, left of City Hall are the B&O buildings, the

Equitable Building. Well, they are all gone. At Baltimore and Calvary Streets to the right is Maryland Trust & Continental Trust. To make a long story short, over one hundred acres and over one thousand buildings destroyed. Twenty-five hundred businesses are lost. The Baltimore Herald was printed by the Washington Post 'cause all the Baltimore papers were burned out. The Herald building was the last to go. Philadelphia also helped to publish the Herald. Jackson, the fire was still burning when the people started plans to repair the damage."

"How far did the fire get?"

"They stopped it at Jones Falls."

Jackson stopped.

"That's when I started for home. I had this terrible feeling something was very wrong."

Jackson waited while Thomas took his coat out of the closet. Someone had tried to clean the ashes of the great Baltimore fire from the coat. Remembering the holocaust downtown, Jackson asked Thomas, "How many people died in the fire?"

"Not a one, Jackson, not a one."

The men were silent as Thomas helped Jackson with his coat. Thomas opened the door. The two brothers hunched their shoulders against the wind and left the parsonage. Thomas slowly closed the door behind them.

Thelma Reeves leaned against the kitchen door and cried softly.

# VIII

Jackson pulled the strip of paper away and slowly opened the weather-beaten door. It creaked. He made a mental note to oil the hinges. The cold wind came inside with him. The rooms were already almost to the freezing point. Jackson quickly closed the windows. He ran upstairs to get those windows closed as soon as possible. The disinfecting smell was still there. He stood in the hall. From there, he could see all three bedrooms. He and Thomas shared the big room, William had the smallest and Mamma and Pappa slept in the room with the largest closet. The brothers had all been born on that old bed. Jackson went downstairs. The eyes on the pictures of relatives followed him all the way down.

The house looked like nobody loved it anymore. How clean it was. No magazines or newspapers. Pappa was always reading something. Jackson began to remember. How did it go? Every room had to be scrubbed. Every piece of furniture, drawers, all the cupboards, floors and woodwork had to be scrubbed clean with soft soap and hot water. All the windows, doors and crevices had to be covered with strips of paper over them. Yes, there on the table, was the metal dish placed in the shallow baking pan Mamma used so often. Rock sulfur, about a quarter of a pound to every hundred cubic feet of air, had been placed inside the metal dish and broken up. A little methylated spirit was poured on it and lit. It was important to make sure the sulfur would begin to burn. The room would then be closed with paper pasted all around the openings, even stopping up the keyhole. It was to be left this way for twelve hours. Jackson surmised the house had been left this way for three days. There was a reason Thomas went through all this. Who would buy a house that had not been disinfected?

Little pieces of childhood came back to Jackson. Mamma holding him while talking to a checkered suited salesman at the door. Mama fanning herself on the porch. Pappa kissing her when he came home from work and Mamma telling him not to do that in front of the children.

There were some strips of rags draped over the chandelier. Jackson began pulling them down. They had the smell of chloride. Suddenly, Jackson needed fresh air and started toward the door. Before he could open it, he heard a soft knock. Mrs. Rogers asked, "You in there, Jackson?"

Jackson quickly opened the door. "Mrs. Rogers. Thank you for comin'. I've been wanting to see you." He embraced her. "You have been such a good sister to Mamma. Always doing for her when you could. I can't thank you enough for helping Thomas with the family. Not many people would have tended them thinking they might become infected."

She patted Jackson's arm.

"No more than she did for me."

Mrs. Rogers airily dismissed the thought of infection. "Thomas said it would be all right. That was enough for me."

"I wish he would have let me help."

"You were too sick, Jackson, don't you see that? My goodness, you might have been more of a burden here. This way you were able to recuperate at the parsonage."

"I wish I had tried harder with Oliver. Clara was so bright, so quick to learn. I guess I expected too much of the boy." Jackson smiled, thinking about Clara. She had been his favorite child.

"With Oliver, it was always dissension and a lot of arguing about stupid little things. You know, Pappa told me it was like that between father and son, 'cause the boy had to grow up to a lot of responsibilities."

"You did just fine, Jackson. You were a good father and you were a good husband."

Mrs. Rogers did not reveal to Jackson she knew about Clarabelle's infidelity.

"Thomas, William, and I want you to take any household goods you want. You are welcome to them"

"Why yes, I would like some things. But don't be too hasty, you don't know what the family would like."

Jackson chuckled, "We know India wouldn't want anything here. You see, I'm thinking of leaving the city."

Mrs. Rogers brightened.

"Along with some household goods, may I have Nola? I am so afraid Doctor Tom will think she would be better off in an institution."

"No, I think Thomas can handle her. He has taken Ella Hanson to do some chores for him. She is learning fast. Maybe he can do the same for Nola. The two girls may be good for one another."

"Oh, no, Jackson," Mrs. Rogers disagreed. "No, please let me take her. She knows me... trusts me. I'm all alone now that your mother is gone. I don't know what I'll do without your Mamma. Let me take Nola. She will be a comfort to me. She is sweet, you know. I'll have someone to care for and someone to do for. You understand, don't you?"

Jackson thought awhile.

"I would agree with you right away, but I think I had better consult with William and Thomas."

Mrs. Rogers tilted her head.

"I'm sure they will agree, too," he added.

"You're so kind, I'm sure Nola would be happier with you than with anyone else. We'll see to it you have enough money to take care of her needs."

"Mrs. Rogers hugged Jackson.

"Don't leave your brothers.," she pleaded. "They'll miss you. Think on it."

"I'll miss everybody, too. Look, I know we, who are Colored, are treated very well in Baltimore. I know I will have difficulties I'm not used to... there are places we are not welcome. I'll have to feel my way around." H

e looked into her sad eyes.

"You see, Mrs. Rogers, in my heart of hearts I have always wanted to be independent. Farming would do that for me. I knew Clarabelle wouldn't want to live on a farm. I don't blame her. You must have a liking for that kind of living. Being on a farm is hard on a woman."

Mrs. Rogers nodded in agreement.

"I won't be far. Just out of the city. And I won't be alone. I have a friend who feels exactly the way I do. He and I have always wanted to pool our resources and be independent. Believe me, I won't be alone."

He kissed her on her cheek. She went to the door, turned, and smiled, "Good Luck, Jackson."

"Thank you."

After she closed the door, Jackson felt elated. She was the first person he had told he wanted to be a farmer. She did not laugh. Baltimore would need workers to rebuild her. He would make a lot of money, save every penny, and fulfill the dream he and Carl Schimmer had shared for such a long time.

They envisioned wagons going to cities in the wintertime filled with fruit and vegetables. They would make large profits since cities need fresh foodstuffs during cold seasons. Carl had been playing with automobiles but surely now he would be ready to partner with him in tilling the soil. He would call on Carl tomorrow.

# IX

Head held high and spirits soaring with the confidence that his decision was the right one, Jackson approached the fence almost defying anyone to stop him. No one did. As he lifted his elbow to lean on one of the main fence posts, he could smell the thrice-worn shirt Clarabelle would have ripped off his back before allowing him to wear in its condition this hot August morning. Jackson narrowed his eyes at the scene before him and became aware of a different odor coming from the lean-to by the muddy ditch. It sickened him. How did Carl stand it? The air wafting oil, grease, and gasoline from the vicinity of the temporary fix-it shop began to anger Jackson. He pulled his chin down and spit. Still there was the taste of gasoline in his mouth just from the smelling of it.

"My shirt smells better than that mess," Jackson thought.

Looking up from his work, Carl spotted his friend. He let go a big smile as he openly waved to his Colored friend. Then, noticing Jackson's eyes looked like smoldering black coals, Carl threw his work aside and hastily walked toward the fencepost. He was sweating. Stick-straight, greasy, sandy-colored hair that defied scissors and comb clung to his flat forehead in clumps. He had a very heavy gait. His heels coming down hard with every step and his arms hanging loosely at his sides lent an odd rhythm to his walk.

Jackson's face softened as his good-natured friend approached him. Looking deep into each other's eyes, the men realized it was time to make a decision about the dream they had shared since childhood. Carl glanced over his shoulder to indicate the messy rubble that comprised the makeshift fix-it shop.

"Vhot you tink, Jackson?"

Jackson's chin started to come up. Carl knew that gesture well. When

Jackson pulled up his chin high, it gave the impression his eyes were looking down at his opponent. That was the start of an attack... verbal or physical. Carl began to talk fast.

"Jackson, come look at vhot I done."

He opened the gate and gestured with both hands as if holding a platter.

"This is all mine now. You also can learn all about automobile fixing and vee get rich together. Chust put some of your money to this business and you vill see."

Jackson was silent.

"Jackson," Carl's voice took on a strange high intonation, as if he did not want to convince his friend.

"Tink about it. Vot you vant vit a farm?"

"Didn't you tell me people always need food in the cities?"

"I haf shifted gears."

Carl laughed at his own joke. Jackson did not laugh. This was too important to him.

"See," Carl continued, "People vill haf their own cars and vill go to farms for a Sunday ride. They vill buy food from the farmer. Oh! Not out in the open," Carl's voice became louder, "und not on de Sabbot."

Carl cocked his head and shook his index finger side to side. He stifled laughter.

"No, but in the back," he flung his fat, greasy thumb over his shoulder.

"The farmers vill not care if it is Sunday. They vill sell for money. They vill sell!"

Carl nodded his head affirmatively and thumped his friend's chest.

"And they vill need me to fix automobile."

Carl became uncomfortable at the look Jackson gave him, so he hurriedly added, "you unt me... fix automobile."

"I don't know anything about fixing automobiles."

Jackson was pleading.

"You told me you were going to teach me all about farming. I don't know anything about fixing anything. I do know a little bit about farming."

"I teach you farming; I teach you automobile fixing. Vhot's the difference?"

Carl shifted his weight

"This is new business unt not everyone knows how to make engines verk. Pretty soon no more horses."

That said, he hitched his ill-fitting trousers and to avoid Jackson's eyes, leaned back and placed both elbows on the top rail, surveying the sky and flicking a suspender.

Jackson, who had been very still until now, slowly straightened up and took two steps away from the fence. He indicated to the people going about their daily tasks.

"Who can buy them? Who can buy the automobile? You see anybody buying automobiles?"

Sounding as if he was trying to convince his friend, Carl's voice became very confidential.

"All it takes is von man buying automobile. Pretty soon, another man gets jealous. He buys automobile. Then, voman says..." Carl's whole face lit up, "Look at that! I vant vee should have car, too!"

He laughed heartily and poked Jackson hard in the shoulder.

"You come in vit me? Your money vill buy tools."

Carl's voice trailed away. He was hoping Jackson would insist on the farm.

Jackson heard the implication. Why did he have the feeling Carl was pushing too hard? Maybe Carl was right, after all. He was about to suggest he think things over when he was rudely awakened.

"All right Jackson, I tell you the truth. Already I haf a partner. I vasn't going to tell you for avile. I take in Hans."

Jackson quickly looked at the shop and, sure enough, there was Hans pretending to work but intently watching the two men. Jackson looked at Carl, who began to blurt everything out.

"I don't know. You see, people tell me that your kind of people don't... you know...catch on to tings?"

For a moment, their eyes met. Then, trying to explain the turn of events, Carl began to make Jackson see the logic of why he asked Hans to be his partner.

"Hans is not goot for fixing tings, but he has goot salesman pitch. People, they like him. He vill be goot for business." Carl, who had been pacing back and forth, now stopped to confront his friend. He was not prepared for the expression of disbelief on Jackson's face.

"Don't look at me like that. I know you for the long time. I know you vouldn't vant to fix automobiles. Vy? I don't know vy."

Carl threw his arms up in the air, "I don't know vy you vouldn't vant inside verk. Can stop ven vant."

Carl expected to see the chin come up.

"Jackson... please..."

Jackson was looking past Carl at the rundown shack that was Carl's dream. Well, who was he to stop Carl from his dream?

"It's all right, Carl."

His voice cracked a little. He tried but he couldn't keep his resentment and disappointment from showing.

"You'll be better off without me. A Colored man is a hindrance. I was hoping to be a silent partner, but..."

"Jackson!"

Carl was beside himself. He didn't mean to hurt Jackson so much.

"It just happened!" he said weakly.

"Oh, I know you don't feel that way about me, Carl. But you know other people will."

Trying to be jaunty about the whole thing, Jackson stood tall, cocked his head to one side, and said, "Why, everybody would have thought I was your servant. I thought a lot about that, too, you know."

Jackson squared his shoulders imperceptibly.

"I'll have to think about what I'm going to do."

The two men locked eyes again. Jackson started to leave. He stopped, turned around, and said, "Oh, Carl, if ever I need a job…"

Then he smiled, revealing his beautiful white teeth, but somehow the smile never reached his eyes.

Carl's eyes welled up with tears.

"Sure! Sure!"

He would have said more but he just couldn't think of anything that would have vindicated his actions. Carl leaned on the main post of the fence and watched his good friend of many years walk out of his life. Slowly, he became aware of the strong smell of gasoline coming from his soiled shirt.

# X

This morning, sitting in his brother's office with a big, cheery smile, Jackson was back to his good-natured self. He had indulged in a good haircut and he could still smell the lavender when he turned his head. Thomas was hard-put to read Jackson's emotional state. Jackson was up to something, that was for sure. Thomas leaned back in his chair, locking his fingers across his stomach in his best professional manner and smiled back at Jackson.

"You lookin' mighty smug, Jackson."

"I've made a big decision, Thomas. I'm going to seek my fortune," Jackson said facetiously.

"Do what? You mean, go away?"

Thomas couldn't believe his ears.

"You mean leave the family?"

"Yes, leave the family."

Thomas leaned forward, "You can't mean that! We all need to stick together. Help one another. And I was hoping you would keep taking care of Nola. She's not much bother, easy to please, what's more, she likes you. Nola sees my white coat and she shies away from me."

Thomas would have had more arguments as to why Jackson should care for Nola, but Jackson raised his hand to stop the flow of words.

"Thomas, I have some money. Not much. Enough to do some traveling. I see I'm not going to make it here in Baltimore. I'm an old man now. Not that I feel old, I don't. But if I'm ever going to do what I want to do, I had better do it now." Jackson watched his brother's face to see if he understood. Thomas was listening hard.

"I cleaned up the downtown area and made a good amount of money wallowing in the ashes. After that... I'll be right back where I started, looking for work every day. I'll be back doing nothing, being nobody, taking care of Nola. Oh, about Nola. Mrs. Rogers wants to take her. Now, she is someone Nola loves and trusts. I gave Mrs. Rogers enough money to feed and care for Nola for about two months. She is already making plans to sew her some new clothes. I was hoping you would see to it that Nola had family around her as often as possible and see to it she is included during holiday seasons. I mean, a week or two at a time. Then Mrs. Rogers won't be encumbered at holiday times. Also, it wouldn't hurt for India to help keep her for a while during those times."

Jackson's face lit up as he pictured the fashionable India taking care of Nola. It was catching. Thomas also smiled at that.

Silence descended in the room. The two handsome men looked fondly at one another. "I understand," Thomas softly said.

Thomas was everything women looked for in a man. Light-skinned, tall, an educated man with professional status and impeccable manners. Jackson, on the other hand, was short, dark, and heavy-boned in the face. Yet, he was the epitome of manhood. Jackson pulled his earlobe. He was a little embarrassed. His brother was so successful and he, who never had the education Thomas had, felt like a loser. If only he could have had the chance Thomas had... but that time had passed. Everyone in the family gave their effort to educating Thomas. Then it was William's turn. Somehow it never occurred to them that Jackson needed help, too. Perhaps it was his easygoing nature that promoted that feeling.

Jackson got up, "Well, I..."

Thomas jumped out of his chair and walked around the desk, "You leaving now?"

There was a slight tremor in his voice.

"Yup, I'm all packed. I hope to get a ticket to as far I can go and still have enough money left over to live off until I find work. I think I'll aim for Ohio. I hear there are farming jobs there."

"Farming?"

Thomas was surprised.

"I never heard you talk about farming."

"Did you ever think I had any ambition?"

Thomas thought awhile. Softly, he said, "No, I never thought about it at all. I just assumed you were happy where you were. Oh, how self-centered I am. It's just that..."

"It's just that it never came up, Tom. Why would it? You tried to pay me back as much as you could while trying to help William. I know you're not paid what you deserve to be paid." Jackson extended his hand. Thomas shook it, then drew his brother close and gave him a hug.

"Remember, if you need anything, there is Western Union."

Jackson gave Thomas a wry smile.

"I don't know when I'll see you again, but I'll tell you this. If I don't do well, I'll be back. I'll write. You keep in touch, too. Somehow, I have a feeling I'm doing the right thing."

"If I'm not prying too much, you have enough money? I certainly can give you some money."

"With what I sold, after paying the bills I had close to one hundred dollars. Mmmm, about eighty-five now. You know, Thomas, I've never been this rich before and I've never been this poor before." Jackson raised his chin. He was in good fighting form.

Thomas watched Jackson go down the stairs and out in the street. Then he was gone.

"God be with you, Jackson."

Jackson stood outside Thomas' office and scanned the skeleton that once was downtown Baltimore. One last look, a deep breath, then gripping his satchel, he started for the train station. Jackson waited for the White people in the line. When he got to the counter, he put a small amount of money through the slot under the window. The man behind the counter leaned forward.

"How far will this get me?" Jackson asked.

The old clerk looked over his glasses, "The next train will be here in fifteen minutes and will leave in fifteen more. This amount will take you to Pleasant Falls. But don't you believe it. You won't like it. It's a burgh."

Jackson laughed, "It's all right. I want to get a job on a farm."

"Whaat! There are all kinds of jobs re-building Baltimore. You'll make more money here than you would working on a farm."

"But I won't learn how to farm. Thanks for the advice anyway."

Jackson carefully put his ticket in his shirt pocket so he could get it quickly when the conductor came by. The sound of the train's engine quickened Jackson's heart. He was actually doing what he wanted to do. As he boarded the train, his thoughts were weaving pictures in his mind between the past and the present. Taking a seat by the window, Jackson could see his neighborhood. Not far was the cemetery. Thomas' family lay there and now his family was interred close by.

Jackson became anxious to leave. He did not want to dwell on the past. The future was ahead. His heart lifted when the train started to leave. Jackson held on to his small satchel. All his worldly possessions were in that old bag. As the train gained speed, the blur of the city turned into fields and evergreen trees. Jackson began to have misgivings. Perhaps he should have stayed closer to Baltimore. The train jerked around the bend. The die was cast.

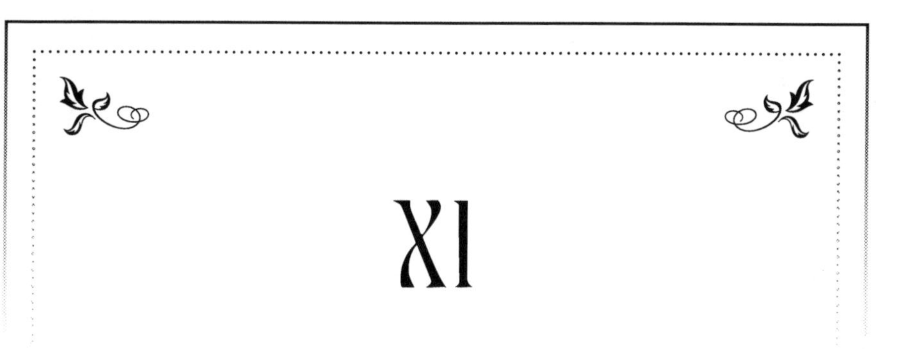

# XI

Anna, covered with shawls, stood in the doorway of her dreary home. She folded her arms across her ample breasts and leaned against the frame. The wind coming into the house made the fire flicker, lighting up her dour face. The cold night air had carried the sound of wagon wheels for quite some time. Anna didn't want company, tonight or any other night. She had been stewing in the predicament of her own making. There was medicine which might have been helpful to Willie, but Anna had not given it to him. He was too far gone anyway, Anna rationalized. Pneumonia was the doctor's pronouncement on the death certificate. Anyway, it was all over. She had the best farm in the whole territory, and she meant to make a go of it. But how? She was a good farmer, she knew that. However, plowing, sowing, and harvesting all that land... She was beginning to get nervous about the coming spring.

The wagon was close now. Anna could make out two exceptionally large horses, probably Belgians. She stood like a stone statue, listening, unsmiling and stoic; her empty eyes followed the dark shadows turning into her farmyard. The creaking sounds of the large wagon stopped and Keith skillfully jumped off. Anna could make out three men. It worried her that she was alone but there was nothing to do except wait and see what they wanted. She would have been more apprehensive had she known Jackson was sitting in back of the wagon. Four men at this time of the night was more of a worry. Anna caressed the gun she held under her wraps and stood straight to meet them. Even when she recognized the figure lumbering toward the porch, her expression never changed. She had been alone from February to this cold September. The depression she felt was not easily overcome.

"Ho there, Anna!" Keith called out.

Anna made no move, nor did she answer his cheerful call, so Keith, coming closer, tried to find a spot of light that would announce to Anna who he was. Anna saw him all right, but she did not give Keith any indication she was ready to become hostess to three men, whether she knew them or not. Keith stepped closer to the door and said, "Anna, you remember me."

It was more of a statement than a question.

"I'm Willie's friend. In trouble tonight. I've got food to bring to Stanton and we had to fix a broken axle. Now we're too late to go on. I was hoping… Please, Anna, could we stay here for tonight? The horses have just about given up and we didn't expect the weather to be so cold. Look," he pointed to Beany, "He hasn't even got a good coat. We all thought we would be in town already. Anna, please let us stay here for tonight."

Anna had been thinking all the time Keith was talking. Come spring, she would need advice and help. Even the best farmer needs more hands than one woman working day and night. Plowing, fertilizing, seeding, and that was just the beginning. Harvesting all the produce was a big job that had to be timed exactly right. Keith had some large equipment that Willie never invested in because the two men worked the machinery together. Anna moved her head slightly as if to say it was all right to enter the house. Keith caught the gesture and was relieved.

"Oh, thank you, Anna, this is good of you."

He turned to the men who were waiting for the decision. "All right my boys, come in and don't forget to thank Anna. Jackson, you fix the horses for the night. Make sure all the produce is covered. Then you come in, too. Maybe Anna will make us some hot coffee. Hers is the best, you know," he called to Jackson so Anna would hear the compliment. All Anna heard was that there was yet another man. If it had not been so dark, Keith would have seen the flicker of apprehension on Anna's face.

Anna did not move out of the way, so Keith opened the door wider and made straight for the fire. There was much activity on the porch as the men stomped their boots clean. Removing their hats, they thanked Anna as they entered the house. Keith nodded his approval to his partners. The men moved toward the fire murmuring their delight to be in a warm room on this cold night. Beany blew his nose and received a quick look of disapproval from Keith. Anna ignored them. She waited, listening to the preparations near the barn.

"Missus…ah," Lemuel Smith dared to speak, "Jackson will be awhile out there."

The night became quiet. Anna was getting chilled, so she began to shut the door when she was startled by a black hand strongly holding the door open. For a split second, Anna lost her composure. She peered in the slit of the door. Jackson met Anna's eyes and for a moment they were both riveted.

"It's all right, Anna, he's with us. He's a good man, Anna, he's one of our partners now."

Keith was talking fast. He did not want to jeopardize the good fortune of finding a warm shelter for the night.

"He'll sleep near the fire. Won't you, Jackson?"

Jackson put on his best Colored man routine.

"O, yaz Ma'am, I'll sleep by the fire and tend it so's it won't go out."

Anna studied the frosted Black face, looking so intently at her. The light from the fire mapped the Negro features. She was repulsed by the wide nostrils watering from the cold night air. All she could see were the whites of his eyes, the outline of a triangle that was his nose and the soft, full lower lip. The rest of his head was a blur, melting into the darkness. Why was her heart beating so fast? She was not afraid of anything, let alone one Black man. Perhaps, it was one man too many, and he was a Negro at that.

Jackson's heart was beating fast, too, but not from fear of rejection; he was afraid of Anna. There was no face to this creature, only a black hole in the twisted shawl held by thick fingers of a hard-working hand. He was overcome by a premonition about this woman. Whether it was a good premonition or a bad feeling of the future, he could not make out. There was an electricity that passed between them. Jackson knew the woman felt it, too.

Anna let go of the door. Jackson sidled into the room making for the fire as the other men had done before him. Anna was aware of his silhouetted form against the fire as she made her way to the stove to make coffee. From the corner of her eye, she watched as Jackson took off his damp jacket holding it to the fire to get dry. He cut a straight figure compared to the other men. Anna never had contact with the Colored people who lived in Stanton or the village across the hill. She knew she did not like their kind. Everybody said they smelled bad. Well, could they smell any worse than Willie? Or herself, for that matter? When was the last time she had filled the tub that hung on the back porch? Anna made sure her gun was secure in her pocket before washing her hands. She decided to feed the men and make them comfortable. Surely they would go to sleep after a warm meal and a cup of coffee. She would lock herself in her bedroom. After all, she did know Keith. He seemed like a decent kind of man. Tomorrow they would be gone. It would be all right.

The men made themselves comfortable in the large kitchen. They smiled at Anna as their eyes met hers while she was busy with the preparations of bacon and eggs. Jackson watched her dark form as she crossed the room to get the coffee. Reaching for the can, Anna gave a side-glance toward Jackson and caught him staring at her. He quickly turned his head back to the fire praying this woman would be generous to Negroes. He was very hungry. Jackson saw that Keith observed the look Anna gave him. He lifted his chin a little as if to question Keith about Anna. Keith pursed his lips and shook his head affirmatively. Then, really addressing Jackson's fears, he said, "Anna, you're all right." Anna turned to Keith. "I want to introduce you to my friends. This is Beany. He don't think so good. He was kicked by a horse when he was just a tyke. He's a good man, though," he added quickly. "Good worker."

"And I sing, too."

Everybody laughed, except Anna who busied herself to keep out of the group. She wanted to keep a low profile, not wanting to be noticed much.

"And this is Lemuel Smith, one of the best farmers west of the river. Take a bow, Lem."

Lem blushed and made a small gesture with his index finger. Jackson was trying to keep a low profile, too, but Keith was in a vaudeville mood.

"And that," he gestured with a wide expanse of his arm, "is Jackson Freeman. Yessir, that's the lot of us."

Keith was feeling at home even though he knew Anna disapproved of their dropping in on her like this.

"Anna, I know Willie always had schnapps. Maybe we can have some before our repast. You know, I remembered he had some in the barn. Or, maybe there's some apple juice that has really gotten good by now. I'll go see, huh Anna?"

Anna was setting the table. She turned to confront Keith. With her hands on her hips, she answered him in a deliberate tone. "I don't think that's a good idea at all, Keith Cailern. The meal is ready, and I think you and your boys had better eat something before you drink anything stronger than my coffee."

Keith was not to be salved out of a drink before his meal. He came forward with a little jig step singing an Irish song he learned in the bars in Ireland. Trying to make Anna dance with him, he put his arm around her waist. Anna wriggled out of his grasp before he would have felt the gun in her apron pocket.

"Just a minute, Keith, I'll see if there's anything to drink in the pantry."

Before entering the walk-in pantry, Anna removed her shawls, hanging them on a peg in the closet. She pretended to rummage around as if trying to find whiskey. When she returned, Jackson saw her face for the first time.

From a distance, she was rather pretty. Her features were small. Her eyes were not cruel, as Jackson thought they would be. They were just sad. Her nose was delicate and straight. As she came closer, he noted the hard lines around a small, slightly crooked mouth, the puffs under her eyes, and the utter granite stoical countenance of the woman. She was short, but a sturdy build made her appear strong and able. A survivor. He felt an urge to make her smile. To have her enjoy the warmth of the room, the food, and the company of four men who were grateful to be in a house, sheltered from the cold night. Instead, he kept physically still and verbally quiet. He was with three men he had met only five days ago in a strange place called Stanton, Ohio.

"No whiskey," Anna announced.

"Well, that's a fine way to treat a friend," Keith complained. "Tell you what, I'll see if Willie left some of his fine whiskey in the barn."

Buttoning his coat, he said, "Oh, the times we drank together after some hard work! Not that coffee isn't good on a night like this, no sir. It's just that we need a drink before your generous meal. Isn't that right, boys?"

Lem agreed by clapping his hands.

"You see how it is, Anna!"

Yes, Anna saw how it was.

Keith was making fun of her just as everybody else had all the years she was Willie's lonely, hard-working wife.

They had a way of doing it, making her feel stupid even if she could prove she was right. These people had a gift of winning any argument. Anna used a different tactic.

"Do what you want. I'm putting food on the table now."

Much to Jackson's relief, she did just that as Keith hurried out the door. Anna filled four dishes, put them on the table, and poured coffee indicating to Beany to help her place them at each plate. Beany was delighted to be given the responsibility and gingerly held each cup carefully until they were in place. Jackson waited until Lem and Beany sat down to eat. He moved slowly toward the table. Balancing a fork on his plate, he took it to his place by the fire. It wasn't long before Keith triumphantly entered the house with two bottles of whiskey.

One bottle in each hand, he held them up in victory.

"Have a drink, boys!"

Happy at his success, he laughed as he spoke.

"Ho, ho, Anna, get some glasses. We'll be warm with drink soon. Get a glass for yourself, too. We want to toast our hostess."

Anna ignored him by putting more scrambled eggs on the table.

Beany's face lit up.

"Wow! Two bottles. Hey, look at Lem. Now, he's gonna wake up, ain'tcha Lem?"

Beany patted Lem's shoulder. Lem blushed with delight. He was not much of a talker, but he sure was a drinker. Anna took four of the smallest glasses she could find from the cupboard. "I'll help ya, missus."

Beany carried them to the table.

"Fill 'em up, Keith."

Keith had been having trouble opening the bottle, but as if on cue from Beany's command, the pop of the cork was heard. Everybody made noises of approval. Anna and Jackson pretended they were pleased. Jackson was afraid the men would be angry if he did not act happy to have a drink. He was quiet, staying close to the wall, enjoying the fire and the coffee

Anna gave him without looking at him. With a full stomach, all Jackson wanted to do was sleep.

Keith ceremoniously filled the glasses giving each person his drink. Jackson balanced his coffee on his plate to accept the whiskey he did not want. Raising his glass too close to Anna's face, Keith gave a toast.

"To Anna, our hostess."

They all drank. There were sounds of "ah" around the room.

"Oh, drink your drink and eat your food. I don't waste food around here, you know."

Anna tried to make the statement sound funny, but Keith caught the anger behind the words.

Jackson sipped the whiskey. It tasted awful. There was no way to get rid of it, so he took another sip. Keith, Beany, and Lem drained their glasses.

"Damn good whiskey, Anna. Why, Anna where's your glass? You can't have us drinking Willie's best and you not even having one drink with us, can you?"

Anna held out her coffee cup. Keith filled it up to the brim. She took a drink while Keith was looking at her.

"Here, my boys, have another."

He filled each glass again.

"Have some more, Anna. I don't like to drink when you don't. How about you, Jackson?"

Jackson gave Keith a crooked smile and held out his glass. "Oh, no you don't. You're going to be one drink behind us. You finish your drink and I'll fill your glass again, too."

Jackson was dismayed at the turn of events, but he did not want to upset Keith. He drank a little more of the powerful home-made brew. It made him cough. Keith pounded Jackson on the back.

"There, that'll make a man out of you," he said as he poured more whiskey into Jackson's empty glass. "Now, drink up." Jackson did as he was told. It went down a little smoother this time.

Jackson felt a little woozy, but he was still smart enough to watch Keith closely. He was the man to reckon with if there was to be any trouble. The subtle way Keith talked down to Anna was beginning to get Jackson angry, and the drinks were taking their effect. He made a decision.

"Say, Keith, you're missing out on a good meal here. Our hostess was truly kind to make such a nice table of food. Better eat it while it's warm."

Keith gave Jackson a quizzical look. Jackson pretended not to notice by drinking the last of his whiskey. Things were beginning to blur. He was so tired and yet he felt exhilarated. Keith poured more whiskey all the way around. Anna put her hand over the top of her cup.

"Just a little more, Anna. It'll warm you up on a night like this."

Anna, figuring she did not have to drink it, took her hand away. Keith seemed pleased about that.

Beany and Lem slowly ate a little of their meal. Beany poked Lem to get his attention.

"Did you hear the one about the niggers on a stormy night?"

Lem leaned forward, "No, I didn't."

"Well, there was this bunch of niggers that was caught in this storm. So, they all went to this house. The people let them come in and soon it was dark and rainy. Then, the wind come up. It was bad! One of the niggers looked outside. He screamed!"

Beany's eyes got bigger as he started to dramatize his story. "'It's a ghost,' he yelled. They all ran and bumped into each other screaming. When they got quiet, they all ran to the window and sho 'nuff, thar was a ghost with long arms out like this." Beany stretched his arms out wide.

He continued, "That ghost would come close, then wiggle back, then come close, then wiggle back, then..."

"Oh, for Heaven's sake," Lem interrupted the repeating phrase, "What happened?"

"Well, them niggers shivered together all night, staring out the window until dawn. And still, the ghost didn't go away, 'cause you know what? It was a sheet hanging from the line." Beany laughed until his face turned red.

Maybe it was all the whiskey he had drunk but it struck Jackson funny too, and he laughed along with them. Keith gave Jackson a look of contempt and curtly said, "What you laughin' about? Ain't you one of them niggers?"

Jackson knew he was in jeopardy. Alert for trouble, he rose unsteadily to his feet, holding his fork and dish as he looked for a place to put them. Anna came to his rescue. Taking them from him, she skirted around

Keith and Lem, who were slopping more food on the table than in their mouths. Anna did not put the dirty dishes in the sink. That would have her going to the wrong side of the kitchen. Her idea was to escape to her bedroom and let the men drink themselves into oblivion. However, she also was a little tipsy now, and made more noise than she intended. Keith looked around so Anna just pretended she was leaning on the old lamp table after putting Jackson's dish on it.

"Say, you haven't finished your drink, Anna. Jackson, pour more whiskey in Anna's cup."

Jackson saw the cup was full, but he pretended to fill it anyway. Anna, not knowing this said, "No, thanks, I've had enough. I'll just go..."

"No, no," Keith boomed.

"...get your blankets."

Anna stood her ground.

From the table Lem's voice came soft but clear, almost pleading, "Keith, I would like another drink."

"Sure." Keith turned in his chair to face Anna.

"See, you mustn't let good liquor go to waste."

Keith inspected the bottle. it was almost empty. He grabbed the other bottle and battled with the cork. Jackson, still standing slowly crumpled to the floor.

His head fell on his chest. It would take a lot to get his chin in his fighting position now. Keith popped the cork, picked up Anna's cup. Seeing it was still filled, he lurched toward her swaying, and breathing hard. He offered her the cup. She quickly turned sideways, afraid Keith would feel the gun. "Thank you," she said pleasantly.

Anna stiffened her face and drank some of it. Keith smiled, obviously pleased. He shakily spilled more whiskey in his glass.

"Ahw... how about us?" Lem held out his glass.

"Oh, yeah," Keith muttered as he poured Lem and Beany another drink.

"How about you Nigg..ah, Jackson?"

By now, Jackson was what his father called "pissy-eyed drunk." Drunk as he was, Jackson now knew how Keith felt about him. He would have to go along with it as his mother had taught him to do. Keith slopped a drink in Jackson's glass, making sure he overfilled it, wetting Jackson's hand and flannel shirt. Jackson looked down at his wet shirt and clumsily tried to brush it dry with his hand. While they were thus engaged, Anna stealthily closed the gap between the men and her bedroom door. Keith stumbled toward the table, put the whiskey bottle on it and plumped down in his chair. Jackson tried to take a sip of his drink but spilled more of it on his shirt. He had never imbibed so much whiskey. A couple of beers on a Saturday night was about all Jackson ever had. Mamma saw to it her sons were upright, law-abiding citizens, clear-headed for church services on Sunday.

"Better eat your dinner, Keith."

Beany always looked out for Keith. Without Keith, Beany had no one who would care for him. Keith gave him a surly look but did begin to eat his cold supper.

"Mmmmm, good food, Anna," he said without looking around. If he had, he would not have seen her. She had slipped into her bedroom and quietly closed the door. She was exhausted. Not only because of the tense situation but this was a late hour for her. She unlaced her high-top shoes, put her derringer under her pillow and collapsed on the bed. The drone of the men's voices soothed her nerves. As long as they were talking, eating, and drinking, Anna felt safe. She pulled her shawl around her cold feet. She lay quietly. Slowly, as her feet became warm, she began to breathe steadily. Her eyes became glazed with the desire for sleep. She listened. Beany was telling another story. The murmur continued for a while, then all the men laughed. Lem's voice was quiet. Anna could not make out what he was saying. When he was finished, they were beside themselves with laughter. The clink of more whiskey being poured made Anna's body stiffen. The last thing she remembered was praying the men would pass out as Willie used to when he celebrated the weekend. Anna fell into a deep sleep.

It was now one o'clock in the morning. Lem and Keith were the only two who could make conversation. Beany had put his head on the table and passed out. Keith and Lem had made several slanderous remarks at Jackson. Keith was about to make another snide aside when he was interrupted. Jackson, his head swimming with thoughts of his lost family and thinking of his beloved Clarabelle, began to sing one of the hymns the choir sang at funerals. The alcohol he consumed put him in a stupor, but it did not affect the beauty of his voice. Keith listened intently and marveled at Jackson. Then, he became angry. Why did this Colored man make him so jealous? Everything Jackson did, he did well. Keith wanted to be the one everyone looked up to. Here was this fellow from... where did he say, Baltimore, besting him at every turn. Keith glared at Jackson.

"Shut up!" he snarled. Jackson went on singing. He was too drunk to know he was in danger of being thrown out into the cold night.

Lem rose shakily from his chair.

"Hey, no."

He held on to the table as he leaned closer to Keith.

"What that guy needs is a good come-uppance. Think of something, Keith."

Lem noticed Anna was gone.

"She left us. She didn't even say good night," Lem said sadly.

Jackson finished his song.

"Don't stop now, Jackson," Keith said as he poured more whiskey in Jackson's glass.

"Here, have another drink."

He winked at Lem. Lem laughed but he didn't really know what Keith was up to. Jackson tried to drink some of the whiskey, but he could not raise his glass. He began to croon an old blues song. Suddenly he stopped singing. His glass fell to the floor. Jackson stared at it with glazed eyes. Slowly they closed and Jackson was in that state of oblivion Anna prayed for.

"Out like a light!" Keith announced to Lem.

Lem's shoulders shook as he snickered over Jackson's plight. Keith, walking very unsteadily, went to the door of Anna's bedroom. Slowly opening it, he peered into the darkness. Hearing Anna softly snoring, he carefully closed the door.

"Tell you what we're gonna do, Lem. We'll put Jackson in bed with Anna."

Lem let out a squeal of delight.

"Hush! We'll put Jackson in bed with Anna, spill some milk between 'em and Anna will think Jackson did IT!"

Lem clapped his hands almost toppling himself. Keith opened the door again. He beckoned to Lem to help him pick up Jackson. Lem tried several times to extricate himself from the table but could not make his legs do his bidding.

"Oh, for Christ's sake! Do I have to do everything?" Keith asked, almost too loudly. He walked over to Jackson and gave him a gentle kick. Jackson looked up with bleary eyes.

"Come on, Jackson, you can't sleep here!"

Jackson smiled as Keith pulled him up to his feet. He half walked, was half dragged into Anna's room. Lem sheepishly sat down. He could hear Keith softly talking to Jackson.

"Now, stretch out and go to sleep." Jackson began to sing again. Keith put his index finger to his lips.

"Hush! Go to sleep! We have lots to do in the morning." Jackson, glassy-eyed mimicked Keith, "Hush!" he whispered and snuggled his head in the pillow. Anna moved. Keith froze. After making sure Anna had not been awakened, he slowly backed out of the bedroom. Lem was still at the table trying to stay awake. This was too good to miss. Keith indicated to Lem to pour milk into a glass. Lem staggered around the table finally managing to get the milk poured. Keith stretched his arm as far as he could as Lem held on to the table stretching his arm to give Keith the glass. Milk spilled on the floor, on the table and all over Keith's hand as he took the glass.

"Go to sleep, you fool. Hear me, Lem? Go to sleep! We must get to town before these two wake up. That way we don't have to give Jackson any part of our profits."

Lem slowly let himself down to the floor. He curled up and dutifully went to sleep. Keith went back to the bed where his two victims were sound asleep. Slowly, he pulled the blanket up and carefully spilled the milk between Jackson and Anna, making sure Jackson was moistened in the proper place on his underwear. Jackson stirred a little at that, however he was in such a deep sleep he did not wake up.

The plan was in place.

# XII

Jackson, even in his sleep, was aware he had a headache. He was not prepared for the hard slap in the face waking him up. He jumped away from the blow, hitting the back of his head hard on the headboard. Stunned by both hits, feeling stiff from heavy sleep, Jackson got up on his knees, lifted his chin, and was ready to do battle. He cocked his left arm around his face, pulled back his right fist ready to strike his unknown enemy. Staring into the gloom of early morning, he groggily turned to the dark figure pulling at the rumpled garment on the bed. Anna, crying and moaning, was clawing at her moist skirt.

"You... you nigger! Get out of my bed!"

She lunged at Jackson with both fists pounding on Jackson's chest.

Realizing the figure was Anna, Jackson protected himself as best he could, letting her vent her fury. Anna became too tired to continue. She looked down at the bed. Covering her face with her hands, she sobbed. Jackson looked around the room, puzzled.

How did he get here? Carefully, trying not to disturb Anna, he slowly got out of bed. When he stood up, the room started to spin around, making his head throb and his stomach tighten. His knees buckled. Hugging the wall with his back, Jackson slid to the floor. He managed to lift his head and look around the room in disbelief. Having regained some strength, Anna crawled across the bed and attacked Jackson again. Both her fists came down hard on Jackson's shoulders and head. This time, Jackson grabbed her hands and held them close to his chest. Somehow, he pulled her off the bed and managed to roll on top of her holding her hands above her head while pressing his knees hard against her knees, making it impossible for her to kick.

Anna became hysterical. She rolled her head from side to side trying to escape. Finally, after using up the rest of her energy, stopped. They were both breathing hard. After they lay awhile, Jackson, still holding her secure spoke to her quietly and cautiously.

"Please, Ma'am, what'd I do?"

Anna turned scarlet with anger and disgust.

"You raped me! I would NEVER consent to... to... you! NEVER! NEVER!"

Anna spit out the words.

"Why would you say such a thing? I don't even know how I got here."

Jackson was aghast at the very thought of raping Anna. His head was beginning to clear. He let Anna go and scrambled unsteadily to his feet. Holding on to every piece of furniture he could, Jackson made it outside to the porch. His effort was too much for his stomach. Clutching the railing he emptied out the poison in his system. Painfully raising his throbbing head, Jackson could see his breath in the cold morning air. He leaned against the pillar and looked toward the place he left the horses the night before. The wagon, the horses and the men were gone. It became clear to Jackson the men had absconded with his Belgian horse. It became clear he would not share in the profits. He wondered just when the men decided to make a mockery of their friendship.

He had trusted Keith. Liked him, even. Jackson couldn't have guessed that Keith would have liked him if he had been an ignorant man.

The cold air cleared Jackson's head and now that he had relieved his stomach, he began to feel better. He found a pan of water with a skiff of ice covering the melted frost. He broke the film of ice, melting it in his hands. It was so bracing on his face he decided to clean his body. Pulling his union suit down past his waist, he shivered with delight as the cold water soothed his bruised shoulders. He was right. Anna was strong. Anna. What was her problem? Obviously the "boys" wanted to pull a mischievous trick. She should know what those men were like. They were her husband's friends, weren't they? Jackson found a large towel on the line at the end of the porch. The sun came out pale and warm. It felt good. Jackson was beginning to feel he could deal with Keith but first he must make it right with Anna. She had been so kind to him and there was still that feeling of wanting to make Anna feel good. To make her smile.

Jackson pulled up his underwear and was surprised at the feeling of wet crust near his genitals. He looked down and felt the spot. Jackson's heart fluttered. Had he... did Keith and his boys watch him have sex with Anna?

"Oh, God, please help me!"

He turned to run into the house to make Anna understand he did not know what he was doing and almost knocked her down.

Her expression was stoic and cold just the way she looked at him last night at the door.

"How long have you been standing there?"

"Never mind. Come with me," she commanded in a husky voice.

Jackson hesitated. Maybe she would take down the rifle off the wall and shoot him. Anna walked past the rifle, through the kitchen and into her bedroom. Jackson gave a sigh of relief and followed her. "What is it Mrs. ah, ah..."

"Mrs. Wilhelm Schein."

"What is it, Mrs. Schein?"

Anna answered by pointing to the bed.

"Feel that!"

Jackson rubbed his hand over the sheet. It felt like the damp, wet spot he felt on his underwear.

"What the hell is it?"

Jackson looked intently into Anna's eyes.

"Please, Mrs. Schein, I wouldn't do anything to hurt you. You were so kind to me. You must know how much I appreciated the food and the shelter you gave me."

Jackson was hoping for a sign of friendship.

No sign of friendship.

"It's on the skirt I slept in, too." Anna said, tears welling up in her eyes.

"Don't you see what's happened?"

Jackson's perplexed look told her he did not see what she meant.

"Come to the kitchen."

Jackson did as he was told, happy that Anna was calm now. "See this? Milk!"

"Milk!"

"Milk?"

"Yes. Milk."

Ana folded her arms across her chest and leaned on the little table.

Jackson's dirty dish was still there.

"And you thought I ..." Jackson decided not to antagonize Anna. He thought about the milk.

"Why would they do such a dumb thing? It would be different if they saw us when we woke up."

Anna stiffened.

"Because Keith wants my farm. He wants my farm more than anything else in the world. He has always wanted to be looked up to in Stanton. Adding my acres to his would give him all the best land in these parts. That's why he befriended Willie. They used to meet at the "Heavenly Divide," Belinda Resnik's whorehouse. Keith always thought someday Willie would gamble away some of the farmland. Willie was too smart for him. Besides, Willie was lucky. He always won. Keith should have known Willie would never put his land in jeopardy."

Trying to make sense out of what Anna had just told him, Jackson went into the bedroom to find his clothes. They were in a lump on the old rickety chair no one would dare to sit in. He dressed quickly and joined Anna.

"I still don't understand," he persisted, "why are you so upset at the stupid joke they played on us?"

"Don't you see?"

Anna's voice became a half-tone higher.

"They rode into town and told everybody I have a nigger for a lover. The whole town will believe it because they want to. The children will follow me and taunt me with their ugly childish sayings. Keith found a way to laugh me out of town so I'll sell my farm. He'll come by and tell me he'll help me out of my predicament. Oh, he'll give me a fair price, I think, but not what this farm is really worth."

Anna lowered her head and caught sight of the gleam of the spilled milk on the floor. Her chest felt tight, but she fought back tears.

After a long silence, Jackson said, "The Heavenly Divide?"

"That's what the men call the fork in the road halfway from here to town. To the left the road takes you to downtown Stanton all the way to the square. Turn right, and you climb the hill to the old Stanton mansion."

Jackson finished tying his shoe. He stood up and came closer to Anna.

"I'm sorry this happened, but if you loan me a horse I'll go into town to see if I can get my share of the money the boys said they would give me. I put up my money for the one horse. I'll at least get that or know the reason why. I have proof of my purchase."

Anna was studying his face as he spoke.

"I'll be sure to put your horse in a shelter so's you can pick him up in case something happens to me."

"You're not going."

"What do you mean? Why not?"

Jackson took a step toward Anna and slipped on the sticky floor. With her back straight, her face looking like carved stone, her hair flying, Anna went into action. She went outside, grabbed soap, dipped a bucket in the barrel of water, and began to scrub the floor. Her soiled skirt flowing in the dirty water did not deter Anna from her goal. Jackson didn't know what to do. He slowly began to clear the table, then the dishes, then the stove. By the time they were finished it was time for lunch.

"Jackson!"

"Yes, Ma'am."

"Throw this dirt from those filthy-minded men away."

Anna could be dramatic, the way she thought a heroine would be in the magazine stories. She had studied the pictures.

Jackson threw the dirty water out over the railing. When he walked back in the house, he surveyed the kitchen. It seemed like an oasis last night. This morning with the sun streaming through the grimy windows it was the most dismal room he had ever seen. Jackson stepped gingerly on the clean floor as he grabbed an old towel to wash the windows. Anna was so pleased she almost smiled.

"Can you milk a cow?"

Jackson stared.

"Well, can you feed horses?"

Jackson looked to one side.

"That's all right, you can learn that. Let the horses out of the barn so they can graze and there is a basket in the chicken coop to put all the eggs in. By that time I should be cleaned up and breakfast made. You've just had bacon and eggs. How about oats, homemade biscuits, and honey?"

Jackson's mouth watered. He was almost out the door when she said, "After we eat, we'll make you a room in the barn." Jackson stopped short, his jacket half on.

"There is a place for cooking. It's not so bad. Then you can go into town and look Keith up."

Jackson was hungry so he didn't contradict her. There would be time to discuss the matter over lunch. He wanted to be rid of the woman once and for all. Jackson did not let the chickens intimidate him. He just shooed them off their nests with an old rag and scooped up the eggs. Now and then he would stop and admire the rolling hills, the dried rows of harvested vegetables, and the line of evergreens in the distance. Someday he would have a farm like this. The warm sun was canceled by a cold breeze and he realized he had been daydreaming. The cold day made him think. Somehow, he had to get a coat. Maybe Mrs. Schein would help him. Surely, Anna had some of Willie's clothes left in the house. Now for some food.

Jackson put the basket of eggs on the table. Anna was nowhere to be seen. It did smell good in the kitchen and he was ready to eat. He called out, "Mrs. Schein?"

She must be making the bed, he reasoned, so he made his way to the bedroom. Anna was staring at the soiled sheets. There was no expression on her face. Tears were streaming down her cheeks, giving her an unreal silvery look.

Jackson cautiously approached her.

"It's all right, Mrs. Schein," he said quietly.

"It's all over now. The boys have had their fun. You mustn't let them get to you."

He wanted to pat her shoulder but thought better of it. Jackson made like a soldier.

"I fought the hens and got the eggs. I didn't know where you wanted me to put them

Anna didn't answer.

"Come now, in a couple of days Keith will have forgotten all about last night."

Anna seethed.

"You still don't know what they did, do you?"

Jackson scratched the back of his head, "What do you mean? People in town who know you won't believe you have a Black man for a lover."

Anna gave a guttural, "Oh," and turned on her heels and went to the kitchen. She started to throw things on the table. Jackson hurriedly opened drawers looking for sheets. When he finished making the bed, he realized how quiet the house became. Jackson made for the kitchen on the run. Anna was sitting at the table waiting for him.

"Where do you want me to sit?"

Then he saw that the table was set for him to sit opposite her.

"Do you want me to say grace?" he asked.

"Do what you want."

Anna folded her hands.

Jackson prayed, "Dear Jesus, bless the hands that prepared this food and keep us mindful of those who don't have as much as we. Amen."

Anna unfolded her hands and for the first time, she really looked at Jackson. Her eyes were softer than Jackson had expected.

"What's your name again?"

Jackson spoke with food in his mouth.

"I'm Jackson Freeman, ma'am. I come from Baltimore. After a big fire I lost my family to an intestinal germ, so I made the decision to come West. You see, I've always wanted to become a farmer. That way I'll be independent. Always have food on the table."

"How did you meet Keith Cailern and his bunch of rowdies?"

"Well, as I was telling you, I have always wanted to become a farmer. Sure, there are good jobs in Baltimore...odd jobs at the docks. Sometimes I even got seven dollars an hour moving goods off the ships. Those jobs didn't last long and mostly they went to the White men. You'd get paid good like that because the job was dangerous. So when I found myself without any obligations, I decided to try to buy a farm. I heard farms were good and cheaper in Ohio. I headed West. That was three weeks ago."

Anna went to the stove to get the coffee. She poured a cup for Jackson. That did not go unnoticed by Jackson.

Jackson continued, "I met Keith by helping get his wagon reloaded after his horse spooked when some kids teased it. You know how kids are. Noisy and running. Anyhow, there was a crowd of people so I went to see what was going on."

"Was this in Ohio?" Anna asked.

"No, a small town in Pennsylvania."

Jackson waited for more questions, but Anna busied herself with her food.

"Beany was saying, 'I tied the rope good.'"

Jackson mimicked Beany's high voice. Anna gave him a look. Jackson was sorry he had tried to be facetious and decided not to do it again.

"A big man I later learned was Keith started to yell at Beany. 'You did not,' he said. Beany was sweating now. 'Do you think I wanted this mess to happen?' Beany said. And what a mess it was! There were bushel baskets rolling and swaying all the while spilling their contents making a vegetable stew on the dirt road."

Jackson laughed. Anna kept eating.

"So," Jackson continued, "I said, 'Need any help?' By now the children were stealing everything they could get their hands on. The big man, Keith, turned around and yelled at no one in particular, 'Hey, anybody, get those kids out-a-here.' He looked at me, 'Can you do that?'

'Sure.'

'Yeah, get what you can from the little beggars.'

'I'm asking for a job,' I said. I knew he didn't have much time to think about it.

'One dollar... get goin', he says.

'Two dollars and I'll get it all back,' I said.

'You think I have that kind of money?'

I stood my ground. We couldn't help but smile at the situation. We liked each other right off.

I started at the outer fringes of the mess grabbing the young ruffians, opening their coats, and emptying their pockets. They ran in all directions, but I caught 'em. One of the young fellows showed me he still had a potato and stuck his tongue out at me."

Jackson smiled hoping to keep Anna entertained as he picked up the dishes and took them to the sink. She looked at Jackson as if to say, 'I'm listening.'

The woman has no sense of humor, Jackson reasoned.

"Anyway," Jackson held up his cup for more coffee, "I began to realize there were three men. Keith, Beany, and a thin man they called Lem."

Anna sat down with her second cup of coffee.

"Go on, I want to hear what they promised you that made you give them your money."

She blew on the coffee.

"The crowd thinned out when the three of them helped me put the vegetables back in their baskets and when we were done, we all laughed. They were nice to me. They treated me as if they thought I was one of them. Negroes in Baltimore who had been out West told me that when they left the city, no one treated them the way Baltimoreans treated us. We have been given many advantages and we appreciate them."

"I liked Keith, so when he convinced me he and the others would deal me in on their profits if I would help them get another horse to pull their large wagon, I wanted to believe them." Jackson leaned forward, "It sounded good to me, Mrs. Schein. I figured since Keith was the leader... well, I trusted him. I'm sorry to say I bought an old Belgian for twenty-five dollars. That was the real reason why we were so late coming into Stanton. That old horse had one speed. Slow. Then, there was this unexpected cold weather. We also had an axle go bad on us." Jackson was quiet for a moment.

"I guess it wasn't the best day I've ever had..."

Anna picked up her cup of coffee with both hands. Leaning on her elbows she brought the cup close to her lips. The coffee was not hot now. Nevertheless, she blew on the rim of the cup. Jackson waited for a reaction to his story but she said nothing. Her eyes welled up with tears again. She just stared out the newly washed window.

Jackson finished his biscuit.

"Could I have more coffee?"

Anna just nodded. He helped himself to half a cup more. "You know Missus Schein, I feel that you take things too hard. Those fellows take things... everything...too lightly... and make jokes."

Anna got up to gather the dishes.

"There are some more things to do around here. I'll do the di..."

"No ma'am! If it's all the same to you, I'm going to Stanton to get my money from Keith."

Anna looked deep into Jackson's eyes. She could see he was determined to leave. Going to the cupboard, she pulled out a drawer, "Here's five dollars.

I'll give you Jocko, he'll get you to town. He knows the road. Jocko is a good horse. Gentle. Mind you," she pointed a finger at Jackson, "put him in Brady's barn at Maple and Main before you try to find Keith. You might try to get Keith off guard in the hotel at the end of Main Street. It's a cheap place. He used to stay there when he was in town. He rented a room there by the week."

Anna waited for a response.

"Well?"

Jackson was speechless. Where did she get off making plans for him?

"Come on."

Anna's voice was now condescending, as if she were speaking to a child, irritating Jackson even more. She put on her stone face, stiffened her back and went out the door. Jackson followed her to the barn, where Anna herself saddled Jocko.

"Mind what I say now. Pay Brady for three days before you do anything else. Hold on to the rest of the money. When you come back, bring some groceries. Whatever meat you like, some cheese and oh, yes, bring some paper. The ones with lines on. I don't read or write too good, but my neighbor helps me with figures."

You don't talk too good either, Jackson thought. He put his hands on his hips, "When I come back?"

"Do you think you can beat up Keith? Or maybe you think he'll give you twenty-five dollars. Get a job in Stanton? Doing what? We have a river but there are no dockworkers here. Besides, you're a stranger in town."

"No, I don't think I can beat up Keith!"

Jackson imitated Anna.

"I'll have to use uh... uh... strategy to get my money back. Then I'll look around and see if there is a farm I can buy, or at least some land, or... or... I could lease a few acres. I'll find work. Don't you worry about that."

"You, of course, know how to tell if the land is fertile, and if the water is good. Do you realize what time of the year it is? You have all winter to learn about farming and I can learn ya. You, on the other hand, will have to work for me. I'm not so bad to work for."

Jackson's face fell. He really had not thought about the time of year, except that in the months that were so cold, he would work for more money. It was true. Anna could teach him a lot. She and Willie were successful.

Anna was beginning to feel sorry for Jackson but brushed the thought aside.

"All right, I can see you know I'm right. You go ahead and do what you must do, and I'll work on your room in the barn. When you come back," Anna pointedly repeated, "we will start farmin' lessons. If you're going to be a farmer, you might as well be a good one. Can you write?"

Jackson nodded he could.

"Good. Come evenin', you can give me readin' and writin' lessons."

Jackson cringed at the thought of spending evenings with this detestable woman.

"Oh, there's a sweater in the stall behind you. Might be a jacket, too. I used 'em when Willie got too fat to wear them."

Jackson looked at Anna in disbelief.

"I'll pay you back! Every penny, woman!"

"Oh, really? With what? Your farm money?"

Anna brought down a stirrup, leaned on Jocko, and squinted her tear-swollen eyes at Jackson.

"You'll pay me back by workin' for me," she repeated. "And don't think because I'm here alone I can't take care of myself."

Jackson threw his eyes heavenward.

Things were not going the way he wanted them to, but perhaps Jesus was showing him the way. He answered Anna with a wry smile and a knowing look.

"I saw you pat your apron a couple of times. I figured you had a small gun tucked away in your pocket."

Jackson smiled broadly at her quick look. He said, "Don't worry, I'll not be back. Anything I should know about this horse?"

"He's a good ride and minds well. You won't have any trouble with him."

Anna started for the house.

"Mrs. Schein," Jackson called to her. Anna did not turn back or give any indication she heard him.

"Thank you, ma'am. Thank you for everything."

Anna kept walking.

"I'll send you the money by mail."

"You'll be back," she said under her breath.

# XIII

Jocko began the ride slowly. The horse was very responsive to Jackson's commands and soon was jogging at a steady pace toward the valley. Starting so late in the day, it occurred to Jackson he did not know where he would sleep tonight. It would be all right. After all, he had money and surely there was a Colored district that could accommodate him. Halfway into Stanton, Jackson came upon the "Heavenly Divide" Anna talked about. He was curious about the Stanton Mansion but kept Jocko left of the divide. The path into town. Twilight was early this time of the year and he did not want to get into Stanton too late to make all the accommodations for the horse and himself. Besides, he did not know how long it would take to get to his destination.

The countryside was beautiful. As the sun set, the long shadows reached out caressing Jackson as he rode in and out of the filtering sunlight. Here and there were neat, clean farmhouses. Cows had been milked and were out to pasture again. Now and then, a dog barked in the distance. The birds were quarreling for space to settle down to sleep.

It was past evening when Jackson crossed the wooden bridge leading into the downtown district. There were thin streaks of light coming from closed stores. The whole town had the look of a fine haze filtering the light. It was going to be an early winter. Jocko took Jackson to the middle of the large square and stopped. West Main was the business district with dry goods stores and a few private houses in between them. Looking East, Jackson noted, was the tacky part of town. There, he surmised, would be the red-light district, cheap stores, and the Colored section. He rode East.

Jackson rode almost to the end of Main Street before he saw any signs of life. There was a glow of what had to be the blacksmith shop. Yes, there was the sign. You could hardly read, "Brady's." He would bed Jocko, then get some information about a room for himself.

Dutch had been watching the lone rider but until Jackson came into view, he did not know the rider coming into town so late was a Negro. As Jackson came closer, Dutch became alert.

"Hold it right there!" he commanded. Jackson dutifully stopped Jocko.

"Get off that horse!"

Jackson did as he was told. Dutch noticed the rider did not act cowed as most Colored men did.

"Who the hell are you and what are you doing on Jocko? Where is the Widow Schein?"

Dutch could be very intimidating.

Jackson thought quickly.

"Ah, Mrs. Schein is home. Sent me for supplies. She gave me money for groceries. I've been working for her ever since Keith Cailern had no need for me anymore. I'm going to work for her now."

Well, Jackson thought, some of it wasn't a lie.

Dutch began to laugh.

"Oh, so you're the Black lover Keith told us about!"

"I'm not her lover!" Jackson bristled, "You're mocking a good woman, sir. You should be ashamed to fall into Keith's trap to make fun of a lone widow."

Dutch stopped laughing. His eyebrows shot up in his hairline. He took a step closer to Jackson, spread his feet and bellowed, "You watch what you say to me and how you say it!"

Jackson did not back off.

"I would like to put Jocko in one of your stalls for the night. I'll pay in advance. He's already been fed. Mrs. Schein will pick him up in a couple of days in case I haven't finished my business here."

His voice carried no concern at the way Dutch spoke to him.

"Hey," Dutch laughed again, "you're all right. What happened? Keith do you out of some money or was it the widow he conned?"

Jackson patted Jocko, "I bought that outfit a horse. All I want is my money."

Dutch held out a friendly hand.

"Everybody calls me Dutch."

"I'm Jackson Freeman."

They shook hands. Jackson looked quizzically at Dutch. It was not often White men were so friendly to Colored men as soon as they met.

Dutch saw the look and began to explain.

"I know a lot of Colored people, Freeman. Working here... Hell, I'm with them all day long. I see the "Chocolate Babes" and the "Church-going Virgins." It's easy to tell them apart. I know the "Sports" and I know the "Good Guys." You a gambler, Freeman?"

"Depends on what you mean by gambling. I never have any money for craps."

Dutch unsaddled Jocko. He happily whistled through his teeth as he put the horse in his stall.

"You know of a room I can rent for tonight, Dutch?" Jackson asked.

Dutch stopped whistling, "Sure." Slapping the saddle over the rail, he folded his heavy arms. Looking straight at Jackson, he said, "Listen, fella, I'm taking you at your word about Missus Schein being all right. You better not be lyin', 'cause if you are, you'll have me to contend with. Now, there is a roomin' house down the street two blocks on the corner. Madge Simpson is a hard landlady, but she is a lady."

Jackson started for the street.

"Hey, if you're gonna look for Keith in the morning, he usually is at the Main Street Restaurant. You can take it from there. By the way, they don't serve Coloreds."

Jackson waved and smiled.

"Hit him a good one for me, too, would ya? Then I'll pick you up and take ya to Doctor Fiske. You'll need him after Keith gets through with ya."

"Thank you for all your information. I don't think it'll come to fisticuffs, though. Keith did this while he was drunk to the eyeballs. He's an alright fella... I think. Oh," Jackson came back to the smitty, "How much do I owe?"

"Fifty-cents."

Jackson dug deep into his pocket and extracted the exact change. He didn't want to flash a five-dollar bill.

"Down the street two blocks on the corner," Dutch repeated.

"There you are. Thanks again, and a good night to ya." Jackson started for the rooming house.

"Good night and good luck to you!"

Jackson kept walking but he raised his hand high to acknowledge that he had heard Dutch. Now, he would get some rest. Tomorrow was time enough to take care of business. Tomorrow he would get started in his new life. His whistling echoed back to Dutch.

Down the street two blocks on the corner.

# XIV

Jackson awoke from a deep sleep. He checked the vest pocket watch he kept hidden in his front pants pocket. "Never show wealth," his Mamma warned him. Luck was with him this morning. He found a twenty-five-cent piece in his pocket. This would be a lucky day! It was later than he thought, so he dressed quickly and hurried down the rickety stairs.

Finding Missus Simpson, he asked if there was a barber shop nearby. Missus Simpson perched her thin hands one over the other at her waist.

"Right next door to this house. It ain't fancy like the one uptown."

"Thanks," Jackson said on the run.

Feeling good after a shave, Jackson walked briskly to the uptown district hoping he would see Keith, get his money, and settle into a permanent room. Madge Simpson's wasn't bad. He could live there while looking for some land to buy. What was it Missus Schein said? 'Look for fertile soil, not too hilly, and water.' Good water and plenty of it was particularly important.

The town was not too crowded this early in the morning. It was easy to find the restaurant. Jackson took a stand across the street. He did not want Keith to see him before he saw Keith. It was past ten o'clock when there was a scuffle at the restaurant's doorway. From where he was, Jackson could make out a waiter pointing a finger at a customer. It was Beany. He was being thrown out of the restaurant. The argument did not last long. Beany made his way toward the river, no doubt looking for Lem. Jackson began to wonder if Keith was in the eatery. He crossed the street and as he approached the window to have a look, he felt a heavy hand on his shoulder.

"Dutch! What are you doing here?"

"I came to watch you get your money, Freeman."

Jackson smiled. He had made a friend. Yes, this was going to be his lucky day.

"Thanks, Dutch."

"Tell you what, Jackson. I'll go in and roust Keith out of his booth. He's probably in there holding court. What do you intend to do?"

"I'll just remind him about the old horse."

"Yeah, then...??"

"He'll give me my money and that'll be that."

"You don't know what he's been saying, Jackson."

"Saying?"

Jackson began to feel uncomfortable.

"Keith has been talking all day about the widow and some Colored man. Everybody is laughing and making jokes. You had better watch yourself or you may be in for some shovin' around. The people in this town don't have much in the way of entertainment, and well, Keith is a likable guy."

"I know. I like him, too."

Jackson gave Dutch a wry half-smile.

"I'll get my money back, you'll see."

"All right, Freeman, I'll rustle him out for ya."

Dutch gave Jackson a wink and disappeared into the restaurant. Jackson leaned against the light pole prepared to wait. It wasn't long before the doors flew open. Keith came out of the building like a rocket. When he saw Jackson, he rolled up his sleeves. He started to dance around Jackson, darting a fist close to Jackson's face. Thus engaged, Keith did not notice Dutch coming out of the eatery. The big smitty placed himself behind Jackson. He stood with legs apart, his huge arms in a wrestling position that made Keith stop in his tracks.

Keith stopped dancing around, threw his head back and laughed.

"Can't you take a joke, Jackson?" he said. Dutch knew Keith was really talking to him and he straightened up a little. Keith patted Jackson on his shoulder. Speaking in a soft monotone, he asked, "How did you get away from the Widow Schein? We wondered what became of you."

Jackson did not know what to make of Keith's turnaround. He only knew he was glad for it.

"You owe me for the horse, Keith. I know you won't pay me the two dollars you promised but that's all right. You gave me a ride into Stanton. That should make us even. I just want what you owe me. I need the money, Keith."

"Why don't you ask Missus Schein for the money? She likes you," Keith said as he looked over at the men who always hung around the restaurant. They all laughed with Keith.

"Mrs. Schein doesn't owe me any money," Jackson replied good-naturedly. Dutch, still behind Jackson, took one step closer toward Keith.

"Come on, Keith," Jackson tried to cajole him, "you'll make it up. I need my chance. Besides, you still have the horse. You can sell him; I can't. Right is right."

Dutch nodded approval to all Jackson said.

Keith was quiet for a moment. He took another look at Dutch. It was obvious Dutch had had enough. Jackson waited but Keith just stood close to him with a wide grin. The crowd started to snicker. Slowly, the snickering became loud laughter. Jackson was beginning to see what Missus Schein meant. It would be a constant challenge to do business in town. Their fingers would always point. Always the whispering behind her back. If he was uncomfortable, just think how hard it would be for the Widow Schein. Jackson pictured Anna walking down Main Street with her head held high and children taunting her as she did her shopping or banking. Again he was angered by the way people treated her. With the anger, Jackson became bolder.

"I thought you were fair, Keith. I need the money you owe me."

Keith put a heavy hand on Jackson's shoulder. Jackson shrugged it off. Keith lost his grin. Now it was Jackson who rolled up his sleeves and ground his fists in a circle.

"I'm ready for you, Keith."

Keith wasn't quite sure how to handle this situation. He put his big grin on again. It was not without cause. Jackson looked rather comical trying to fight the big Irishman. The men who were milling around the two of them were laughing out loud and egging Jackson on. Keith was beginning to get embarrassed.

"Aaw, c'mon Jackson, let's be friends," he said in a good-hearted way.

"You want your money? Well, I don't have all of it right with me, but I can give you..."

Dutch crouched as if to spring on Keith. Keith began to talk fast.

"Hey, these fellas are my witnesses. You'll get it all tomorrow."

Jackson kept rolling his fists as he had seen Joe Gans do when Gans boxed at the arena in Baltimore. The crowd stopped milling around. This was getting serious. Keith threw his head back and laughed.

"I can't give you what I don't have, now can I?" Keith pulled out a ten-dollar bill and handed it to Jackson. "Where are you staying?... with the Widow?"

Jackson stopped in his tracks, Dutch straightened up and waited.

"No," Jackson replied, "I'm at the Simpson boarding house."

"Well, all right." Keith said brightly.

"I'll get the rest of the money to you there."

He looked over Jackson's shoulder at Dutch.

"I really will!" he said to Dutch. Dutch nodded his head imperceptibly.

Jackson came down off his toes.

"Fair enough."

Jackson extended his hand. Keith shook it, but really he was making a contract with Dutch.

"Well, I wouldn't have believed it," Dutch said to Jackson. "You really did it."

The men were disappointed there wouldn't be a bloodbath and started to disperse.

"Better be on our way, Jackson. It's time for lunch and I don't like to eat alone."

Dutch put his arm around Jackson's shoulders and steered him toward the East side of town.

When they reached the Square, Jackson stopped and looked at Dutch.

"You might as well know now; I'm not going back to the Schein farm."

Dutch put his huge hands on his hips, "Oh, no?"

Jackson started to tell him about his dream of having a farm of his own. About his wanting to be independent and not having to wait for jobs to be filled by White men before he got a chance. Could Dutch understand his situation?

"Well, you might as well know a few things yourself. Let's sit on the bench by the statue."

They sat down, leaned back, and surveyed the town. Dutch sat, bending forward and leaning his elbows on his knees. When he finally spoke, it was as if he were speaking to the ground. "See, Jackson," he started, "I've always kinda looked after Anna. "You hear me? She must never know I care for her! She doesn't know that, so don't you go telling her." Dutch leaned back, folded his arms over his chest, and gave Jackson a hard look.

Jackson cocked his head.

"Are you in love with that woman?" he asked incredulously.

"Well, I used to dream about her. You should have seen her when she was young. You shoulda seen me, for that matter!"

Dutch was quiet for a while. When he spoke, he had a catch in his voice.

"I never had the nerve to call on her. When she married Schein I told myself I couldn't compete with his wealth. Time went on and soon I was old and alone. She'll never leave the farm. I'm not a farmer. It wasn't meant to be."

Jackson stood up.

"I'm going to have lunch. Thank you for helping me. Tomorrow I'll have my money, then I'll be ready to buy my own farm," he said proudly.

"I don't think you understand, Freeman. You are going back to the farm. Without me, you won't get your money. Keith is afraid of me, not you."

Jackson knit his brows.

"You helped me more than I thought. No wonder Keith settled so quickly."

"And for that, I want your promise to stay at the farm, help Anna, take care of the stock this winter, and stay until the next harvest. She'll pay you well. I know Anna. She's fair. She never had pay for what she did for that ugly old man. She can't run that farm herself."

"I don't care. I don't want to be out there all by myself with that old woman."

Jackson spoke a little too loudly. Several people turned their way. Jackson sat down on the bench again.

"How can you like that cantankerous female?"

"Oh Freeman, you should have seen us when we were young."

Jackson looked at Dutch. Yes, he would have been a handsome young man. Leaning back on the bench, Jackson began to think about his days with Clarabelle. Waiting for her to give him that smoldering look as she walked by. He told his Mamma, 'That's the girl for me.' He followed her home one day, to a ramshackle old house by the river where water rats roamed at random. No words were spoken. She openly invited him to make love to her. Thinking of the consequences, Jackson had hesitated. Clarabelle took his hands and rubbed them over her body until Jackson wilted into her arms. They were beautiful then, too.

Dutch jumped up, giving a pat to Jackson's knee as he did. "We have to have lunch before I collapse. I don't lug all this weight around by missing meals." Jackson got up and joined him.

They made quite a pair. Jackson svelte and handsome, walking like a cat, and the big brawny smitty lumbering down the street next to him. The town was now teeming with people, horse-drawn wagons, and vendors plying their trade. To Jackson, it looked quaint. He was used to skyscrapers, paved roads, newsboys hawking the trade papers, and beautifully dressed women. As they made their way down Main Street, Jackson saw a realtor's sign.

"Would he be a good man to do business with, Dutch?" he asked, pointing to the curled cardboard in the second-story window.

"Won't do you no good right now, Freeman. You're going back to the widow."

They were both quiet all the way back to the blacksmith shop. Jackson watched as Dutch made ham sandwiches.

"You like ham?"

Jackson nodded he did, although he wasn't hungry anymore. He was tired. Dutch noticed the difference in Jackson's attitude.

"You'll feel better after you eat something."

He handed Jackson a cup of coffee.

"Come out here. We can sit outside to get away from the smell of the horses."

He gestured for Jackson to sit on one of the stools and put the food on a small table peeling paint.

"I call this my back-dirt. It's just a strip of green between the shop next door and my place, but you know, it's my favorite spot." The two men ate in silence.

"Jackson..."

Jackson looked at Dutch.

"I mean it. Don't make any plans you can't keep. I've been thinking about it and I've come to a conclusion. I'm going to give you the money Keith owes you and send you on your way. You should make the farm by late afternoon."

Jackson began to object.

"Listen," Dutch leaned closer to Jackson, "You do this for me, and I'll help you in every way I can. I'm well-known in this town. As a matter of fact, I thought of going into politics once, but I have an illegitimate son and that might stop everything. Still..." Dutch shook off the thought.

"Anna has been laughed at all her life. Her father stuttered. He was made fun of every time he opened his mouth. Took good care of Anna 'though he didn't send her to school. Guess he figured the kids would be cruel to her. He was probably right."

Dutch heaved a big sigh.

"I used to watch her come into town. She was so proud and pretty. No one dared to make fun of her when Willie was around, but the minute he left the buggy..."

Dutch became quiet remembering days gone by.

Jackson studied the man who befriended him. He began to think Anna...that was the first time he used her first name...Anna and Dutch were right. The small plot of ground that yielded tomatoes, lettuce, and herbs for Clarabelle was hardly what you would call experience in farming. Perhaps a season as a hired hand would give him time to learn how to be a successful farmer. It was as much a surprise to Jackson as it was to Dutch when he got up and announced, "All right! I'll spend a season at the farm. I won't let that woman get the best of me. I'll do only what I want to do, and she'll have to pay me something for my time." Jackson felt the hand of Jesus pointing the way.

Dutch jumped up and put his heavy hands on Jackson's shoulders.

"You won't be sorry, Freeman," he said with much sincerity. "Saddle up and I'll get your money."

Jackson hurriedly got Jocko ready and waited for Dutch to get through waiting on two customers in the barn. Dutch emerged with the money and the two men shook hands.

"Jocko knows the way home. Just give him his head. Oh, and when you bring Anna into town, people will talk. Remember, talk doesn't hurt anyone. She's used to it. You'll have to get used to it, too. If you run into trouble, just send any kid to find me." Dutch paused. "I wish I was going with you."

"Have you seen Mrs. Schein lately?" Jackson asked.

"Oh, yes, I know she isn't taking care of herself. But then, neither am I."

He patted his stomach.

"Good Luck, Jackson."

Jackson gave Jocko his head.

# XV

Anna stood up from her bent position. She looked around for Jackson, who was nowhere to be seen.

"Jackson!"

Where in the world can he be, she wondered. Then from a distance she heard him call out to her.

"Anna, I found lots of wood! It's just there for the taking." He trudged over the hill with his arms full of small, even-sized pieces of wood that would fit in the fireplace.

"You can't bring those pieces of wood close to the house." Anna said sarcastically.

"That wood is full of vermin!"

"It's wood." Jackson insisted.

"You want wood-eatin' ants in the house?"

Jackson dropped his arms quickly. The wood crashed to the ground.

"It's all right," Anna said calmly. "You didn't know."

Jackson walked toward Anna.

"Everything I do is wrong."

Anna thought to make light of it because he was so dejected.

"Don't be so dramatic. That's what you're here for, to learn."

Jackson started to walk to the house.

"The winter wheat looks good," Anna called after him. She admitted to herself he was learning about crops and how to grow vegetables, and he was also helping her to read and write. Perhaps he was doing too much. There were other things to learn, however. Like how to live on a farm. Anna decided to make an especially good dinner tonight. She followed him to the house.

Jackson stopped to wait for Anna.

"What do you make of these kinds of clouds?"

Anna looked up.

"Looks like a lot of snow. We better get home."

They walked in silence, their breath melting together in the cold air. As they approached the house, Jackson turned to go to his room in the barn.

Anna stopped.

"Where are you going?"

"I wish I were going home for Christmas," Jackson said softly. "It's the first Christmas that, well, that my family..."

He could not finish saying the dreadful words.

"Since February and all that summer, I was busy getting things in order. I worked some on cleaning up Baltimore to make more money. My thoughts were to leave and get my own farm, as you know. I know we have arguments but I'm grateful for your counsel, the money, and your good food. Now that winter has set in, it doesn't take much to finish my chores. Our lessons go quickly of an evening. I come to my room and just stare at the fire, remembering my wife, my children, all the good times. When I left downtown Baltimore with all the river rats that were scurrying about trying to get out of the way of the flames, I didn't even know my family was sick from that damn germ and suffering so horribly."

Anna pulled her shawl around her neck, "Well, it's just you and me this Christmas. Why don't you come in with me and teach me some more spelling? I studied my lesson good... eh... I don't remember which word to use."

Jackson tried to decide which was worse, feeding Anna words to spell or sitting alone in his room in the barn.

"You help me spell, I'll teach you about potato borers." Anna ran to the house. It was settled.

"I made coffee cake."

Her coffee cake was damn good.

The following morning, Jackson and Anna made their first trip into town together since Jackson had begun living in the barn. Anna asked Fred Miller to bring a few things now and then. However, with Christmas coming she knew Fred couldn't do as much shopping. Jenny had lost a baby and she needed attention. Anna visited Jenny once, but with her lessons and Jackson wanting to know more than Anna could teach him, there wasn't much time. Now there was no putting it off anymore. Anna needed supplies.

Jackson looked at the list Anna gave him.

"It will be quicker if you take one side of town and I take the other," Anna told him.

"Maybe, maybe!"

Anna put her hat on carefully so as not to disturb her newly coifed hair.

"What will be, will be."

They rode into town. No one noticed them at first. Jackson parked the buggy in a convenient place facing the right direction for when they left the downtown district. They jumped into action, Jackson hurrying to the grocery and hardware shops and Anna to the department store. She was waited on by a clerk who did not recognize her. What fun she had! It had been a long time since she shopped for anything new. A beautiful dress, gloves for herself and Jackson, a couple of bells to put on Jocko, and she splurged on a nice flannel shirt for Jackson. Finally, she purchased two pillowcases as a gift for Fred and Jenny.

Mr. Nickols, who owned the store, came over to Anna as she was paying her bill.

"Well, well, well, who have we here?"

Anna blushed but stayed calm.

"I know I haven't been shopping much lately, Mr. Nickols, but then I haven't been shopping anywhere else, either."

She tried to be cordial, "Business good this Christmas season?"

"Mrs. Schein, I appreciate you don't come here in my shop no more. I don't want trouble."

"Trouble? Why would you think I would give you trouble?" Anna stood toe-to-toe with Nickols.

"I have always been a good customer, haven't I? What is the problem?"

"Missus Schein, the whole town knows you and that nigger live together."

Anna took one step back and caught her breath.

"You don't ask, you just go. Please, I don't want no trouble." he said again.

"I'll thank you to keep a civil tongue in your head!"

Anna could hardly get her breath she was so angry.

"Jackson works for me, Sir. He is not my 'lover' as you indelicately put it. I need help on the farm! Are you going to help me? Is anybody going to help me? No! I have to hire help."

Anna was close to tears.

"We hear from people who know what you do. Please. Go."

Mr. Nickols was nice but adamant.

Anna's hand shook as she dug in her purse to pay for her purchases. While waiting for her change, she noticed a small crowd of people she recognized outside the door. The clerk hurriedly handed Anna her shopping bag and her change at the same time. Anna did not hesitate. She straightened her back, held her head up high as she always did to show pride and with a flourish of her shawl, left the store. The group of people, mostly women, followed her as she walked back to the buggy. There was no place to hide from the murmuring behind her back.

Jackson was ready for her. As soon as she entered the buggy, he slapped the reigns and Jocko jerked into a trot.

"Did you get everything on your list?"

Jackson glanced at Anna. She was stoic. He could feel her coldness to the situation. It was her way of getting above it. He admired Anna for that. Jackson was not so sure he could have lived the way she did all these years. He was always the happy-go-lucky kind of person. Well, on their way back home Jackson wanted to make her smile again.

"Back to your old self, Anna?" He patted her hand.

"When we get home, we will study some more. I want you to help me to write sentences correctly."

"You know, Anna," Jackson laughed, "there is such a thing as being too smart for your britches!"

Anna caressed her packages. She did get some pretty things and she did manage two Christmas gifts for Jackson. Soon they would be home, the trip into Stanton forgotten.

The next three weeks before the holiday, Anna and Jackson quarreled and bickered over nothing. Part of the reason was that Jackson had written several letters to Thomas but as time went on and he had not gotten a response, he became rather hard to live with. Jackson kept saying the post office was not delivering his mail on purpose. Anna reminded him that was not allowed to happen, besides the weather made traveling just about impossible. Two blizzards in two weeks made the roads impassable with high snow drifts. Jackson fussed and fumed over everything until Anna finally quit talking to him.

The day before Christmas, Anna saddled Jocko and told Jackson to go into town to see if any mail had come for him. She watched sadly as he zigzagged between the drifts. He left her without a word.

That night, Christmas Eve, Anna was alone. The tight feeling in her stomach came back again. The house was so quiet. Only the fire spoke to her and that was a hiss. She stared vacantly at the house Jackson made more livable by adding shelves, painting the furniture, and making a beautiful bookcase on one side of the fireplace. She thought she would braid more of the rug she started. But no, her heart was not in it.

Anna went to the bedroom. She put away the two packages she had wrapped for Jackson and let out an audible sigh. Jackson, of course, did not know about the presents. The way they had been arguing, Anna guessed he would never have suspected such generosity. Slowly, quietly, sadly, Anna closed the bureau drawer. With a heavy heart she began Christmas dinner.

Anna made a fish stew with herbs and cubed potatoes. Needing more milk, she put on her shawl and started for the Spring house. Halfway there she noticed a light in Jackson's room in the barn. Not knowing what happened in town, Anna decided not to bother him. On second thought, who was he not to tell her he was home safe and sound on such a night as this? He knew she would worry... or did he?

Anna went through the side door of the barn, checking stock, feed bins and the cleanliness of the barn. Jackson was a good worker. Everything was perfect except... Jocko still wore his saddle. That could only mean one thing. Jackson had gotten his mail! After taking care of Jocko, she went back to the house with her pitcher of milk.

Standing in front of the window, she waited for the first star to appear to begin her dinner as was the custom her father followed. Anna would celebrate Christmas Eve by dining alone.

# XVI

Anna knit her brows and through clenched teeth she tossed her words up the stairs, "You can rummage around Willie's room all you want, none of those clothes are going to fit you. You're too..." She thought better of it and said, "you're shorter than Willie was. And skinny," she added.

"Oh, for heaven's sake, woman, leave me be," Jackson retorted. He was standing naked in the middle of Willie's room. Clothes were strewn everywhere. He caught sight of himself in the oval ivory framed mirror that stood in the corner of the room. Even through the months of dust, he could see himself full length. He was muscular and firm. The skin on his body was lighter than his face and had the same smooth texture. The sun outlined the muscles he had earned from all the chores of lifting bails, chopping wood, and beautifying the house. Jackson closed his eyes, lifted his eyebrows, and pulled his chin up. "Anna could do worse," he thought.

He fingered the clothes he thought would fit. The shirts he had put on the bed were his size. Apparently, Anna's stingy husband kept everything he had acquired throughout his entire life. Of course the socks would fit. Now for the trousers. Willie had always been portly, so that might be a problem. A vest would be nice. The jacket Jackson found was too large, but worse luck, it was white. Jackson leaned over the railing, "Anna, can you make this jacket smaller in the shoulders?" There was no answer. "Anna. Can you make the waist smaller in the trousers? How about the length? Anna?"

"Oh, for heaven's sake, Jackson! Leave me be."

Jackson could not see the smile creep over Anna's face.

He pulled the trousers on and carefully walked down the steep stairs. He was holding the jacket. "See? This pair of black pants would be good for many occasions and if you can fix the jacket, too, I can go to the church Fred told me about... maybe even make some friends. It's still a long way 'til Spring." He waited. Anna was thinking it would be nice to get rid of him occasionally even though he kept to himself most of the time now. There was a coolness between them. They just did not get along anymore. Even the lessons were not going well. Anna never did give Jackson the Christmas presents she bought. Now she would give him the gloves. If he was going to look smart driving the surrey, he had to have gloves.

"Yes, I can sew those clothes for you. I'm not a tailor but I'll do the best I can." With that, she began to make herself a cup of tea.

"Thank you, Anna." Jackson was elated. He wanted so much to be with people who understood him. The church sounded like something of a miracle.

Anna started to heat the water for tea. While at the stove, she looked at Jackson who was in the middle of the room holding about four inches of material on either side of the pants and standing in the ends of the pant legs. She couldn't help smiling.

"What do you think?"

"I think you look silly."

Then Anna did something she had not done for a long time. She laughed until she bent over.

Jackson was a little hurt.

"What's so funny?"

Ann, still laughing, could not speak. She pointed a finger at him. He looked down at his feet. They were in the pant leg and it looked as if he had no feet. Anna's laugh was so melodious and infectious, Jackson began to laugh, too.

When Anna caught her breath, she said, "Well, if you want them I'll try to fit them to you." She went to the cupboard to get her sewing kit. As she began to mark and pin, Jackson, thinking she held the trousers, let go of the excess material. The trousers rode down his body, crumpling at his feet. Anna turned crimson and turned away. Jackson quickly drew up the pants holding them tightly. Anna started to pin the trousers again, but she could not continue. She began to laugh again. Jackson looked at her with disdain. Then he looked at her as if he saw her for the first time.

"Anna," he reached for her hand. She looked up at him and he decided not to touch her. He began again.

"Anna, I have given a great deal of thought to your predicament. And mine too, if you please. I know how we can stop all that scandalous talk in town."

Anna stopped laughing.

"I know we haven't been getting along lately but we do well together in the fields and we both have learned a lot, haven't we?" Anna thought about it and nodded her head in the affirmative.

"We both know we will make a lot of money," he looked heavenward, "God willing and good weather this summer. I had a friend, Carl. We were going to pool our money and buy a farm in the outskirts of Baltimore..." Jackson thought he better not mention Carl's thinking Colored people were too lazy to be good workers. "Instead," Jackson continued, "he became interested in automobiles. I guess it's the growing business of today. Carl and his buddy, Hans, started fixing automobiles. Well, I didn't want to do that so, I decided to leave and start a farm myself."

"What about your family?"

"I had a wife and three children. My whole family, including Mamma and Pappa died of an intestinal germ. My brother is a good doctor and he could not do anything for them."

"Your brother is a doctor?" Anna was impressed.

Jackson was holding a wad of material in front of the trousers while Anna pinned the back. She did not think he looked funny anymore. He looked vulnerable and sad, obviously wanting commiseration. Or was it her farm he wanted? She squinted her eyes trying to figure him out. Anna punched the needle she was threading into the pin cushion. "Is that why you're always asking me about my farm? Where it begins and where it ends? You want my farm?"

"I have a proposition for you, Anna. A fair one."

Anna got out her cup and saucer, opened the tea canister, looked at Jackson and asked if he wanted a cup of tea by tilting the canister with a questioning look. Jackson nodded affirmatively. After pouring the hot water into the cups, she put her hands on her ample hips and asked, "Well, what's your fair proposition?"

Jackson sprang like a tiger toward the table. "Those men are... even now, as we stand here... laughing at us. How they got away with their prank and how they convinced everybody you are some kind of a slut because living with a White man in sin would be just as bad for you as living with a Colored man would be..." Jackson always wanted to point that out to Anna. "Don't you want to do something about that?"

"What am I supposed to do about it? The whole town has been laughing at me all my life. Making fun of my father because he stuttered. Making fun of me because I'm ugly. But oh, when they needed me to help the mid-wife, or bathe someone who was sick, you know who they were praising? Willie! 'What a wonderful wife you have' they would tell him! The only person who is nice to me is Jenny Miller. Which reminds me. I must visit her. She must be so sad, losing the baby." Anna looked out the window toward the Miller farm. "I don't trust her either. As a matter of fact, I don't like her." Jackson raised an eyebrow. "She's too, I don't know... has no backbone." Anna sat down to her tea. Curiosity getting the best or her, she bent forward a little and asked, "How did you meet Fred? How come he was nice enough to tell you about the Colored church?"

Jackson sat down to drink his tea. "Can I have some sugar?"

Anna straightened up. For a moment, they looked deep into each other's eyes. It was the first time neither one of them looked away. Anna did find Jackson to be fascinating. The way he spoke in a soft voice that somehow carried far even if he was in the field. She had been told his kind of people were lazy and indigent. Here was a Colored man who seemed ambitious. Was she wrong about this man who walked like a cat?

On the other side of the table, Jackson was trying hard to read Anna's mind, but as usual, she was an enigma to him.

"Please?"

Anna took the lid off the sugar bowl and gave Jackson her spoon. He dug into the bowl putting three heaping teaspoons of sugar in his cup. Anna stiffened at the amount of sugar he used and quickly put the lid back on the bowl.

"Well," he began, "Fred and I were working close to our farm's... er... your farm-line, when I noticed he was trying to dig a tree stump. I offered to help. He was mighty glad to have an extra hand 'cause that stump was wide and deep."

Jackson smiled as he remembered the event. "I told him to sing along with me...did you know he has a voice almost as good as mine?"

Anna smirked good-naturedly.

"We sang and grunted that old stump right out!" Jackson took a sip of tea. "Tea is good, Anna. Then, we talked a little and one thing led to another and I mentioned I played the piano, led our church choir and did some singing."

"I know," Anna interrupted, "I heard you and your drunken friends."

"They are not my friends!"

Jackson hit the table with his fist. Anna leaned back in her chair, narrowed her eyes, and took a sip of her tea.

"You know what they did to us. We'll never be able to show our faces in town again unless we skulk around hiding from everybody. And I know you're still smarting about Mr. Nickols."

Anna put her cup down. She could see Jackson was getting truly angry. Jackson persevered, "You see how they fixed it so they wouldn't have to pay me? They saw a chance to embarrass you into selling the farm and cheat me out of my money, too. Well, they had to pay me. Now, we have to do something about our reputations." Jackson's voice grew louder as he rose from his chair. "We have to do someth..." Jackson's trousers began to slide down again. He quickly sat down.

The two people who were such misfits sat quietly staring at one another. Anna's face took on the stoical look she used to cover her thoughts. Finally, she raised her cup. Just as she was about to drink her tea, she looked over the brim of the cup at Jackson. The look put Jackson on alert.

"What's your 'fair' proposition?" She took a drink of tea.

"Marry me!" Jackson made it a demand.

Anna choked on her tea. She dropped the cup hard on the saucer, stiffened her back and with hatred in her voice screamed at Jackson, "Get out! Get out! Get out!"

Jackson put his hands up as if she had a gun on him.

"If you don't like the scheme, all you have to do is say 'no' and we'll forget the whole thing. Now, do you want to hear my proposition or not?"

Jackson knew she had to calm down first.

Anna was shaking as she stomped toward the door. Her finger

pointing to the barn she screamed, "Get out!" She planted her feet firmly, ready to fight if that would become a necessity.

Jackson stood up, this time he had a grip on Willie's trousers. "I am going upstairs to put my clothes on. We're going to talk this out." He started toward the stairs, turned back, picked up his cup and drained the tea. He looked at her with a twinkle in his eyes. She would make some man a damn good woman, he wanted to tell her. Instead he said, "Tea was good, Anna. Thanks." He carefully went up the stairs. Anna standing by the door with her finger still extended watched the arrogance of the man going to Willie's old room.

Hearing Jackson absorbed with his clothes again, Anna picked up her best cup. She turned it over and over, looking for flaws. No, not a mark on it. With a sigh of relief, she brought all the dishes to the sink. Washing her dishes first, she then put boiling water in the cup Jackson used to let it soak. Perhaps he was right. Marriage might be a solution to their dilemma at that. What could it hurt now? She owned everything. Jackson could not get his hands on her property and maybe people would leave them alone. She gave a grim look to the noise upstairs and sat down to wait for Jackson.

She heard the loud thump of the trunk Jackson had been raiding. He rushed down the stairs.

"Anna! Anna!"

He cried out.

"Your name isn't Anna! It's Annabelle!"

He ran to show her the wedding papers he found in the trunk.

"What's the matter with you? I know what my name is."

Jackson looked at Anna somewhat dazed.

"I don't know why I... I guess I just...well, your name reminded me of my wife's name, Clarabelle. It's an omen, Anna."

He looked triumphant.

Anna patted his arm. She had never given him any solace, but she could understand his loneliness.

"I understand, Jackson," she said, "I have a present for you." She disappeared into her bedroom. Jackson looked at the legal paper he showed Anna. She was so young when she married. Perhaps she was not the mean old lady she has made herself out to be. If she had gone to school, she might have been a different person, but she didn't. Anna came into the kitchen with a box.

"I had trouble finding them."

She held out the beautiful leather gloves she had bought him for Christmas.

Jackson was astonished.

# XVII

Jackson's heart was pounding as he jumped off the buggy. Some of the congregation were already noticing a stranger in their midst. He handily took care of Jocko, then pulled off his beautiful leather gloves. Jackson knew he looked very handsome in the clothes Anna so meticulously fitted to him. His overcoat hid the white jacket, but he had trouble keeping Willie's large brimmed hat straight on his head. Anna had tucked paper inside the brim and it seemed to work but it was still a worry. He nodded to several people he passed on his way to the lovely church.

"Good morning. Good morning."

Jackson tried to take in several people in each of his greetings.

"Mornin'," replied some of the parishioners. Jackson hoped the paper Anna put into the under-brim would hold up. Just to be sure, he did not doff his hat. He merely touched the brim as he greeted the minister.

"Jackson Freeman, Sir," he said loud enough for those nearby to hear.

"Reverend Harley Williams," the minister replied. "Welcome, brother, welcome." They shook hands. Reverend Williams noticed the hand he shook was a hard-working hand. Jackson was aware the minister was giving him the once-over as was every available girl who attended services that morning. Everyone noticed Jackson was alone. Perhaps he was single.

The church was small, exceptionally clean, and inviting. The white interior emphasized the black skin of the people dressed in their finest. The children's faces were shining, but their eyes were downcast or looking up at the ceiling. Jackson knew they were bored. He remembered Clara and Oliver at that age. He wanted to hug the little ones, to feel a child in his arms again. He tried not to think about his loneliness for his family, he had a mission here.

Jackson was beginning to feel at home with his Black brothers and sisters. It was a good feeling. Anna was far away and out of his mind, for now. Somehow, as he sat down, he began to think of the fire and how he never saw his children after the devastation. He never saw Clarabelle again, never kissed her goodbye. He shrugged the thoughts away. He needed a friend, and that man in the pulpit would become his friend, he schemed.

Jackson gingerly put his hat on his knee during the service. He caught a glimpse of paper peeping out of the brim and tried several times to tuck it back in place without success. After a while, he gave up and decided to hold the hat over his heart with his left hand for the rest of the service.

The beautiful voices singing the hymns surrounded him. Anna had a grating voice even when she was in a good mood. Could he ever teach her not to be so guttural? Jackson's heart soared as he joined in the singing.

At the end of the service, The Reverend Williams shook Jackson's hand heartily, "So glad you could come this morning', Sir. So Glad! Where are you stayin' in these parts? We would like to see more of you, Mr. uh, Freeman, is it? Always happy to have a new member." The large bill Jackson had placed in the basket as it was passed was noticed by the Reverend. "We're not a rich church but we're better off than most churches around here. Where are you from, Mr. Freeman?"

"Baltimore, Sir. I've been meaning to get out of the city and into the country all my life. Always wanting to farm and be independent. But you know how it is Reverend Williams, we all get into a rut and it's hard to get out and do something different." Jackson noticed a beautiful, voluptuous woman sashaying from one group to another, making small-talk and trying to keep from leaving the church grounds so that she could be introduced to Jackson. Finally, she could stand it no longer and made her way to the Reverend!

"Don't mean to interrupt you, Reverend," she smiled, holding the collar of her dress as she bent forward a little, "but I'm just not sure when the meetin' of the Society To Clean The Parish is to be and I wanted to be sure not to miss it. You'll excuse me for a moment, won't you?" She locked eyes with Jackson. Jackson got the message and looking at this handsome woman, he was tempted. He felt himself get warm all over and knew his cheeks were becoming a bronze color. How long had it been since had held a woman in his arms?

Emma had dressed very beautifully this morning. Her blue taffeta skirt billowing by the two petticoats underneath was the talk of the women of the congregation. She wore a gold pin at the end of her neckline, which was as low as would be allowable for church services. A blue and white hat sat straight on her head emphasizing her large eyes. There was a natural beauty-mark under her right eye that was more noticeable when she winked, when she told a mischievous story or while repeating gossip. That eye narrowed before she turned away from Jackson, just perceptible enough to make a man wonder what it meant.

"You see, Reverend Williams, I'll be entertaining my sister, Feeny and her new husband soon, so I would like to get my part of the church work over before that time. You understand."

"I do indeed. Please excuse me, Mr. Freemen, while I check the dates. Oh! Let me introduce you to Mrs. Beech. This is Jackson Freeman from Baltimore, Emma. If you keep him company, I'll be right back with the information."

Jackson was disappointed. He wanted the Reverend to ask him to stay for dinner, but now he knew Emma Beech would try to get him to go to her house for a repast. And if he made an excuse, he would not be able to stay long enough to make a friend of the Reverend.

"Baltimore," Emma murmured, "I have heard it is a lovely city, Mr. Freeman."

She was careful not to gush. Just the right amount of nicety. "I have never lived in a big city. I'm just a country girl. I guess I'll always stay that way. I..." If she noticed Jackson's quick look at her, she didn't let on and kept right on her course, "...don't know what I would do if I had to leave this place. I'm sure if I would leave, I would be lost, lost, lost."

Jackson smiled to himself. Lost! This woman is never lost. She knows just where she is all the time.

There are times when things go right. This was one of them. The Reverend had posted the dates Emma wanted on the vestibule wall and as he quickly read the working times, he nervously took several glances out the door to watch Emma ingratiating herself to Jackson. That girl is the devil's helper, he thought. He knew of her escapades. The Reverend had kinfolk in Saint Louis, and he heard about Feeny soliciting candidates for another husband for her sister.

Harley Williams needed a friend as much as Jackson did. Most of the people here played checkers and talked farm talk. One look and he knew Jackson was more educated than anybody with whom he had been associating. The Reverend hungered for a friend on a higher plane. Not that he did not like the people here. He did. They were hardworking with aspirations of owning their own farms instead of working for the White landowners.

One more look out the door. Emma was laughing easily with Jackson. Come to think of it, the Reverend had a sister who was ready to marry and coming to visit him any day now. That thought hurried the Reverend out the door and he began talking from the top of the steps.

"Yes, I have the date, Emma. It's a week from Monday, nine o'clock and bring your own lunch. The ladies of the Bethel will bring casserole dinners for the evening folks. The church will provide the beverages. We'll be glad for your help, Sister. Anything else you need to know?"

Emma turned to the reverend. Her face was radiant.

"Thank you, Reverend."

Then, laughing, she said, "I have just asked Mr. Freeman to have dinner with our family and he is hesitating. Now, you tell him he'll enjoy himself at our place. We won't bite him."

She threw her head back and laughed again. Jackson thought her laugh was beautiful. Not today but soon, Emma Beech. He let her see his approval of her womanly beauty.

The Reverend was beginning to feel the electricity that was building between them and he quickly tried to quench the fire. "Why Emma, I've already invited Mr. Freeman to dinner and he was trying to let you down nicely. Ain't that so, Sir?"

"Well, yes."

Jackson's heart soared. He did it! He would get to know Reverend Williams, make him understand that he was sincere about marrying Anna Schein.

Emma pouted, trying not to show her temper. The Reverend won this one and the look on his face told her that. She extended her gloved hand to Jackson, who did not shake it but held it fondly. "I hope to see you again, Mrs. Beech."

"Emma please, Mr. Freeman. Call me Emma." She smiled and quickly turned on her heel toward her surrey. Emma never stayed long in a place of defeat.

Jackson's eyes followed her to her buggy. The Reverend caught the look. Jackson could not cover up his interest. "Well Reverend, you caught me. But it's always nice to see a beautiful woman, isn't it?"

Turning Jackson around toward the house, the Reverend said, "Emma has a way with her. Widows always know how to make a man feel welcome. Best you bring your wife with you the next time you come to church."

"A widow? Well, I know how lonely that can be. I have been a widower for over a year now. That is not long enough to forget a terrible time for me, Reverend. Sometime, if I stay here and we become good friends, perhaps you'll be able to help me. Right now, I'm going to enjoy this lovely day."

"And a good dinner, Mr. Freeman. My girl puts a good meal on the table come Sabbath. I hope you like pork roast, chitlins, and buttered greens. No one cooks better than Vivian."

As they started up the steps on the parsonage, Jackson looked up the stairs and saw the Reverend's girl All of fifteen, Jackson thought.

Vivian dressed exceptionally well for a servant in these parts. Her hair was beautiful, pulled back with a large braid ending at her shoulders. She had a small cropped nose and a very full cupid's-bow mouth. Vivian smiled when she saw the two men approaching her. Her dimples were deep and although her teeth were uneven, it didn't detract from her smile. She considered herself lucky to be working for the Reverend and was perfectly content in the big house. This could change. Who was this stranger?

"Vivian, we have a guest for dinner."

Vivian made a small almost imperceptible curtsy, spun on her heels, and ran to the kitchen. Her heart was beating fast. Why? perhaps her friends were right. Maybe she should stop reading those romantic novels. Was there such a thing as love at first sight? In her young mind, Vivian was a beautiful heroine waiting for her knight in shining armor. She sat down with a thud.

"Mr. Freeman never even noticed me," she whispered to herself.

# XVIII

Anna stood in the middle of her dusty bedroom looking at herself in the milky mirror. She had not taken care of herself over the years. Her face was still pretty, nevermind her age. She was older than Jackson, how much she was not sure. He always was clean and shaved. Always dressed nicely after he was through working. He was city folk. Anna sniffed at that. She studied her hands. They were large and puffy from field work. She had not done any housework since Willie died and the house looked it. Jackson had cleaned Willie's upstairs bedroom and it was nice. It made Anna feel he was censuring her. He had made a mess trying to make some of Willie's clothes work for him, it was true. Perhaps he was just making up for that. Anna decided to clean her room.

She needed more light. Putting one knee on the carefully made bed, Anna leaned across it to open the old piece of cloth that substituted for a blind. Pulling hard at the material, it gave way and she fell face-down on the pillow Jackson had slept on when Keith had put him to bed with her. She quickly got up. Anna had never used that pillow since that time. It was as if she could feel Jackson was still lying there. Angry at herself and at the situation she was in, she stood on the bed and yanked at the cloth one more time. It was so old it shredded, leaving the nails exposed.

Even though the window was high and small, the light poured in, revealing the accumulation of a year's worth of dust. This was not the way she had lived before Willie died. What had happened to her? Looking around, she began to remember all the lonely nights she had spent lying in her bed after Willie's footsteps ceased upstairs. When she thought he was asleep, she felt safe. She would sneak into the kitchen, make herself a cup of tea, eat cookies or bread and butter sandwiches, and make beautiful stories in her mind.

The night shielded her movements when she would pretend she was a beautiful stranger in Stanton who lived in a lovely house. The men in her dream life were big and strong, always fighting over her favors. Here she had been in a dream world, but no more. Jackson had talked about making the bedroom larger. Anna envisioned two beds, but did Jackson? Well, he better! He was, even now, negotiating with some minister to marry her. Was she doing the right thing? Jackson said it was the only way. But was it? He mixed her up! On the other hand, Anna had the feeling that he would make them both rich. After all, wasn't that what she really wanted? He would do all the work and she would do all the negotiating, since he was a Negro. He said it would happen if she would do everything he told her to do. Jackson said she was smart. Her lessons proved that. All she had to do was believe in herself. But could she?

Anna's shoulders drooped as she slowly sank into the bed. She did not believe in herself. Her eyes traveled slowly around the room. How ugly the house was. Now she was seeing the rooms through Jackson's eyes. That could be changed but how could she change herself? She took all her clothes off and looked in the mirror. It was not too much of a revelation. Anna knew she had a mature body. Her breasts sagged a little and there was a thicker waist, but wasn't that normal? Her legs were good; her arms, were a mite heavy. That was from hard work. Most of the women she knew of her age were not beautiful. They just had nicer clothes. Nicer shoes. As she turned her head slightly, her hair tumbled in front of her shoulders. As thick and beautiful as her hair was, it was tinged with grey and lay in clumps because it was greasy.

Anna plunged into action. No Negro was going to be cleaner than her. Or better dressed, for that matter. She cleaned the house. Found a piece of material and quickly made a lovely curtain for the bedroom, folding it over the nails that were already there. Rummaging around the trunks, she found a forgotten bedspread, new sheets, and a pillow which had a slip on it reading "I awoke and found that life was duty."

"How true," she thought.

Tired as she was, she did not stop. There was another trunk with clothes she'd not worn for years. Would anything fit? There was a pretty petticoat, lisle stockings that had been carefully mended at the heel, and a box. She opened the box and stared at the contents. A lovely pair of slippers. Tanned with age, buckles tarnished, spool heels. Her wedding shoes. A rim of tears began to form as she picked them up, picturing her wedding day. It was a stormy Friday. Everybody said it was a bad omen. The marriage would be miserable. They were right.

These memories gave her new vigor. She washed her body and then her hair, rinsing the soap out many times as the girls in the city did. Putting on a clean petticoat and a newly found chemise, she went outside into the sunshine. The day was beautiful! Anna felt revived. Her hair was brown, and the grey gave it a smoky-silver look. She tossed her head, feeling the water dripping on her shoulders and back. Running in the sunlight with her arms outstretched, she felt the warmth and it made her feel better than she had ever felt before.

Anna had a contralto voice and she began to sing the hymn Jackson had taught her. She stopped abruptly. Why did she think of that old hymn? She sat on the ground near the brook. The cold water felt wonderful. Spring chores were around the corner. There would be no time for frivolities. Anna put cold mud on her face, she let her head fall back to face the sun. She could feel the mud drying and making her face itch.

What else do the beautiful women of the magazines do to become more desirable? Anna got up and walked to the stream where the water was clear. Cupping her hands, she rinsed off all the mud. The front of her dress became wet and cold. Her nipples began to stand out. She folded both hands over her large breasts to warm them. A strange wave of emotion came over her. She had been content never thinking of a man in "that way," as young girls in her school days used to say. She began to feel ashamed of her feelings. If only a prince would come on a white horse and whisk her away. The word "white" began to mean something to her, too. Damn Jackson! No! Damn Willie! If only she had not married him, she might have married a man she could love. At the time, she thought it best to have a home she felt comfortable in.

Slowly, Anna started back to the house. Her petticoat clung to her buttocks and the back of her legs. She had never been aware of her breasts moving as she walked before. Suddenly, she wanted to be the most beautiful woman in the whole world. The desire became so great, it made the world stand still for a moment. Anna raised on her toes and let out a horrible guttural scream before running back inside.

She slammed the door behind her. The afternoon sun sent long shadows in the house, making everything glow. Anna admired the cleaned rooms. With a Mona Lisa smile, she went into the bedroom and took a long time at her toilette. When she was through, she could not help thinking how pretty she looked. Then she destroyed her perfect "look" and put on a plain dress. Jackson should not know how she felt about her looks or that she wanted to be beautiful. He should not notice any change in her. She would make a Sunday dinner as usual. He would be full of his church experience and she would dutifully listen. But in her heart, Anna was happy with herself for the first time in her life. Things were changing for the better. Today, Anna wanted to feel religious. She would ask Jackson to help her with the Bible. She knew he would.

# XIX

Jackson sat at the large table aware of the beautiful crocheted cloth. Clarabelle had such a hard time learning the craft because she hated to crochet or knit. She did manage a bedspread and dresser cover. Jackson remembered the first time she graced his bed. The wedding had been a happy family affair, everybody wishing them the best. For the most part, it had been a good marriage. What went wrong? Jackson wished he could ask her just that one question. He knew he was not the Casanova his brother Thomas was. Jackson's sexual desires were accommodated by one of the girls in the house by the railroad tracks. He kept that a secret. When he married, he never touched another woman. Not to this day. He thought Clarabelle was as true to him as he was to her. Was Henry White such a good lover? How and when did he entice Clarabelle?

"Have some more meat, Mr. Freeman."

"Thank you. Please, call me Jackson."

The Reverend smiled and nodded as he passed the succulent roast. Jackson let the Reverend talk about the farms, the farmers, and their problems. It seemed their biggest problems were keeping body and soul together during the winter months. They were aware the cities needed vegetables and fruit all the year long, not just when they were plentiful. So they tried to keep enough food as they could in cold storage cellars. Of course, by the end of January the fruit begins to wither and the vegetables would all be gone. The women fared better by taking in sewing and doing housework for the White women. Things did not change in the Spring. Farmers start all over again.

Vivian fluttered around Jackson and brought in the dessert, a lovely raisin custard. Jackson ate in a gentlemanly manner even though it was hard not to tear into the food. He had never had such a delicious meal.

"My, my, what a wonderful meal and such a lovely dessert," Jackson exclaimed.

Vivian beamed. The Reverend took a quick look at her. He did not want anything to spoil his way with Vivian. She was young and eager to have him make love to her for the favors he could provide. Her life was comfortable with him. If he were to marry such a young thing, the congregation might frown on it. There was always the problem of a pregnancy, but so far so good. Perhaps it was not a good idea to have Jackson here as a friend. Perhaps it would be better to meet him in the church office. There they could have a drink and talk, play chess, or they could just walk, weather-permitting.

The Reverend offered Jackson a cigar. Jackson raised a hand, "I never smoke, but it doesn't bother me if you have an after-dinner cigar."

The late afternoon sun filtered through the heavy curtains, sending long shadows over the room. The Reverend's cigar smoke wafted lazily toward the ceiling. Jackson was at peace. Spending time with his brothers and sisters was just what he needed.

"This is a lovely home, Reverend Williams and you have it so tastefully furnished."

Jackson's eyes twinkled, "Being head of your church hasn't been a poverty commitment to you, has it?" The Reverend smiled at the remark, revealing his good sense of humor.

Jackson studied the imposing man sitting across from him. No fool! He had already deduced that. Sophisticated, that was evident, but was he liberal enough to understand what he wanted him to do? Would he really know what he and Anna were experiencing from the townspeople? And more to the point, would he marry two people who needed each other for their own purposes? Jackson had to make a judgment. He observed the reverend more closely. The face of the man was rather angelic, which was very advantageous for a Colored man ministering to the sick and poor. His skin was light and his features were more Indian than Negro, but his preaching was powerfully evangelistic.

Harley Williams had never gone to seminary school. He sold his services to the church by sheer charm. No formal education had he. He was a self-made man in every way. Never showing himself at a disadvantage, he never divulged his real childhood, when he traveled with a con man who played minister at crossroads. If you knew how to do it, a traveling minister could always get a following, come up with a few shekels and possibly a warm meal. Harley began to study the Bible. He watched how rich people behaved. He became very polished. Harley did not want Jackson to know any of this. He especially did not want Jackson to know about Vivian.

The Reverend wrapped his lips around the cigar, turning it first one way, then another with his thumb and index finger. Taking the cigar out of his mouth, he leaned forward toward Jackson.

"Tell me about yourself, Freeman, you are from Baltimore? Were you there during the great fire? Tell me about it. We got a lot about it in the newspapers but it's not like hearing it from a person who was there."

Jackson began talking about the fire, reliving those horrible thirty-six hours. As he spoke, Vivian sat close to the door in the other room. She opened the door a crack and became hypnotized, not only by the story of the fire, but by the storyteller. Vivian admired Jackson's beautiful voice, the way he used his hands and the cock of his head. Yes, there was such a thing as love at first sight. Fairytales do come true.

Noticing that Jackson was reliving a bad time in his life, the reverend poured him a glass of wine and offered some crackers and cheese. As Jackson drank the wine, he felt more relaxed and continued talking about the horror of the fire. Vivian moved, making a slight sound. Suddenly, Jackson became alert. This sentimental journey into the past was not what he wanted to talk about. What he said here today might make a great difference in the future. Jackson decided not to go into his homecoming after the fire. That could be the subject for another time.

"Freeman, I've been a minister for a long time. I feel there is something more here."

"Well yes, Reverend." Jackson grew silent. The cool spring breeze billowed the curtains into the room. Williams started to pour more wine in Jackson's glass. Jackson indicated he did not want more and stood up.

"Funny, Reverend, I never loved my father in life as much as I did after he died. I began to understand him. Why he stayed in the background. It was the easy way out. Let Mamma be the one to work, scold, plan. You know, keep the family together. He worked hard and brought in as much money as he could. Rather than argue with Mamma, he leaned back and let her do the rest. I don't intend to live my life that way."

Jackson's eyes flashed angrily; he could not hold back his passion for respectability.

"I will have what I want. I will get it."

He sat down. Taking the last sip of wine, he carefully put the glass down on the table. Jackson crossed his legs, folded his hands across his well-filled stomach and said, "I didn't mean to go into all that. I'm grateful you listened to me. I guess I needed to tell someone. Thank you."

Harley began thinking he was too hasty. Perhaps he misread Jackson's calm, clean-cut appearance. He would have to watch what he said to Jackson.

"It is amazing what thirty-six hours can do to your life," Jackson continued. He did not tell the Reverend about Clarabelle or Henry White. She was dead. God rest her soul. He made a point of looking at his vest pocket watch, which he was wearing in Willie's vest.

"Reverend, I must not take up too much more of your time."

The Reverend Williams crushed his cigar out, stood up, and extended his hand. Jackson sincerely shook his hand and warmly said, "Thank you for a fine meal and a lovely afternoon. Be sure to tell Vivian what a good cook she is for one so young." They walked to the door,

"You have really helped me sort out those terrible days. I've held everything inside for so long, I didn't realize what a burden it had been."

As they reached the hall, Jackson carefully picked up his hat so as not to disturb the rolled paper inside the lining. Reverend Williams put a hand on Jackson's shoulder and ushered him outside. Vivian scooted upstairs as fast as she could to watch Jackson get into his buggy. Jackson was at a loss as to what to say so that he and the Reverend could spend more time together. He did not need to worry.

The Reverend looked up at Jackson and with a wave of his hand he said, "Perhaps the next time you come, we can play checkers. Do you play chess?"

Jackson nodded.

"Good! We can get into some politics. We have to fight for more education for our children, don't you agree?"

Jackson nodded again, this time picking up the reigns slowly, getting Jocko ready to go on their way.

"I have books, Mr. Freeman, you may borrow them anytime."

Jackson was elated. His smile was broad and genuine, "Jackson! Call me Jackson!" he said over his shoulder. "See you next Sunday! And thank you, again!"

And with that, he happily slapped the reigns putting Jocko into a snappy trot. He relaxed. As he raised his hat to put it on his head, all the papers flew out and the hat wound up over Jackson's ears. He laughed heartily, threw the hat up and caught it. It had served its purpose.

From the upstairs window, Vivian watched as the papers wafted gently from one bush to another. She cocked her head.

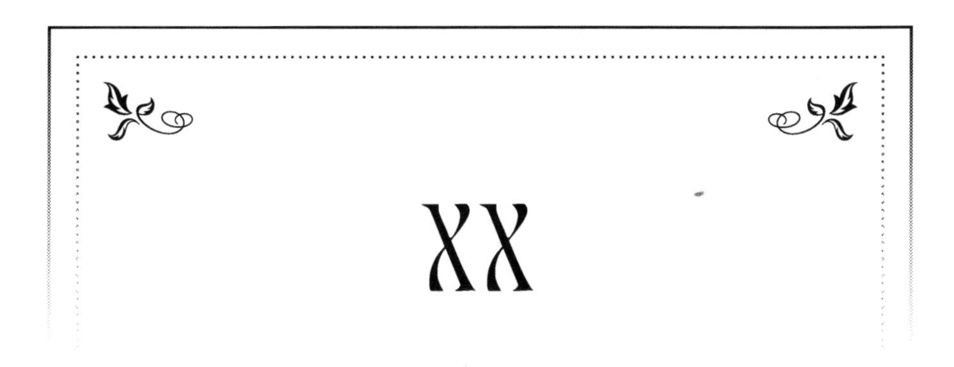

# XX

Reverend Williams studied the checkerboard; Jackson studied the Reverend. Of all the times he wondered how he would approach the Reverend about marrying Anna, he never dreamed it would be the Reverend himself, caught in the dilemma of his own making, who would give him the perfect opening. Jackson felt something was bothering his new friend. The Reverend was losing badly, which was strange, for the man was a good player. Jackson himself was also having a hard time keeping his mind on the game. Always trying to get on the right side of the Reverend, Jackson gave him all the time he wanted. As a matter of fact, Williams took so much time, Jackson's mind wandered. He had learned a lot since last September when he first set eyes on Anna. How do you take care of the animals? You keep to the most boring routine and the barn (always the worst chore) had to be kept clean at all times. He had refused to take care of the chickens. He hated them. This was not farming the way Jackson had imagined it to be. Now crops, that was where the money was. He was learning about crops from the church congregation. How gratifying it was to know that he really did have a love for the soil, but more than that, he was becoming an exceptional farmer. Even Anna said so.

The Reverend put his hand to his mouth and coughed, breaking Jackson's reverie. Still, the man did not make a move on the board. Jackson looked around the comfortable room. He enjoyed his visits away from Anna and her demands, feeling at home with his new friends. Jackson knew the Reverend tried to keep him interested in coming to church every Sunday so they could talk politics, gossip, and review the news of the week. Playing board games or cards was not Jackson's favorite pastime but if that was what the Reverend wanted to do, Jackson complied. The Reverend took great delight in winning. Jackson let him.

"Your move, Reverend."

"I know!"

"I think I've got you this time..." Jackson hid a smile.

"Maybe not, Jackson, maybe not."

"I haven't seen Vivian today... she all right?"

"Yes, she's fine. There! Let's see you cope with that move! She's gone to see her mother. She lives over the boundary into the other county."

"I see. Well, now I do think I've got you... oops... I can't do that, can I?" Mmmm, then I'll just have to render you helpless here and take your last king!"

"Don't have my mind on the game, Jackson."

The Reverend stood up and stretched. Jackson moved just his eyes to look up at the troubled man.

"Oh, not to take credit away from you. You play a mean game. It's just that I… Damn it, Jackson, I'm worried."

When he saw the look on Jackson's face, he added, "Or did you already know that."

"No."

"Well, I am. The truth is, I have been with Vivian. You understand what I'm saying?"

Their eyes met.

"I guessed it."

"She hasn't been... you know... willing lately. I've been wondering if there was another man."

Jackson leaned back, "Did you ever stop to think she might be pregnant?"

Reverend Williams sat down hard and clenched the arms of his chair.

"I've thought about another man. If she was pregnant, I would be proud to marry her and tell the congregation we were married a long time, 'cept she was so young we kept it a secret 'til she understood more about being a preacher's wife. Why wouldn't she come to me? She knows I would give her everything she needed. Oh Jackson, if she is with child, my child, I would be the happiest man in the world. Don't nothin' come closer to Heaven than a man has his own child."

The Reverend held his hand over his eyes and leaned on his elbow. Jackson tried to guess his age. Probably late thirties. "Having Vivian was the best thing that ever happened to me," he said into his cuff. Then he straightened up, looking Jackson in the eye.

"I know she looked at you in that special way women have, and you are much older than I am, so it's not my age she dislikes." Williams leaned forward, putting his hands flat on the table, and looked hard into Jackson's eyes.

"You been with Vivian?" he demanded.

For a moment, Jackson was taken aback. Then he threw his head back and laughed.

"Reverend Williams, I'm not that much older than you. And as a matter of fact, I've been having my own woman problems. I was hoping you could help me!"

The two men laughed heartily, and the tension vanished as quickly as it had begun. They became quiet, each with his own thoughts. Jackson saw his opportunity. He slowly stood up, walked to the other side of the table, folded his arms, and faced the Reverend. He leaned on the table and for the first time called the Reverend by his given name.

"Harley, we can help one another. I can do what you cannot do. I can find Vivian, see what the problem is, perhaps even bring her back to you. In return, you can do me a great favor."

Harley looked perplexed, "What can I do for you, Jackson?"

"We won't talk about that now. It is rather involved. Only you can perform this service for me. When I return, whether or not Vivian wants to come back, I expect to cash in on my favor."

"What's the mystery about? And how do I know you are not the one responsible for Vivian's disappearance? I know she was happy with me until you came along. Never wanted to leave this house! Why, she loved every piece of furniture, polished and cleaned this place like it was her own. Only when you came along did I see a change in her."

"It's not Vivian I've been seeing. I have made overtures to Feeny. By the way, what kind of a name is Feeny?"

"Baby talk for Josephine."

"Oh, I wondered. To make a long story short, I have not gotten what I want from her. She's too busy telling me about how wonderful Emma

Beech is. The widow is after me hard. I don't want to get into anything permanent with her."

"Well, I'll be damned! I never would have guessed it," the reverend said with great relief. He stood up in front of Jackson who was still half sitting on the table and now didn't have room to stand but had to look up at the towering figure. Bringing his face close to Jackson, he said, "And I was wanting my daughter to meet you. She stayed in my wife's hometown to get an education. Justine has been dead for fifteen years." The Reverend shook his head in disbelief.

"You see, Jackson, even I had designs on you! I tried to keep you away from the Widow Beech and all the time it was Feeny you were after."

"No Harley, that is not my problem. I want to get married and I want you to perform the ceremony. No questions asked."

The Reverend straightened up.

"As long as it's not Vivian, I'll do it. I promise you when you return, with Vivian or not, I'll marry you to your gal! Who is it? One of the pretties in the choir?"

"No questions asked. Deal?"

"Deal."

# XXI

Arbour Road looked more like an alley than a street. Jackson held the paper closer to his eyes. In the fading light, he read again the scribbling on the soiled sheet of paper. Arbour Road, that's what it said. Jackson began to realize Vivian was not staying with her mother because this part of town was...unless her mother was...surely that was not the case. Jackson entered the street thinking he wasted money trusting the man at the bar who told him where he could find Vivian Coleman.

"Hey, Mister, got a nickel for a cup of coffee?" a disheveled man asked. Ignoring the plea for money, Jackson crossed the street. One-three-two Arbour Road was standing between two empty lots. A dim light in an upstairs window softly glowed through the dirty glass. The first floor of the building had been a store of some kind. It was dark. Jackson went to the side door and knocked. No answer. The knob turned hard, but the door was not locked. Making his way up the dark, dismal stairway, Jackson thought he heard a small voice. He called out "Vivian!" No answer. "Vivian!" He was at the top of the stairs in suffocating air. There it was again. A thin voice came from the room where the sparse light streaked a path from the bedroom into the hall.

"Azalea?"

"Jackson Freeman."

A slight gasp, then a voice filled with tearful grief pleaded, "Go back! Don't come in here, I'm sick."

Jackson opened the door with his foot. Vivian was lying on a dirty disheveled bed. Her hair was matted and frizzy spreading out like a twisted black halo on the pillow. She heard the door open and pulled the limp covers over her face. When she spoke her voice was muffled. "Mr.

Jackson, please, please! Azalea wrote to the Reverend telling him I'll never come back."

Jackson pulled Vivian into his comforting arms and sat on the bed.

"Vivian, what's the matter?"

She hid her face in his chest. Jackson cradled her and began to croon a soothing hymn. Tenderly, he smoothed her hair. Finally, letting herself go limp, Vivian felt safe enough to fall into a fitful sleep. Leaning against the headboard, Jackson slowly raised his feet on the bed. summing up the situation, it was obvious this was not a place that was used for entertaining men. Why were the windows closed on such a warm night? Who was Azalea? Jackson felt Vivian's forehead. Fever.

In a little while, Vivian stirred. She looked at Jackson with dark sunken eyes. She admired him the first time she saw him at the rectory. He always was kind to her and always complimented her. What must he think of her now?

"Don't you know, Child, everyone is wondering where you are? Why didn't you send word to the people who love you that you didn't meet your Mamma? Where is she? I can fetch her for you."

Ignoring all the questions, Vivian began babbling. "I'm gonna die!" She shook her head affirmatively, "I know it. I'm being punished. God is punishing me for wanting big, beautiful house and pretty clothes. Mamma told me I'd come to no good." With clumsy fingers, Jackson tried to wipe the tears streaming down her frail, frightened face.

"What is wrong with you? What hurts? Have you seen a doctor?"

Vivian hid her face with her thin trembling hands. "I let Reverend Williams... we... I let him in my bed." She clutched Jackson's coat. "I don't want nobody to know..." She had exhausted the last ounce of energy she had. Her hands became limp. Letting go the lapels of Jackson's coat, she sank into Jackson's chest.

Jackson patted her as he spoke, "Reverend Williams will do right by you, Vivian. He loves you. He wants you home. This can all be remedied. All you have to say is that you were so young, you didn't want people to know you and the Reverend were married 'cause he's so much older than you."

"I hate him! I hate him for doing this to me. I never thought about being with him." She spoke through her tears, "He offered me so much and he's gone a lot, you know, ministering to the people. It was like I lived in a dream world... I, I used to pretend..."

She was gasping for breath now. Twisting in his arms, she held her head up to get some air. There was an odd odor when she moved. Jackson laid her down.

"You rest, child. You're too tired to think now. This Azalea, is she taking care of you? I'll find her to tell her you're coming with me." He spoke to her as one speaks to a sick child. In a melodious singsong, he reassured her. "We'll get a good doctor. Why, in no time at all, you'll be feelin' fine." Then, with a smile in his voice, he admonished her, "You want a healthy baby, don't you?"

"Ain't gonna be no baby."

Suddenly, Jackson realized what the odor was. He was no stranger to birthing. With one yank, he pulled the covers off the bed. No wonder she covered herself in this heat. She lay in a pool of blood. Vivian raised up on one elbow.

"I'm goin' to die."

She tossed her head like a spoiled child, "I don't care."

Jackson darted for the door to procure a doctor. He stopped short... what or who was standing there. He felt relieved when the apparition moved. Azalea walked into the thin light. She stood close to the bed, her eyes never leaving Jackson's face. Without looking at Vivian, she asked, "Who is this man?"

"It's all right, Azalea, don't be scared. This is Jackson Freeman, all the way from home. I know him well. He thinks he can help me. Did you bring me some water?" All the time she was speaking, Vivian clawed at the covers trying to hide the horror of her condition.

"I left the tray in the hall when I heard a man's voice. I'll fetch the water and clean sheets now. I'll be right back."

Before Azalea could move, Jackson grabbed her by her shoulders. "Who is the best doctor in these parts? Get him!"

This stranger frightened Azalea. She was glad to get away from the situation and fairly flew down the stairs. Jackson went back to Vivian. "Where are your things?" She stared at him. "Your traveling bag?"

"At the hotel."

Leaning back against the pillow, Vivian gave Jackson a small smile.

"I'm not going anywhere. Azalea will take care of me to the end."

Her attitude infuriated Jackson.

"What hotel? Where did you get such a nurse? Who is that woman?"

"I took a room upstairs from the bar called Adagio's. As for Azalea, my sister got her for me. My sister has gotten rid of lots of babies and..."

"What! You had an abortion?"

"When I knew for sure, I made her tell me where to get Azalea."

Vivian screamed, "I didn't know what else to do!"

"You let that dirty woman scrape your insides in this filthy mess of a room? Are you crazy?" Jackson wanted to turn her over his knee and spank her but when he looked at the sweet face wracked in pain and misery, he quietly said, "Get some sleep, my dear. I'll get a doctor."

He waited until Vivian relaxed and went to sleep. Tiptoeing around the bed, he put the pitcher of water and a glass near her. He tried to open the window, but it would not budge. Not wanting to wait any longer, he ran down the stairs to find a doctor. Nobody was on the street. Looking down Arbour, Jackson saw a sign dimly lit by the gaslight on the corner. He ran to a decrepit tavern. The sign read 'Pappa Dinks.' He prayed there would be someone who could help him. Jackson straightened his clothes before entering. He didn't want to look panicked.

The bartender wiped his hands on a dirty towel, "What's your drink, Mister?"

"Gin. Gotta good doctor nearby? Mind you, a good one!"

"Well, Doc Straw-Hat used to be good. Retired now and makes his home in the middle booth right over there." The bartender put a drink down in front of Jackson, "Two bits."

Jackson paid for the drink.

"Doc Straw-Hat? He got a real name? I want a real doctor. I have a sick girl on my hands. There's a dollar in it for you. Give me the name of a good doctor."

"If you got a girl in trouble," the bartender leaned over the bar, "I'd keep it to myself it I was you. The men around here don't like strangers. Or have you noticed?"

Jackson had not noticed. He was too intent on his mission to think of anything but getting a doctor for Vivian. The bartender straightened up and wiped the scarred top of the bar. Jackson saw the men taking quick glances at him from time to time.

"This Doc-uh-Straw-Hat, is he a good doctor?"

"The Doc is all right, Mister. Oh, he may be a little tipsy all the time, but he sure took good care of all the girls around here."

Jackson gave the bartender a dollar and tried to look nonchalant as he carried his drink to the middle booth. Doc knew he was being talked about and was ready for Jackson.

"Doctor?"

"Doctor Straw-Hat." He extended a pudgy, sweaty hand.

"Jackson Freeman, sir."

"Well, I can tell you're not from around these parts. Sit down and enjoy your drink. Best thing about the night is a good drink and a good woman."

Jackson smiled. Inside, he wanted everything to go fast but he had to be sure this man was not an incompetent doctor. Taking a sip of a drink, he wished he had not ordered, Jackson began to wonder if he was doing the right thing by coming here at all.

"I have a sick girl, Doctor. She got into trouble and how she ever got this Azalea woman..."

"Azalea!"

"You know her?"

"Take me to your sick girl, Freeman!"

Doc drank the last of his drink, finished Jackson's gin and grabbed his bag, which was always on the seat next to him. He moved fast for an overweight man, all four feet, seven inches of him.

They were sweating profusely when they reached the top of the stairs. No sound came from the dimly lit room. Doc unbuttoned his sleeves and pulled them up as he dashed about preparing to attend to Vivian. Opening his black bag, taking out the necessary medicines, he placed them within reach on a clean towel. Jackson was relieved to see him go about his doctoring in a very professional way. Getting this doctor was not a mistake.

Straw-Hat examined Vivian.

"Lord, in Heaven above," he exclaimed.

"Open the windows, Freeman, we need some air in here. Bring the light closer, too."

Jackson wrestled with the window, even though he knew how hard it was to open the last time he had tried. They were painted shut so many years ago, it would have taken a crowbar to open them. Not wanting to take too much time with something that could not be done, Jackson rushed to give Doc more light. He stood back, waiting to see if he could be of more help. "Is there more water in the wash bowl?"

Jackson looked in the bowl on the stand.

Yes, but how long it's been here, I don't know."

"It's just to wash her. I'll use alcohol where I need it."

Jackson looked but could not find anything to wash Vivian with so, he began to look in the drawers of the dresser. There he found Vivian's purse and a few personal belongings. She did have some beautiful handkerchiefs. Jackson quickly folded a couple and made a washcloth of them. As he washed Vivian's beautiful body, Doc pushed her legs apart and began to probe. Jackson could not help feeling a need for a woman. She was a beautiful girl. And…

Oh, yes, he better remember she was Reverend Williams' girl.

Vivian awoke screaming but Doc, not seeming to notice, kept working on her. Jackson heard a slight "Oh." Azalea had returned with more water, clean bedding, and towels. She quickly put things in their place. As she walked in and out of the light, Vivian strained to reach her. "Azalea. Azalea."

"I'm here, Child. I can't help you now. Doc Straw-Hat, he'll do it. Don't you be scared. You do like he say."

Jackson had a good hold on Vivian. She was wriggling in his arms. His clothes were wet with the sweat from the two of them. Finally, Doc was finished. Vivian became calm again as Jackson gently placed her on the clean pillows Azalea had exchanged for the messy ones. The two men held Vivian up and Azalea put a clean sheet on the mattress. She also picked up all the messy bedclothes and cotton swabs off the floor. Azalea handed Doc another clean sheet to use for a coverlet and started to back-up to be near the door. All three of them looked down at the unadorned beauty of the nude figure. Jackson removed his shirt and was about to put it over Vivian when Doc remembered he had the sheet to cover the girl. Jackson hung his shirt on the end of the bed. He bent over Vivian, smiled, and nodded his head as if to say that everything would be all right. Her dull stare frightened Jackson. "Doc, is she dead?"

"No, Freeman, she isn't dead. But she'll have one hell of a long recovery. Don't expect she'll be going anywhere for a long time."

Jackson straightened up. "How long, Doc? I have business to attend to. I can't just sit here."

Doc studied Jackson's tired face.

"Well, there's the bar, there's gambling, and there's women. Good ones, too."

Jackson's face turned bronze. Doc had noticed his desire for a woman.

"It is awfully warm in here. I can't get this damn window open."

Doc walked over to help Jackson. Both men worked each side of the frame as quietly as they could and finally the window opened a tiny crack. Jackson let his temper get the best of him. He grabbed one of the dirty pillowcases, wrapped it around his fist and knocked out the glass from one window. The sweet cool morning air slowly wafted into the steamy room, encircling the two weary men.

Heavy blackness before the dawn hovered over the ugly crossroads below. Some of the dilapidated houses had lights on for those who were going to work in the field. Jackson had a pang of guilt. Anna would be getting breakfast and sitting all alone at the table. He knew that she relished making meals for both of them. She even enjoyed arguing about what they would do that day. He was not used to an argumentative woman. Clarabelle and his mother always tried to be cooperative, setting a good example for the children. Jackson got that same feeling he had during the fire. He could hardly wait to get back to the farm to his intended "bride." This was supposed to be so easy. Pick up Vivian, bring her back to the outskirts of Stanton, and Reverend Williams would owe him a wedding.

Now that he had been cooled by the breeze, Jackson put on his shirt. As he moved to button the sleeve, he realized how tired he was. "Sun's coming up, Doc, can I buy you some breakfast?"

Doc Straw-Hat noticed how tired Jackson was.

"Nope. But you can buy me a drink tonight."

He put his arm around Jackson's shoulders, "We'll be good friends by the time your little girl can travel." He turned to Azalea, who was cowering against the wall.

"Azalea, you take good care of her, you hear me? Next time anything like this happens, don't wait. Call me. I'll have the sheriff after you and that is a promise. You stay here and the minute you think something is wrong... you... call... me. I'll stop in to see her at noon. Keep her as cool as you can."

Doc threw the dirty water out the opening of the window and pouring clean water into the basin, he washed his hands. Jackson took his turn, then he threw his water out the window also.

"Wait an hour or so before you get more clean water, Azalea. If there is no change in our little patient, then you can leave her for a few minutes."

With these words of caution, Doc closed his black bag, straightened his straw hat, and prepared to leave.

Jackson studied Doc's puffy face. The hazy light coming through the dusty windows was just strong enough to reveal large pores, red veins around the nose, and the Irish twinkle in Doc's bleary-blue eyes.

"You're a good man, Doc. Thank you for everything. I'll contact Rev…uh…the person who sent me to get Vivian. Then, I'll have to make this time profitable. He turned to Azalea, "I'll pay you when I take Vivian off your hands, and only if you take good care of her."

Azalea nodded approval.

"When you bring Miss Coleman more fresh water, bring her a little soup."

Azalea's lips turned up at the corners. Jackson was too tired to notice the leer in her smile.

"One other thing, Azalea," the Doc cautioned, "keep your hands clean."

Azalea had had enough. She turned on the doctor.

"Why you treat me like I was stupid? I know what I do. I been mid-wife for many years, now. My Mother teach me good."

"All right, that'll be enough."

Doc was too tired to be tactful.

"You did a stupid thing here, didn't you? Didn't you!?" Azalea gave him a twist of her head.

"I want you to know you will be paid well, but you must promise you'll not say a word about Miss Coleman and the reason for her illness."

Jackson had not thought about that. He was grateful Doc mentioned it.

Azalea made Doc wait for her answer. She folded her arms and slowly walked to the window. The day was unfolding bright and hot. She needed the money so better not let this opportunity slip through her fingers.

"I'll do right by your girl," she promised. Jackson was pleased. Now he felt Vivian was being taken care of and he could look for a hotel or a boarding house for himself. He wished Simpson's was just around the corner.

When the two men felt they were presentable enough for a restaurant, they went downstairs. As they reached the last step, Doc turned to Jackson, tucked his chin in his collar and asked, "What is your connection here? You a relative or are you responsible," he looked up at Vivian's room, "for that?"

Jackson looked sharply at Doc Straw-Hat. He raised his chin high. Doc saw Jackson's nostrils flare.

"Just asking'. I like to know all about my patients. You know, Jackson, she may not make it."

Doc watched Jackson's eyes widen. It was obvious he had not thought Vivian would die.

"Doc! How bad is she? I'll have to know when I contact...her family."

"She is young and strong."

"But...?"

"These things can go either way."

"But she'll be all right?"

"Yes, I think she'll be all right. She has lost a lot of blood. That'll be what will take the time to build back up." Doc patted Jackson on the shoulder.

"Now, for heaven's sake, get a room and get some sleep."

Jackson leaned against the wall.

"I guess I'm too tired to do anything but rest. I'll go back up and sleep on the floor 'til I feel better."

Doc watched Jackson wearily climb back up the stairs, then headed for Pappa Dink's.

Jackson cautioned Azalea not to speak. He stretched and sat on the floor. Leaning against the bed, he tried to make himself comfortable. Vivian moved slightly, making Jackson's heart beat faster. He closed his eyes remembering her beautiful body and drifted in and out of sleep.

# XXII

Vivian opened her eyes halfway. Through the blur she saw a white wing flit past her face. It came again, this time going the other way. She closed her eyes. There were small noises. The sound of a starched cotton skirt. Bracelets. Where was she? Vivian opened her eyes again. Azalea bent down so Vivian could see her.

"Vivian. You up, child? How do you feel?"

Vivian licked her lips. They felt dry and crusty.

"More water? Yes, that is so good for you. Doctor Straw-Hat was real pleased you took your broth so nice this afternoon. You're gonna be all right, Miss Coleman."

"I have to use the bed pan."

Vivian began to take the covers off. Raising up on one elbow, she saw the room start to go around but the urge was too great. She started to crawl out of bed.

"No! Don't get up! Doc says you mustn't move much." It was too late. Holding on to the side of the bed, Vivian squatted on the chamber pot. As she began to void, the pain was so great she screamed. Azalea held her until she was finished then, she carried Vivian back to the bed. "now, I'll check on your dinner for tonight. It's a nice vegetable gruel. You know, something you can eat that won't fill you up much."

Azalea took the chamber pot with her. In the hallway she surveyed the contents. Not too much blood. Good. Through the door she said, "Get some more rest. I'll be back as soon as I can. Don't you get up without I'm here to help you. My goodness, it's hard to make you mind."

With that reprimand, Azalea went down the stairs to the outhouse behind the old empty store.

After draining the pot, she walked to the street where children were playing. She beckoned to one of the older boys.

"Here is three pennies. Go get Doctor Straw-Hat. Tell him Azalea wants him. Hurry."

The boy ran to Pappa Dink's, where the doctor was having a drink with Jackson. He shyly approached the doctor. "I'm s'posed to tell you... ah... oh, Azalea wants you. She told me to hurry."

The boy quickly ran out of the bar, knowing his mother forbade him to be there.

Doc and Jackson rushed out of the bar not knowing what to expect when they reached Vivian. They ran up the rickety stairs and made straight for the bedroom. They were relieved to see a big smile on Azalea's face.

"She's up Doc, and she urinated," Azalea announced triumphantly.

"Where is it?" Doc asked.

"I threw it to the outhouse."

"I wanted to see it! How much blood was in it?"

"Not too much. 'bout half and half. I checked."

"Well, I'll have to rely on your report."

Doc turned to Jackson.

"It looks good, Jackson. She is very weak, though."

"How bad is it?"

"Don't know yet. She seems to be quiet and that is a good sign. Now, if we can get her to eat solid food, we just may have a good chance. She lost so much blood she is going to have a hard time building it up again. You all right, Jackson?"

Jackson was feeling better than he had for days. He gave Doc one of his smiles "that could light up the skies at midnight," as his mother used to say.

"I'm very hungry, Doc, that hole of a bar down the street serve dinner?"

"Hell no! You don't want to go there for dinner. We'll wait for Azalea to get back with Vivian's repast. Then," he winked, "I'll take you to a good place for our evening meal."

Azalea, who had been resting on her laurels as a nurse, heard what the doctor said and hurried to the other room, where she had made a makeshift kitchen, to fetch Vivian's dinner.

"Got a girlfriend who cooks, Doc?"

Jackson smiled as he pictured Doc with one of the ladies of the evening. Before Doc could answer, Azalea shuffled into the room with a dish of vegetable soup. As she prepared to feed Vivian, Jackson noticed how clean she was. A new dress covered with a starched apron; her black hair carefully braided into a soft bun at the nape of her neck reminding him of his beautiful Clarabelle. Azalea had powdered her face and was wearing large gold hoop earrings. A lovely ivory fan Vivian had mistaken for the wings of a white bird, hung from a thin braided black cord. Easier to use when fanning Vivian. Azalea resembled a voodoo woman whom Jackson had once seen in a Baltimore bar for Negroes in one of the worst sections of town. The voodoo woman gave him a strange feeling, something about her was frightening. Azalea, on the other hand, was not that kind of woman. She wanted desperately to be accepted.

Doc bent down close to Vivian. "Vivian, open your eyes."

She opened her eyes. Doc could see the listless, hopeless look of someone who wanted to give up the fight for life. He had seen it many times.

"Am I going to die?"

Azalea turned quickly to the bed to chastise Vivian sternly. "Don't talk 'bout dyin', child. No one talks 'bout dyin' round me. Do you understand?'

"Azalea!" Doc brought her up short. To Vivian he said, "Don't worry about a thing. I want you to eat as much as you can, nap, and let Azalea help you when you wish to move about. I'll visit you again tonight and I'll be here several times a day until you are well. Be a good girl, do as I say, and in no time you will be going home with Jackson. Won't that be nice?"

"Yes, Doctor," Vivian answered vaguely.

"Mr. Jackson..."

Jackson hurried over to the bed. Gently taking Vivian's hand, he said, 'I'm here, Vivian. I'm right here."

"I want a minister, Mr. Jackson."

Jackson gave Doc a quick look. Doc pursed his lips, closed his eyes, lifted his head, and gave a quick nod. you know, it's going to be a great day. I can just feel it." He looked at Doc for conformation.

"Ah, yes, I'll attend to that. Sure. But

"It certainly is," Doc said sincerely, "a good day."

Vivian nibbled at the vegetable soup Azalea offered her. Doc gestured to Jackson to back out of the bedroom, then followed him out. From the doorway, Jackson took another look at Vivian. Azalea caught the concern. She smiled at Jackson. He smiled back at her, making her feel warm all over. Quietly she thought, "I'll take good care of your girl, Mr. Jackson Freeman."

# XXIII

Jackson followed Doc across Arbour Road. They walked between two houses, through two backyards, and wound up at a cottage surrounded by a meadow. Doc stamped his feet, shuffled his shoes across a reed mat and opened the door. Jackson watched the ritual and smiled to himself, but he cleaned his shoes in the same manner. When he entered the house, he could understand why Doc was so careful about meadow dirt. "What a beautiful house, Doc!" he exclaimed. "Why it looks like a cottage from one of my children's fairytale books.

Doc was pleased Jackson appreciated the beauty of his home. "My wife loved this place. I was a successful physician, then. When she died in childbirth, I went crazy. Drunk every day. When I came out of my mourning, I found I had lost my friends, my reputation, and my practice."

Jackson nodded his understanding and was tempted to tell Doc about losing his family. He decided not to be too personal. "Well," Doc continued, "I've been half drunk ever since. Occasionally, though, when I'm sober, I come here and think about Emily and wonder what my life would have been like if the baby had lived. You have a family, Jackson? Children?"

"No Doc, I'm quite alone. I lost my family except for two brothers, a sister-in-law, and their children."

Jackson wanted to get off the story of his life, so he changed the subject. Rubbing his hands together, he said brightly, "What are we going to have for dinner, Doc?"

"I have it all right here. You will see how quickly we will fix our meal. Everything is ready in the ice box. Which reminds me, I had better spill the water out of the holding pan." Doc reached under the ice box, pulled out the pan that held the melted ice water, threw it out the back door and quickly put it back in its place. Doc winked at Jackson as he opened the ice box door and pulled out a pot of potatoes already peeled and immersed in cold water. Reaching in again, he brought out chicken which was cooked and ready to eat. Making a fire in the stove, he returned to the potatoes and began to cut them in very thin slices.

"What are you doing?" Jackson asked.

"You're in for a treat." He put more wood in the stove.

Jackson quietly watched as Doc finished slicing enough potatoes for the two of them. By then, the stove was working hot, and Doc put an iron skillet on the burner. He proceeded to put a good amount of oil in the pan. After the oil was at a hot temperature, he carefully put the potatoes in the skillet. They fried into a delicious hard round wafer. Doc carefully pulled out the potatoes with a slotted spoon and put them on newspaper to drain off the excess oil. Doc poured the oil into a small bowl and put the chicken in the skillet to warm. He placed silverware on the table, a napkin and two dishes he proudly picked up from the sideboard. Holding them up for Jackson to see, he said, "Emily's favorite serving dishes." He put the potatoes in a fluted bowl and the chicken on a flat oval dish. "Now, I want you to try this, my friend."

"Sure smells good." Jackson started to taste the potatoes.

Doc held up his hand to stop him. "You have to put some salt on them." Jackson did as he was told, then he tasted the new way of cooking potatoes. "Well? What do you think?"

"It's just about the best potato I ever tasted!" Jackson exclaimed. "What made you think about fixing them like this?"

"As you know, if you have a large farm, you have to hire people who will help you harvest."

"No, I didn't know. I assumed neighbors helped each other."

"Oh, I'm talking about the big farms." Doc licked his fingers. "There is a man west of here. I've brought his babies into this world and got paid well for it. He has about 100 acres. Now, a lot of it is in trees for lumber, but a lot of it is in vegetables for the big cities like Pittsburgh and the other small cities along the way. Miners and people who live in the manufacturing towns, they don't do a lot of farming. Oh, maybe lettuce or maybe green onions in the summer. Of course, they always plant herbs and such but not eggplant or say, sweet potatoes, stuff like that.

"Anna, the widow woman I work for, never told me that. How do the farmers get their wares to the cities?"

"Like you do. Big wagons. And I'll tell you something else. The big guys are talking about buying cars and filling their farm goods in them and riding to different places to sell their vegetables and fruit. They would do it now 'cept there aren't any good roads. He already had one tractor with a motor. Does a good job, too. I tell you, it's the coming thing."

Doc wiped his hands on a napkin. "What's the matter, Jackson?"

Carl was right. He was better off in the automobile business after all, Jackson thought. He leaned over the table, "But where did you hear about cooking potatoes in this way?"

"Oh, right. You see, the people who come to harvest live in the fields in huts. They don't have too much, ya see. They were cooking their potatoes this way. When I asked them about where they got the idea, they told me about this chef, an Indian fellow, in Saratoga Springs. As the story goes, it seems a customer was in a hurry and asked the chef, who was... I wish I could remember his name... if he could prepare a quick dinner. Well, the chef had had a lot to drink and got madder than a wet hen. Now, this was way back about thirty-nine or forty years ago so you know this chef must have been good for a restaurant owner to put up with him like that. The place was known as THE place to go in the area."

"You remember the name of this restaurant? Is it still there?"

"No, I wouldn't know if it's still there, the name of it was never told to me. The eating place was in the Moon Lake House Hotel. I suppose that's where the racing gamblers stayed. Anyway, this…oh...it just came to me...his name was Crum. George Crum."

Jackson repeated the name of the chef and the name of the hotel.

"As I was saying, the man who was in a hurry demanded a quick dinner. After the chef calmed down, he took the potatoes he was going to French fry and sliced them down even thinner. Putting them in the oil, as he would have the French fried, he came up with 'potato chips,' just like the ones I made. The customer was delighted. The next day, the restaurant put the chips out on the counter and put up a sign next to them, 'Help Yourself'." Doc finished his last chip.

"You know why? I'll tell you why. 'Cause when people ate them, they became thirsty and bought more beer. Now, that's smart, right?" Doc ran his tongue over his teeth. "They are popular in New York."

Jackson went to the stove.

"Let me see if I can do it."

"What? Make potato chips? Sure you can. It's easy! Here, I'll put the oil back in the pan. Now, cut the potatoes real thin but try not to break 'em. You want nice, big pieces."

Jackson broke a few pieces before he got the hang of it, but soon he had a nice stack. Jackson put them in a strainer and slowly lowered them into the hot oil. The crackling sound of the oil made Jackson feel apprehensive. He watched the slices curl into crisp wafers.

"That about does it, Jackson."

Jackson lifted the potatoes and placed them on the newspaper. "There, you did it. See, it's easy. Just watch you don't get burned."

Jackson took a good look at the thin wafer. They were very crisp. He salted them and put a few in his mouth. "These are very good." Jackson's eyes glazed over.

"What are you thinking about?"

"Oh, nothing. I was, ah, thinking that people who made chips would need a lot of potatoes, don't you suppose?"

"Yes, I suppose they do. Say, we better get back to Vivian. I want to check up on her. She's not out of the woods yet."

Although Jackson was anxious about his ward, he tarried at the table. He took a handful of crisps and left the house with his host.

Doc was very talkative and pointed out places of interest to Jackson. There was where the new schoolhouse was going to be and did Jackson hear about the new laws governing traffic regulations for the coming influx of cars? He explained the new thing called X-ray. It would revolutionize the way doctors treated patients. Did Jackson hear the new singer Burt Williams on the phonograph?

Jackson wondered how long it had been since he had read a decent newspaper. He felt as if he had been on an island away from all contact with the world.

"No, I don't know Burt Williams, Doc. Who is he?"

"On the stage in New York. He's a Negro, Jackson. I guess he's a big success. I wouldn't know anything about him except I was in New York not too long ago. Got a sister there. She wasn't feeling good, so I went to visit her. While I was there, I subscribed to a good newspaper. If you want, I can give you some papers and new magazines to read while you're here. It might be a good idea for you to subscribe to some kind of reading matter."

Doc stopped walking. Jackson passed him a few steps and turned around to look at him.

"I don't mean to be, ah, you can read, can't you?"

"Oh yes." Jackson smiled. "I can read. My family is very well-educated. My children spoke French. I taught them to read everything they could get their hands on. My son wasn't too happy about studying, but you know how us boys can be." Jackson laughed remembering Oliver and the discussions they had about his lack of keeping up with his classwork. Jackson refrained from telling Doc about his brother being a doctor, too.

Doc was puffing a little as they crossed the street. Jackson stopped to survey the crossroad town. Doc waited for him to catch up, not realizing Jackson was biding his time so that Doc could rest for a while before climbing the long stairway. As they stood by the door, Jackson confronted Doc.

"How bad is it really? I must write a letter and I want all the information I can get."

"This isn't your girl?"

"No, this is not of my doing. Vivian ran away from a good home and people who love her. Now, I must bring her back to loving arm and make good my promise. I promised I would persuade her to come back home."

"I would have bet she was your girl. It's obvious to me she has feelings for you."

"No, she trusts me."

Jackson was uneasy about the way the conversation was going. He wanted no information about Reverend Williams' role in the matter to leak out. He must always be above reproach .

"Let's see how Vivian is doing this afternoon. Maybe you can tell more about her condition after you examine her. I must get a letter off soon."

Doc nodded his understanding about the situation and slowly started up the long stairs. Jackson began to feel very tired. He too took the stairs slowly, all the while praying Vivian would recover and he could bring her home. What a triumph that would be.

# XXIV

Three weeks later...

*Dear Harley,*

*I hope you are well. We have had ridiculously hot weather and a drought. Everyone is praying for rain. If you have any influence in Heaven, now would be the time to use it.*

*Doctor Straw-Hat and I have moved Vivian to the back room of a hotel. She made the move without any harm to her health. I'm sure you will be glad to know that. I have the front room. It is a good arrangement. Her room is dark and cool. My room gets very warm by mid-afternoon.*

*Vivian seems to be physically healing very well. On the other hand, she doesn't respond to any friendly conversation. I have tried everything, even stooping to jokes I read in the magazines near the hotel desk. She is not interested in her looks or her condition, and only speaks when she is spoken to. I am worried about her mental capacity to understand how serious her condition was. The doctor seems not to worry. He thinks she will become more herself when she heals. The doctor said that losing a baby is very traumatizing to a woman.*

*You must feel deeply saddened by the loss of your child. I know what that feeling is, Harley. You will have to heal, also.*

*I will need more money, I'm sorry to say. I hope that will not be too much of a burden on you. Vivian will need new clothes and a shawl for traveling. Her shoes are good.*

*As soon as Azalea can get things together, I'll make arrangements to bring Vivian home on a train that does not stop for the milk cans. It won't be long before she will be well enough to make the trip home.*

*Your Servant,*

*Jackson Freeman*

*P.S. Please write any news about Anna Schein and how the crops are growing. She won't write. She is angry I am gone so long.*

Dear Jackson,

Enclosed is a money order which I hope is sufficient funds for clothes, food, doctor bill, and train tickets.

I feel very strongly that if you can get Vivian to agree to come home to me, I can bring her out of her lethargy. Love is a powerful emotion. My love for her will ward off anything to hinder her recovery.

As for Anna, I heard Jenny and Fred have been helping her with the farm. She is much maligned in Stanton. Now that you have left, people are laughing at her saying she can't even keep a "nigger lover." I have not seen her, but Feeny (who knows everything about everybody) saw Anna at a corner grocery store at the crossroads. Feeny said she was surprised at her beauty and her lovely figure. Anna had a "radiance." That is what Feeny called it.

I'm counting the hours when I shall see Vivian again. Also, as soon as you come, I'll marry you to your sweetheart. I am anxious to know who she is.

Very Sincerely Yours,

Rev. H. Williams

*Dear Harley,*

*You will be happy to know we are coming home next Tuesday. Vivian does not seem to care where she is. In a way, it helps me as she does not oppose me in any way. Azalea wants to come with us, but I put a stop to that. Vivian leans on her too much as it is.*

*Also, Doc Straw-Hat has used her on many occasions as a nurse and from the looks of things, she will be a big help to him. I am happy for her. What's more, she has become a good influence on Doc, as he is not drinking so much and has been cleaner in his attire. Would it not be strange if they fell in love? It is just a thought. Of course, he would not marry a Negress. He was so in love with his deceased wife, Emily.*

*My best to you and your sister, who must be with you by now. I am looking forward to meeting her.*

*Your Servant*

*Jackson Freeman*

# XXV

Jackson helped Vivian off the train. She looked around the familiar station. It was the first time Jackson saw Vivian take an interest in her surroundings. The porter put all the suitcases on the station porch and Jackson handed him some money. The porter smiled, bowed, and handily hopped on the train step.

"There it is Vivian."

Vivian looked where Jackson was pointing.

"There's the reverend's surrey."

Clem, the reverend's all-'round boy, climbed down to help with the suitcases.

Jackson gently drew Vivian into the surrey. Several people recognized Jackson. Thinking he and Vivian were married, they made knowing glances at one another. It gave Jackson great pleasure to ignore them. "Go slowly, Clem, we don't want to jostle Miss Coleman."

"No sir!"

The ride to the minister's house seemed long to Jackson. He was anxious to see Anna. He had written to her about the delay, but since she had not answered his letter he only hoped she understood about the situation. He could only guess though, and he felt it was not a good sign.

Finally, as they rounded the bend, Jackson saw the church. He touched Vivian's hand.

"We're home, Vivian. See, the Reverend is waiting for us on the porch."

Vivian blinked her eyes to hold back her tears. Reverend Williams held on to the railing of the porch hoping no one would notice he was a bit shaky. He came to the surrey and held out his arms to her. She let him put his hands around her small waist to help her down. No one spoke.

Clem took the bags into the house. Vivian followed him. The Reverend looked up at Jackson who had stayed in the surrey.

"She needs a lot of rest, Harley, but she is young and strong. She healed beautifully. We were lucky with our doctor, I can tell you that. There are some things she should not do. No work for about three weeks and sit-baths, but she knows about that. No sex, Harley. Not for a month. Take it easy and I think she'll come around. I'll fill you in later but now I must get home to Anna. Poor woman, she must think I've abandoned her."

The Reverend did not answer for fear he would break out in tears. Instead, he mouthed the words, "Thank you," and shook Jackson's hand.

Jackson smiled broadly.

"C'mon, Clem," he called, "Take me home!"

# XXVI

Anna stood in the middle of the bedroom. She gazed tearfully in the mirror. She was more beautiful than she ever was when she was young. The wedding gown from the Sears and Roebuck catalogue caressed her mature body in the right places. Her hair, in an upsweep coiffeur, showed off her high cheekbones, which were now flushed with the thought of the upcoming event. Why was it when she was with Jackson, everything she was doing seemed to be the right thing to do and when he was not around, this feeling of uncertainty came over her?

"Anna!"

Jackson was getting anxious. If Anna backed out now, how could he explain it to Harley? No one must see that his bride was White until the end of the ceremony.

"Don't forget to put on your white gloves."

Anna picked up the white gloves from the dresser. Her hands shook as she pulled them on. Placing a small brimmed hat carefully on her head, she reached for the veil she had taken off her first wedding gown and wrapped it several times around the hat. She would pull it down before entering the church. Her gown had a high collar that came up to her chin so it would hide her white neck. Taking one last look at herself, Anna felt she was ready. She wrapped her shawl tightly around her wedding dress, so Jackson wouldn't see it, and came out of the bedroom into the kitchen. The click of her high heels turned Jackson around. "I'm ready," she said.

Jackson's heart was pounding. Now, for the first time, he had second thoughts about this arrangement. Would Anna treat him with the respect a woman should treat her husband with? Then he remembered all her kindnesses, even when she was angry with him. As she brushed past him, he wanted to put his arms around her to reassure her he would do his part.

She was out the door before he had a chance to say anything. He closed the door. Anna stood by the buggy waiting for him to help her. This was his chance to tell her how lovely she looked. Instead, he helped her up to her seat, took the reins, and gave a flick of the leather, making Jocko start with a jerk. Anna raised one hand to make sure her hat was secure. Jackson swallowed hard and said, "Sorry."

Anna had not spoken during the ride but when she saw the lovely church, she straightened up.

"Why, Jackson, it's a beautiful church. I pictured something very rundown and... well, I've been told Colored people are lazy. The ones I see in Stanton are always dirty."

Jackson turned the buggy in to the churchyard and stopped. "Did it ever occur to you that the reason they are dirty is because the work they do is dirty work?" Anna's cheeks turned pink. Jackson had made his point. "You see I'm clean, don't you?"

Although Jackson's case was well taken, Anna became warm with anger. She decided not to pursue the subject when she noticed a young girl standing on the steps of the church.

"That's Reverend Williams daughter, Alma. She took care that everything will be legal."

Jackson helped Anna out of the buggy on the side opposite the steps so she could fix her veil over her face. Anna kept her head down as she held her skirt up a little so as not to drag it on the path.

Alma dutifully gave Anna a bouquet of flowers Jackson had requested and introduced herself to the bride. Reverend Williams arrived with Vivian, who was dressed like a bridesmaid. It was the dress Harley bought for their wedding. Jackson was pleased to see her looking so happy and well. Harley must have been right, his love for Vivian was mighty powerful. She smiled at Jackson, "Now, Mr. Freeman, you must go into the church and wait for your bride."

She spoke to Anna, "This is my husband, the Reverend Harley Williams, who will preside over the ceremony."

Anna held out her hand. The Reverend shook Anna's hand and saw her white skin between the long sleeve and the glove. He made no outward notice of it. Harley followed Jackson into the church. He had made a promise and he meant to keep it. There would be time to talk about this situation later.

As Jackson and the Reverend waited at the altar, Vivian poked her head into the church and raised her hand for Alma to start the music. She then helped Anna take off her shawl and Vivian put her arm around Anna and gently started her down the aisle, then she hurriedly ran in front of the bride and proceeded to be the loveliest bridesmaid Anna could have had.

As they approached the altar, Alma soft pedaled the music. Still, the Reverend did not start the ceremony. Finally, Anna could stand it no longer. She whispered to Jackson, "What are we waiting for?"

"Clem. He will be my best man. Vivian and Clem will be our witnesses. They will sign the marriage certificate." Jackson had not anticipated any hitch in the ceremony, and now he was not sure Anna would go through with it if she had any reservations about the marriage. She must not have time to think.

The sound of running footsteps were reassuring and soon Clem came through the church door. Quickly taking his place next to Jackson, he accepted the ring Jackson gave him and without making a sound he mouthed, "Sorry I'm late."

The Reverend took over.

"Shall we begin?"

Anna, Vivian, and Jackson took their positions.

"Dearly Beloved, we are gathered here..."

All through the ceremony, Anna could not stop shaking. Her flowers trembled even though she held them tightly to her waist. The Reverend met Jackson's eyes several times during the ceremony. Neither man showed what the other was thinking. Jackson knew the Reverend was suspicious of this marriage, but he was being true to his word. He would marry them. Jackson would explain when they were alone.

It was over.

Anna took a deep breath but did not remove her veil for the nuptial kiss. She would not have stood for that. Jackson gave her a quick hug. That would have to do, he thought. All the papers were signed, given to the right parties, and tucked into pockets. Alma hugged Anna, the Reverend shook hands all around, Vivian patted Anna's hand, and Clem bowed gracefully from the waist. There was yet another obstacle. The Reverend turned to Anna and brightly said, "We have a surprise for you, Vivian baked a wedding cake. We have a nice wine to toast you on your wedding day, so won't you all come to the house and have some refreshments?"

Jackson gave the Reverend a hard look.

"We must be getting back, Reverend. I did tell you that, didn't I? I'm sorry you went to all the trouble, but I specifically mentioned that we would have to start back right after the ceremony. There is no one at the farm and we must tend to things. Animals and so forth."

That said, Jackson turned Anna around and firmly started for the door. The Reverend and Alma followed them as far as the porch steps and watched Jackson help Anna into the buggy. Jackson quickly mounted the buggy, but not wanting to seem too much in a hurry, he gave his friend a wave. With a jovial, "Thank you for a lovely wedding, Harley!" Jackson gently flicked the reigns, starting Jocko on the way home.

Anna lifted her veiling, knocking her flowers to the ground. Jackson stopped Jocko and quickly stepped down to retrieve the bouquet. He noticed a running figure coming toward them. "Anna, pull the veil back down. I think Vivian is running toward us. She has something in her hands."

Vivian was out of breath when she caught up to the buggy.

"I just couldn't let you go without giving you your wedding cake!"

She took a few more breaths, "I want to wish you and Mrs. Freeman all my best!"

Anna stiffened. That was the first time anyone called her Mrs. Freeman. Many things popped into her head. Did she have to change her name at the store? Yes! she hadn't thought about changing her name. Well, she would let things stay just as they were. She would not even think about such things. Anna leaned forward. "Thank you so much for everything, Mrs. Williams. You are most kind."

"You must come to visit me when Mr. Freeman comes to visit my husband. I would be most happy if you would."

Anna looked at Jackson, bewildered. "Oh, we certainly will, Vivian," Jackson said, not very convincingly. He stooped, picked up Anna's flowers, quickly boarded the buggy, and bent down to receive the wedding cake from Vivian's eager hands. Then he noticed Alma had followed Vivian.

"I wanted to wish you good luck."

"Thanks, Alma."

He would have snapped the reins. However, Anna's hand on his shoulder stopped him. He looked at her quizzically. Anna stood up in the buggy and threw her flowers to Alma. Alma caught them handily. Vivian beamed with delight. Alma stared at the flowers with tears in her eyes. She had caught the bouquet.

Jackson put the wedding cake on Anna's lap and flicked the leather strap sending Jocko into a light trot.

"It was a nice ceremony, don't you think, Anna?"

Anna stared ahead at the road.

"Don't you think they are nice people?"

Anna looked down at the beautiful wedding cake.

"They went to a lot of trouble to please you, Anna. I hope you will remember this as being a beautiful wedding day. Together, we'll make it big. Wait until you hear about my plans for us! You'll be surprised and proud of your husband!"

"What do you mean, your plan? I thought our plan was to have the most successful farm in the county. I mean to keep you to your promise. If you don't believe me, just try to get out of your promise to me."

Anna's eyes narrowed.

"Get home as fast as you can. We'll have to have hay to gather in the coming weeks. Then, there is all the lumber. We got to make the house bigger..."

"Oh, don't worry about the hay, I've taken care of that."

"What do you mean, you've taken care of that?"

"I mean I have taken care of the hay. It's in the barn loft and we don't have to worry about it. I just did it on my own. One more thing out of the way."

"Oh, you fool! I told you not to do anything without my knowing about it."

Anna was screaming at Jackson.

"Don't you know what you have done? That hay is not dry enough to put into the barn. The moisture can cause spontaneous combustion! Get to the barn as soon as possible!"

Jackson could not believe his ears. He had never heard about moisture in the hay, although he always wondered why farmers did not pick up the bales for a while after the hay had been cut. His heart pounding, he coaxed Jocko into a gallop. "Hold on, Anna, we'll get there as soon as possible."

"We don't have to get there this minute.," she shouted. Jackson slowed Jocko to a trot.

"But we'll have to do something about it soon."

Anna had been nervous and all she wanted was some rest. She leaned back. Just before Anna closed her eyes, she noticed rolling black clouds in the distance. Straightening up she cried, "Oh, Jackson!" He looked at her, then he followed her gaze to the sky. "We'll have to do something this very day..."

"What can we do?"

Jackson was beside himself. Why had he not asked Anna what to do about the hay?

"Anna, I'm sorry. I thought I was doing something that would please you. Tell me, what can we do?"

"You're not going to like it." Jackson heard her cold voice making him feel worse than ever. "We're going to have to use your lumber. We're going to have to lift the hay and force the boards in between the hay. That way, the moisture will be absorbed by the wood." Anna took off her hat, rolled up her sleeves, and bid Jackson, "Hurry!"

Jackson's large nostrils flared.

"You're not going to use my lumber!" he shouted.

"I'll fight you on that one."

The buggy rounded the hill and finally the farm was in sight. "Hurry Jackson, the winds have picked up. We can't let the wood get wet."

Jackson stopped Jocko at the pile of lumber. Quickly jumping off the buggy, he was ready to defend the taking of his precious hand-picked boards. Anna jumped off the buggy, picked up her skirt, tucking one side into the waist, as she always did when working in the fields, and ran up to Jackson. She doubled up her fists. With great force she pounded his chest pushing him backward. Jackson eluded her for a while, but she was adamant. They would use his lumber. Anna kept coming at him, sometime hitting him, sometimes missing him. It was more than his ignorance about farming. He realized she was taking out her frustrations on him. He knew the marriage did not sit well with her, nor did she want to give him his wedding night. A fight over the lumber and working the boards into the hay would tire them both and there would be no celebration of the nuptials this night.

Jackson side-stepped a fist to the chest and grabbed Anna by her wrists making her stop the brawl in the field. She was breathing heavily.

"Anna! Stop this."

She leaned against the pile of wood they were fighting over. Jackson felt sheepish. He never fought a woman before he met Anna and now this was the second time she used her fists on him. "Look, Anna, if it's that important, then...then we'll do what you know is best. Mind you, I'll have to replace the lumber and I expect you to give me the money to do just that!"

Anna stood up.

"I know you have the money."

Anna looked away from his dark gaze.

"We'll settle that at a later time. Now let's get to work before the rain hits." Jackson looked up as he spoke and was amazed at the turbulent clouds, "Anna," he shook her shoulders, "Look up!"

As Anna looked upward, the wind picked up carrying Anna's veiled hat high into the air. With their emotions at the breaking point, Anna and Jackson laughed at the sight.

"There are cotton work gloves somewhere, I'll get them. You bring the boards in the barn and place them every so often. Then, we'll pull up the hay with the pitch forks and ram the boards in between... here and there. I feel sure it'll work.

With all the anger vented, the newly wedded couple set to work. Standing below her on the ladder, Jackson held Anna at the waist while she plunged the fork deep into the hay. He then, gave her a board, and pulled up the handle of the fork while she pushed the board in as far as she could. They would come down off the ladder and Jackson, climbing back up, pushed the wooden board deep into the hay. They worked tirelessly for about an hour. By now, the heavens were cruelly punishing the earth with fingered lightening and baritone thunder. The wind grew ferocious. The barn doors were banging as they fanned open and closed. Jackson hurried Jocko into the barn and closed the doors, enveloping them in darkness. He released Jocko from the buggy and bedded him down in the stall for the night. All the animals were nervously moving about. Anna surveyed the fruits of their mighty effort. She was satisfied.

Jackson watched Anna from behind the buggy. He had felt her body, working at great length, to right his wrong. They had reached their goal. She was one hell of a woman and he wanted to possess her. A great compassion, for surely it was not love, came over Jackson. He watched her large breasts heave as she caught her breath. Anna felt his eyes on her. She turned to meet his gaze. Lightning splattered the inside of the barn.

For a moment it seemed as if the whole world stopped. The wind ceased its moaning; not one bird screeched in protest against the oncoming storm. The silence was ominous. There was just enough light to outline Jackson's silhouette.

A ribbon of lightning broke the impossible peace, illuminating the interior of the barn. For a split second, Jackson saw Anna, uncertain and feral in her dirty and torn wedding dress. Her eyes were wide with terror as she ran toward him. And he, thinking she was frightened of the storm, drew her to his breast.

Anna threw her arms around Jackson, not taking her eyes off the large post behind him, for there stood Willie! His hat seemed to be down over his face but there was not denying it was Willie. Anna began to tremble. Jackson drew her in closer, enfolding her in his willing arms. A tremendous thunder followed, roaring through the barn, shaking its very timbers. The wind responded in kind, picking up with renewed vigor. The barn's double doors rattled and tree branches whipped against the windows and walls, desperate to get in. Another outbreak of lightning. This time, several quick zigzagging eruptions of light made it easier to distinguish forms and outlines. Anna threw back her head and laughed. There on the post, resting on a large hook, was Willie's coat on an old tired hanger with his worn-out crushed hat hanging limply above the collar. Jackson felt her relax in his arms. Thinking he had helped Anna get over her fright, he began kissing her. Staring at Willie's form, Anna kissed Jackson as if to imply to the specter 'This man is a better man than you could ever have been!'

She wanted to reward Jackson for that.

Jackson slowly wrapped his hands around Anna's body. He groped clumsily at buttons and succeeded in unwrapping her from her wedding dress. Anna responded willingly in front of Willie's ghost, letting Jackson do whatever he pleased. He led her to the hay and playfully, but as a man in power, pushed her down. Looking around for something to keep her warm, he pulled Willie's coat off the hook and wrapped it around her shoulders. He undressed himself and covered her nakedness with his own body and put his arms around her. They melted into the hay, disturbing a Daddy-Long-Legs spider.

Jackson did not question Anna's sudden attitude. He wanted to be a loving husband with a willing wife. It had been so long since he had held a woman in his arms, but he did not hurry his lovemaking. His large cool lips softly kissing Anna's lips, neck, and shoulders made her writhe with desire, driving Jackson insane with passion. Another hard and fast bolt of lightning revealed her glazed eyes. She was ready. Jackson slowly opened her legs. Another clap of thunder, which neither of them heard but both felt, finally ushered in the drenching rain that pounded on the windows and the double-doors of the barn. Now Jackson was in charge. Anna lifted herself, allowing him to put his arms underneath her. She began to feel his shoulders, the muscles of his arms, all the while fantasizing she was the heroine of made-up stories.

Jocko moved nervously in his stall. Outside, the rain began to play a steady drumbeat on the roof and hit the ground with force. The spider tried to cross to the other side of the barn just as a tongue of water gushed from under the doors, carrying it away.

Jackson and Anna became one.

# XXVII

Jackson carefully led the horses over the brook. He had a full load of the best vegetables in the whole county, maybe in the whole state! There in the wagon was the accomplishment of his hard work of the summer. Since last September, Anna had talked of nothing but how to weed, seed, and plow. How to read the clouds, the feel of the air, what the wind would bring coming from what direction, how much and which fertilizer to use on which vegetable and best of all, what to do when all the work would bend his back and cramped-up the muscles in his legs.

Anna knew her farming, all right. Now, if only she could forget his blackness, she would be a good lover. He could feel it coming. He often thought about the night in the barn with the thunder and lightning, the rain beating on the roof, the smell of the hay. But most of all, the smell of Anna's wetness. That night, she was what every man wanted in his bed. Why? Was it the storm? No. Anna was not afraid of anything. Then what happened after that? She just didn't want to show she liked it, Jackson surmised. She had been cool to him ever since. "Well, I want more than what she's been giving me!"

Jackson said out loud to the horses.

He picked out the smooth places in the path to accommodate the wagon and reached the triangle. That place in the road people called "The Heavenly Divide." The road Jackson was on bent to the left and ended at Stanton while the path which veered to the right and up the hill led to the old Stanton mansion, once the showplace of the territory surrounding it. Barton Todd Stanton was the catalyst that brought about the rise of the small community in the valley where the river ran smooth and clear. Barton Stanton convinced the powers-that-be to let him bring a wagonload of prisoners from New Jersey to the area he founded. If they would build the city according to Stanton's plans, they would become free men.

The raggle-taggle group were not the worst offenders of the law. They were in prison for not being able to pay their bills and were happy to chance the wilds of Ohio to start a new life. Even though Stanton was a religious, rigid, and relentless taskmaster, the men admired him and depended on his instructions, and that is what had been necessary to create this thriving city nestled strategically at the bend of the river.

Jackson stopped the horses. The hush of the late afternoon enveloped him. Only the occasional rubbing of the horses' reins was heard. There it was. "The Heavenly Divide." He didn't know how long he sat there in the coming evening trying to make up his mind whether to go to the left or go to the right. Riding his eyes up the hill, he could just make out a small portion of the mansion. It was getting dark and chilly. Jackson pulled up his collar. One by one, the windows began to light up and yes, there was the distinct tinkling of a piano. The bordello was coming alive.

Jackson looked back at his life since he left Baltimore. It was almost a year ago he had played the piano, sang in the choir, and conducted the singers when the church organist was not able to play for the service. Now he was singing at the Crossroads Tabernacle and listening to Reverend Williams' sermons with no wife at his side.

His wife. He had to wait until Saturday, after they both bathed, to have sex. Anna would not change that schedule. Jackson pulled his mouth down at the corners at the thought.

He was beginning to feel comfortable with her in the bed. Jackson smiled. She was quite an armful but somehow she fit him well and despite her reluctance for her own pleasure, she was a good lay. Things could be better, but they could be a lot worse. A spanking good breeze brought him out of his reverie. His thoughts gathered like a storm and he realized he angry. He had led a grey life all these months, ever since leaving Baltimore. So, why he hell not! Jackson counted the money Anna had given him with which to make change. Not very much, but maybe enough. He deserved to be a bon vivant, even just for one night. Jackson whipped the horses into action, giving them enough of a start to get the wagon up the hill. He took the path to the right.

When the wagon was safely over the hill, Jackson slowed the horses down to a walk. He was glad Anna had showed him how to work with the big Percheron horse team before he left. Otherwise, maneuvering them and his great load in the wagon up the hill might have caused him a lot more trouble. Since he didn't want anyone to see him or the big load of vegetables he was bringing to town, he quickly turned the wagon to the back of the large barn. Once the horses were comfortable, he checked the cotton covering that shielded his beautiful produce. It was dark now, but the grounds of the mansion had been turned into a fairyland by torches lighting the way to the house, illuminating tips of the branches of the old trees and revealing the back of the mansion where the Colored servants were milling about in different stages of inebriation. Jackson spoke to the first man who gave him a friendly smile. "Where does a fella get a good drink around here?"

"You never been here before?"

"Nope."

"Hey, you're in for a treat! Here, have some of mine."

He poured whiskey from a small bottle into his own glass and offered it to Jackson, who drank it down in one gulp. He hoped this would give him a lift. Succeeding in not making a wry face, Jackson raised his eyebrows as if to say the whiskey was good.

"Warms you up, doesn't it? That'll be two bits."

The man leaned forward making his hat tip back and fall to the ground. He unsteadily picked it up. He held on to Jackson to get his money. Jackson held out ten cents. Holding the coins close to the man's face so he could see the amount, Jackson waited to see what the man would do.

"All'll, right. That'll do seein' as how you're a stranger in these parts."

He put his hat on, reached for his glass, and began to fill it up again.

"I guess I don't want any more of that stuff, uh... but there are other things here, right?"

"Oh, sure. Hey, tell you what. Get Vilma. She's the best. 'Least she was a couple of years ago."

The man stared into the black night reminiscing. He lost his balance and fell on Jackson's shoulder. Looking up at Jackson he winked and said, "I can't afford a gal tonight, but I get paid tomorrow."

"Who do I see about Vilma?"

"Oh yeah, well since you're Colored," both men laughed, "you go to the back kitchen. Sully will take your money and tell you which room and which wench. Watch him. He's mean."

The drink made Jackson feel warm all over. The bright lights, people laughing, some singing with the piano, being with his own kind of people, it all made him feel good about the decision he made to party this night. There were ways to make up for the money he would spend. Anna didn't have to know everything. The swaying figure beckoned to Jackson who quickly followed his mentor of the evening.

Jackson found himself in a large old room with peeling wallpaper, sawdust on the floor, paint barely clinging to the walls and a huge heavy wood bar on the far side of the room, obviously not in use anymore. The man let Jackson past him but lingered in the doorway, his watery eyes searching for Sully.

"Sully, That's the one you want to see. Sully don't like it when I come in here with a little drink in me. G'wan in."

Just as the piano struck a loud fanfare, the man shouted something Jackson couldn't hear. Then he turned and disappeared into the night, leaving Jackson alone in the large room just as the main room of the mansion went dark. A burst of applause lured Jackson toward the black opening. A bright spotlight shown on musicians starting the show for the evening. Two violinists, a trumpeter, and an exuberant drummer now joined the piano-man playing songs Jackson had never heard before. He peered through the doorway and his eyes widened as he took in the large room for the White clientele.

Jackson had not seen such opulence since he left Baltimore. There was an ivory-colored ruffling of cloth caught with a huge pompom emanating from the center of the ceiling and fanning out to the corners of the room. The walls were covered with a deep red and white velour-like wallpaper in a design of embossed medallions. The carpet was an even deeper red, just large enough to accommodate the diners' area making the white damask cloth on the small tables look like mushrooms. Jackson was still taking in the beautifully dressed men and women when he became aware of someone shouting at him.

"Hey, you!"

Jackson turned toward the deep bass voice that boomed at him and was surprised to see an unusually small man. Thin, very black, with a bony face topped by iron gray hair, and a little bow-legged. When he put his hands on his hips, his spreading fingers looked like spider legs. It was no wonder the man who befriended Jackson was afraid of him. This man was evil.

"You mean me?" Jackson sized up his situation. "Watch him, he's mean," went through his mind. With a deep sigh, Jackson walked over to Sully.

"Stay outta there. Who do you think you are?"

"Sorry, I was just looking."

Jackson smiled his "light up the sky at midnight" smile and kept on walking until he was uncomfortably close to Sully. He raised his chin. Sully didn't give an inch, but Jackson made his point.

"I'll be with you in a minute. S'all right to look in but keep out of the doorway."

Jackson hurried back to look in the main room standing back a little. He wanted to see the show but most of all, he wanted to hear the music. Getting more accustomed to the darkness of the room, he noticed that there was a slight elevation of about two feet making a sort of small stage. The curtains on the right side of the room parted and Belinda Resnick made her entrance.

And what an entrance it was! The Madam knew how to work a crowd. The applause was deafening. Jackson folded his arms across his chest and waited for the entertainment of the evening, hoping Sully wouldn't tell him to leave. He was lucky. Sully was busy counting money, his favorite pastime. Belinda, the very picture of a woman on the cover of 'Police Gazette' magazines, was light on her feet as she strolled through the crowded tables greeting her patrons on her way to the center of the room. When she got to the small stage, she hiked up her dress just high enough for the audience to see her tiny feet and pretty ankles and she raised her voluptuous body to take her place on the small platform. The applause rose higher before the room fell silent in anticipation.

Belinda turned, the dress did not. Instead, it folded around her body, outlining her hips and shapely legs ending in an open fan at her feet. She slowly raised her eyes as she deftly untied her royal blue shoulder cape and sensually let it drop to the floor revealing her low-cut white-puffed-sleeved blouse tucked in her blue velvet skirt. The make-up she wore was as white as her blouse, making it difficult to see where the blouse actually began. Her beautiful breasts were high, supporting a bib of glistening jewels that rose and fell as she spoke.

"Hello, everybody!" she called out melodiously, "are you getting your money's worth?" She tossed her hair, a mass of dark ringlets held by glittering combs on either side of her head to keep it piled high on top while the rest of the curls cascaded down her back. The musicians began an improvised musical accompaniment and Belinda spoke above it.

"You are in for a good evening. We have some new songs for you. But first, how about an old favorite?"

Everybody applauded. Belinda nodded to the orchestra which then switched the vamp to one of the favorite songs, "You Naughty, Naughty Men." Belinda crouched and with one hand on her knee, one finger on her chin she began to sing. "I will never more deceive you, or of happiness bereave you, but I'll die a maid to grieve you, oh, you naughty, naughty men..."

Jackson was surprised at the beauty of her voice. She knew how to sell a song, knew how to work the crowd. She must have been great in her day.

"All right, now, that's enough gawking. What do you want?" Sully's voice sounded off key against Belinda's mezzo-soprano.

"Vilma."

"How much you got?"

"How much money do I need?"

"You ain't got that much."

"Well," Jackson pulled out his money and showed it to Sully, "Who can I get?"

Sully hesitated, looked Jackson up and down, counted the money again, then with a wry smile said, "Carola Bennett." Jackson waited for directions. Sully threw his thumb over his shoulder, "Not from the inside. You go up the stairs from the outside. It's way in the back. Here's your receipt. You know how it works? You give this to her then she gives it back to me. You've got an hour."

Men were beginning to come in to negotiate with Sully. They were now milling about, waiting for Sully to furnish them with a woman. Jackson tried to act nonchalant as he took a long look through the door to the main room. Belinda was swaying as she was singing the latest hit from Eddie Leonard, one of the last of the black-face minstrels.

"Ida, sweet as apple ci-i-i-der..."

Sully closed his scrawny fingers around Jackson's money and with a nod of his head, gestured to the side door. Jackson hurried out of the old bar room into the cold sweet air. Walking around the back of the mansion, he found the old back stairs. As he climbed to the landing, Belinda had everybody singing another new song.

"Sweet Adeline, you're the flower o-o-f my heart, sweet Adeline."

Jackson waited until the song was finished, then proceeded to climb to the top of the steps toward the light coming from a lantern which cast an eerie pall over the white-washed door. He didn't know it then, but when that door opened his life would be changed forever.

The lantern began to sway and the door flew open. A young black boy tried to run out but was unceremoniously yanked back in by a thin scantily clad woman.

"Did you hear what I said?"

"Oh, Ma!"

The woman shook him.

"Yes, yes, now turn me loose," he cried.

Jackson leaned against the rail to clear the way. The woman, noticing Jackson, lightened her grip and the boy leaped into action running down the stairs two at a time.

Jackson's eyes followed the boy as the night swallowed him up, then he turned to Carola Bennett.

Carola was quickly putting on a faded kimono when Jackson reached the door, so he waited to be invited into the room. She posed herself on the cot she used for a bed.

"Come in."

Her voice was inviting. As Jackson stepped through the door, he had the same feeling he had as a young man entering the ramshackle house by the tracks. He felt ashamed of his sexual desires, still he wanted it so badly he went through the act pretending it was true love. Jackson had closed his eyes against the sight of the middle-aged whore who gave him more than his money's worth. Even so, he always wished he had not used her when it was all over. When he laid Clarabelle down, he knew there would be no more visits to the whorehouse he hated so much. Well, then, what was he doing here and why was he so uncomfortable?

He knew the answer to that question. Clarabelle was equal to his passion; Anna was cool to his lovemaking. It was as simple as that. He wanted to be faithful to his wife but for heaven's sake, only on Saturday!

Carola was only a silhouette in front of the kerosene lamp, so it was hard to see her clearly. Jackson handed her his receipt. She put it in her pocket and immediately went to work. Carola let her hands play along his shoulders, down his arms, then with her fingers opened wide, she slowly slid them up his body from his stomach to his breasts and back to his shoulders underneath his jacket. Rounding his shoulders again, she slid the jacket off and let it fall to the floor. Jackson wanted to throw caution to the wind and have a night of ecstasy, but he became ill-at-ease when Carola came near him. Was it the smell of medicine? Why was there only one lamp lit? Why was there no friendly conversation before the intimacies? What was the hurry? He turned her to the light. Carola was not aware her sleeve had come up as she caressed her client, so she did not realize Jackson's motive. She simply tried to keep in his shadow. This angered Jackson and he roughly grabbed her upper arms pinning them against her body, then partially lifting her he thrust Carola toward the light. She wrenched herself away from the lamp, but Jackson was too quick for her and he pulled the kimono down to her waist. Even in the dim light, it was evident Carola was mighty sick. There were multiple sores on her swollen neck, which was covered with white make-up and several strings of cheap beads. She tossed her well coifed head high, put her hands on her hips and held a sensuous pose. "Take a good look at what you almost got," she said with a sneer as she let the kimono fall to the floor. The bravado did not work, and Carola slowly wilted under Jackson's sharp look. She curled one arm around her beautiful breasts and hid her face with her other hand.

Jackson did not know how long he stood watching Carola. He waited until he could move without shaking. Then he quickly scooped up the kimono and wrapped it around the trembling woman.

"How many men are you infecting?" he asked in a calm voice.

"I have a son!"

"So do the men you infect."

"I have to feed and clothe him and, and he's just wild... you saw him! I have no other way to, to, oh, why don't I just die now?"

Carola pushed her arms into the kimono, wrapped it around her thin body, and threw herself down on the bed. Motioning toward the door, she said, "You can go now. I'm sorry I don't have enough money to reimburse you."

Her eyes became slits as she stared at the floor. Jackson started to leave. Carola very coldly stopped him by saying, "I wouldn't anyway, I need every penny I can get my hands on. I have a small account in the bank for my son. It won't go far and maybe he'll squander it, but at least I did my best. What he does after I'm gone, I can't help. Sully said he would keep an eye on him."

"Sully?" It was more of a statement than a question. Carola's face was peaceful and serene. Like a statue. She made no attempt to hide the tears that streaked her make-up. "What's his name?"

"Samuel Bennett. It's a good name."

"Yes, can I have him?" Jackson froze. Why did he ask that? It just popped out of his mouth and he was as surprised as Carola at the request.

Carola became alive. She dug in her pocket to find a handkerchief. First using it to wipe her eyes, then to smear off her make-up, and finally to clear her nose. She didn't see Jackson smile at her sympathetically. Looking up at him she half smiled and said, "Oh, it would be wonderful for Sam to have someone to look after him." She knit her brows. Her face became heavy with concern. Was this man a good man? She must not make a mistake. Carola feared Sully would make Sam work at the whorehouse and keep the money Sam made for himself. Even the small amount she had put in the bank could be filched by this greedy man. Miss Belinda, as the girls called her, had helped Carola obtain a lawyer, but was he reliable? Her greatest fear for Sam was that he would be put on a farm and treated worse than the animals. "Are you married?"

Carola's eyes were pleading, please God. be married.

"Yes, I'm married."

Jackson thought it best not to tell Carola his wife was White. Oh, Dear God! Anna! He felt a tingling at his temples when he considered what Anna might say.

"We don't have any children. I lost my children almost two years ago. So you see, there would not be any sibling rivalry." Carola searched Jackson's face for some signs of lying; she found none.

"We have a beautiful farm up-river and have the best crops in the County. You can ask anyone. I'm taking some vegetables to Stanton this weekend. You can see for yourself."

Jackson gestured toward the window.

"I'm Jackson Freeman. The town is waiting for my red tomatoes, green peppers, and the third pull of lettuce and..." Jackson stopped mid-sentence. Carola was smiling broadly. She looked scared, happy, and perplexed all at the same time. Jackson lifted his chin high. He was going to win.

"Tell you what. Let me take him to Stanton. I'll buy him some new clothes. I'll teach him how to sell vegetables while I hawk them. I'll give him fair wages and feed him, then I'll bring him back to you in a couple of days and if he and I get along he can come to the farm and work."

Jackson was talking fast now.

"He can see you on weekends if he doesn't like being with me and my wife. After a fair trial, mind you, he can always come back here."

"Why would he do for you what he won't do for me?"

"Because he needs a father. Someone who can needle him into doing the right thing by laughing with him. Our kitchen is warm and inviting with good food. Why, he would have an upstairs room all to himself."

Carola was taking in everything Jackson's words painted. The home she wanted her son to live in should be like that.

"I lost my son. He would be about Sam's age now."

"What about your wife? Would she accept Sam?"

"She is a good woman."

Jackson did not lie. He knew Anna to be a good woman.

"She is as lonely as I am."

That was not a lie either, Jackson consoled himself.

"How do I know you'll treat him well?"

"You don't! You have only my word. You must trust me, a complete stranger. Carola, you have to trust someone."

"I can't just give him to anybody! I can't just let anybody take him. I'm mulatto. Colored people shun me and White people shun me. I don't know where to turn anymore. I know how he will be treated after I'm gone. Like an animal. And he is so wild now, I dread to think of what White people will do to him without me to intervene."

Carola began to feel faint.

"Please, sir, in the drawer there are some pills and an orange, my one luxury."

Jackson pulled out the drawer. Pills rolled around between two oranges. He picked out one of each, poured water from a pitcher into a filmy glass and gave it to Carola. Jackson sat on the vanity chair and peeled the orange. She exchanged the glass for the fruit. Carola held the orange in her lap and stared at the floor. There was silence.

Jackson picked up his jacket. He stood up.

"Do you have a choice better than the one I'm giving you?" Carola, tired and beaten, looked around the faded room and quietly said, "No."

Jackson smiled his midnight sky smile. He knelt in front of Carola and tilted his head so he could look up into her eyes. "Well then, take a chance with me."

She studied his face. Jackson stood up and brought Carola to her feet. She started to speak, but the momentous decision was too much for her. She threw herself at Jackson and putting her arms around him, she sobbed. Jackson hesitated, then pulled her to him. If there was one thing he understood, it was the loss of a child.

Carola drew back and cried again.

"I think I'm close to the end," she said quietly. She walked to the cot and picked up the orange.

"I may not be here when you get back. Miss Belinda wants to help me by putting me in an institution where there has been some success with... you know. But I said I wanted to go to the house on the hill. I know I'm too far gone.

"If she knew Sully was using me, she would kill him. Miss Belinda is a fine woman. She has helped me a lot."

Jackson waited for her to finish a section of her orange. She continued, "I wanted to watch Sam grow up. Hear his voice as it changes to a man's, watch him walk, see how he uses his hands, how he'll make decisions."

It was obvious to Jackson that Carola was not speaking of her son's attributes, she was seeing his father.

"Oh, never mind, he shows me hate! I know he loves me. He knows what I do, I do for him. He hates that, but not me." She looked searchingly at Jackson.

"Surely, not me."

"No, of course not. A boy always loves his Mamma," Jackson said reassuringly.

"You love your Mamma, Mr. Freeman?"

Jackson looked up at the ceiling and closed his eyes against the last time he saw his Mamma in the church pew holding little Clarissa.

"I was Mamma's favorite."

He smiled, leaned back against the wall, opened his eyes, and focused on the broken chandelier that hung useless since there were no candles to light in the holders. Now that he was used to the darkness, he could see this obviously had been a beautiful room at one time. The drapes and wallpaper were faded and had a tired, worn-out look. Everything in the room was ugly. Jackson had enough sadness and gloom. He started for the door. "I have to get some rest so I can get to town early tomorrow."

Carola quickly took Jackson's arm. "Mr. Freeman, take him!"

For a moment, Jackson and Carola silently looked at one another. Even in the cold light of the kerosene lamp, there was goodness and sincerity in his face. She became convinced she had made the right decision.

"Take him, Mr. Freeman, I'll trust you to do right by my son. I think it best you go to Stanton alone. I'll prepare Sam. He must get used to the idea. On your way back, you stop here and I'll have Sam's things ready. He doesn't have much."

Then, remembering Jackson had said he would buy Sam new clothes, she added.

"You'll still get him some new clothes, maybe?"

"Oh, of course."

Jackson's mind was going a mile a minute. He tried not to show all the mixed emotions he had. He opened the door and turned to say something eloquent but when he saw Carola in the full light of the lamp, he was stunned into silence. The tears that had streamed down her face made a ribbon of "clean" through her make-up outlining the bones of her face. She was at peace and the calmness in her breast gave her the look of the Mona Lisa. God had given her rest from her greatest worry. "And good food, Carola, I'll see to that. Good food."

"You'll give him good schooling. Reading, writing and make him learn numbers?"

Hell, I'll even teach him French, Jackson wanted to say but he resisted.

"When I get through raising your son, Ma'am, he'll be a gentleman of means, that is if he applies himself. I told you I-er-we have a large farm and I intend to be a rich man one day."

The light went out in Carola's eyes.

"I'll never see him grown up. The doctor said..."

Carola's face turned into stone. "I'm so scared."

Jackson's heart went out to this woman he would never know. There was only one chink in this liaison. How could he explain Sam to Anna? Lately, he thought, Anna seemed so far away. Jackson remembered the wild, willful look in Sam's eyes as he wrenched himself loose from his mother's grip. Jackson could not explain his asking for the boy. A son! It was the right way to go!

"Carola," Jackson hated to give her more hurt. "You knew what your chances were when you took up this profession." Jackson opened the door. The night breeze made the kerosene lamplight jump and flicker. Shadows played on Carola's face tracing the hollow of her cheeks, the curve under her eyes, and the rise of her collarbone. She stoically walked to the door as any hostess would to say good night to her guest.

"I loved him with all my heart. We were to be married in New York and I believed everything he told me."

She was now standing in the bright moonlight. Placing her hand high on the door she began to slowly close it, forcing Jackson to retreat backwards onto the small landing. Carola looked like a green goddess made of stone. Her lips barely moving, she softly said, "Sam will be waiting here for you Sunday morning." With that, she slowly closed the door.

The picture of Carola standing in the doorway was so beautiful that Jackson's brain made a negative of it. He was viewing a woman who considered herself already dead. Jackson stood looking at the dilapidated door without really seeing it. Some of the whitewash from the door had shaken loose and burst into stiff falling snowflakes shimmering in the moonlight. He watched the white confetti of paint waft down and settle on his shoes.

The night air was cold now, awakening Jackson to the lateness of the hour. He flew down the stairs, his heart bursting with happiness. Belinda was finishing the evening's entertainment by singing "Aura Lee." Jackson burst into song with her as he crossed the yard. Looking up at Carola's window, he caught her watching him leave. She quickly closed the drape. He heard her in his mind, "I'm so scared."

Jackson would always remember Carola when he looked at her son. That was something Anna must never know.

# XXVIII

Jackson uncurled himself in the wagon. He had fallen into a very deep sleep for several hours. It was still quite early. Good. He hadn't overslept. Stretching felt good and he stood up to bring back his circulation. As he walked to the outhouse, he stole a quick look at Carola's window. The drapes were still drawn. Everything was still. The backyard of the Stanton Mansion, which looked so inviting last night with all the lights flickering and people milling about, the piano tunes drifting through the house, was now a sorry mess of bottles and debris. Did last night really happen? A little smile stole across Jackson's handsome bearded face. Last night he became a father. At least that's the way he looked at it.

Jackson took special care shaving. He wanted to look good for the city folk in Stanton. As he began his ablutions, his mind wandered back to Baltimore. He must write a letter to Thomas and tell him he is all right... and married...and a new father! So much has happened these past few months. Also, he must bring Anna something. Specifically a present that would not seem like an olive branch. He settled on stationery. A new pen, too. She would like that.

Jackson surveyed his face in the cracked mirror of the outhouse. He was satisfied with his looks this morning. Bright, shining, mischievous brown eyes, smooth dark skin, graying hair at the temples, and a thin, strong neck perched on top of a straight, muscular body. He was doing all right for a man of his age. Shaving woke him up, making him move faster. After he took care of the horses, he checked the precious cargo. Everything was all right. Jackson handily hopped to his seat and whistled the horses to begin the trek to town. He did not notice the three men laying near the barn. They began to awaken as the noise of Jackson's preparations infiltrated their slumber.

Villon Wreak got up on one elbow just in time to see Jackson veer his wagon around the barn and carefully steer his cargo to the winding path which would take him back to where he had made his momentous decision the night before. "The Heavenly Divide." Wreak watched as Jackson applied the brakes to help the horses hold the wagon from free-falling down the steep grade.

"What the hell's a Colored man doing with that big a load?" Villon jumped up, brushing his clothes and spitting the foul saliva from his mouth. He grabbed his dirty hag and ran over to his friends, who were still sleeping. He nudged Jay with his foot. Jay Norton grabbed Villon's foot, throwing him to the ground. They pummeled each other until Jay's older brother Emery pulled them apart.

"What the hell's the matter with you two?"

This was not the first time Emery lost his temper with his brother or Villon.

"That stupid brother of yours will feel my heat if he's not keerful, Emery."

Villon sneered as Jay got up to confront him.

"Take it easy, Jay. I didn't mean nothin' by it. I just wanted to tell you what I saw! That's all. Quick, c'mon, look down the road."

Villon and Emery walked to the hill.

"So what! There's a guy with a wagon!" declared Emery.

"A Colored guy!" said Villon.

Emery turned in disgust.

"Emery, what's a Colored guy doing with that big a load?" asked Villon. Emery thought about that. Villon smiled, revealing broken, tobacco-stained teeth.

"There's three of us and one of him and we can scare the bejeezus out-o-him and git whatever he's got in that wagon. Better yet, we can even sell the horses," announced Villon with a smile.

Jay had walked toward the hill and heard the last comment Villon made. Always ready for a skirmish, Jay ran back to his horse and began to saddle up. Emery called to him, "Not so fast, Jay, we have to have a plan."

Jay laughed, "We can plan as we go, Emery, he ain't gonna go fast with that big a load."

For a moment, they looked at each other. Then all three began to ready their horses.

Jackson settled back and let the horses do their work. The day was starting with a gray sky. The clouds were thin and wispy, like feathers wafting through the heavens. Lack of sleep and all the excitement of the night before began to catch up with him; the rocking motion of the wagon put him into a dead calm. His eyes were slits. Watching the road was hypnotic. Jackson moved into a more comfortable position. As he did so, he was awakened from his lethargy by the sound of a pair of horses near him. He cautiously looked back to see Jay Norton and Villon Wreak pacing themselves to the speed of his wagon. Emery was a little behind, not really wanting to participate in the burglary. Let the "young bucks" do the fighting.

Jackson began to think, if the riders were friendly, they would have passed him. Alert now to the danger, he didn't waste any time. He made a loud kissing sound and the horses responded by getting into a nice rhythm, but Jackson knew he couldn't sustain such a fast pace for long. His only hope was if someone would come the other way and scare off the marauders, so he persevered even though the boxes of vegetables were violently shaking. He couldn't think about that now. Jackson held on to the reigns as tightly as he could, but his hands were not accustomed to the severe rubbing of the leather straps. He wished he'd remembered to bring the gloves Anna had given him. What could these men want? Jackson had felt the difference in his new surroundings. Stanton people were not like Baltimoreans. In Baltimore, Negroes were treated with a little more respect than most other cities gave them.

Despite all the dirt the wagon was spraying up, Jackson took a concentrated look at his pursuers. He wanted to remember who they were. He had to take a look back. His own horses and the creaking wagon shut out the noise of the men's horses, making it hard for Jackson to know how far back they were. Wasn't anybody coming from Stanton this morning?

"Help me, sweet Jesus!" Jackson prayed. He had seen what happened to Colored men when they were taken by the Ku Klux Klan. God only knows who and what these men were. Jackson thought he was running for his life. He would make a good run for it.

It was at a point where Jackson thought he was ot-running the men behind him that the wagon wheel on the right went over a large rut in the road. Jackson was hurled into the air. He fell, flailing his arms for something to hold on to. Falling between the horses, he managed to grab a handful of one of the horse's manes. Try as he might, he could not lift his leg over the horse's rump and he slowly began to slide toward the blurry earth below. He quickly realized he would slide beneath the animal's belly and would not be able to hold on. There was the possibility of being crushed by the galloping hooves or the wheels of the wagon. Getting into the rhythm of the moving muscles of the horses, Jackson had time to gage when the opening between the horses would occur. He closed his eyes and getting as close to the ground as he could, he let go, clearing both the hooves and the wheels. He hit the dirt road hard and turned a somersault after clearing the wagon wheels. His right shoulder dug into the dirt giving him great pain.

Jackson raised his head to see where the riders were. The two who had come close to reaching him were bearing down hard on him and since he could not move, Jackson covered his head with his arms and waited. They skirted around him and whipped their horses to overtake the wagon. Soon the wagon and riders were out of sight. Jackson waited a long time before trying to move. He didn't think his bones were broken even though moving was painful.

Everything was gone. There would be more vegetables to sell to defray the winter costs but the humiliation of being robbed by thugs started Jackson's heart pounding for revenge.

Feeling a little dizzy, he waited awhile before moving again. If only someone would come. He looked at the shadows and figured it to be about nine o'clock. He should have been set up in Stanton by now. What was the trio going to do with all those vegetables? Probably throw them away and sell the horses. Jackson decided not to think about the incident and figure out how he was going to get home. He was closer to the Stanton mansion than to the city so, he started to get up to see if he could walk there. Carola would help him.

Jackson twisted to his left side, his good side, raised his knees as far up as he could and with all his might pulled himself into a crawling position. He moved very slowly to the grassy area to avoid the stones on the road. So much effort made his stomach feel queasy, but he continued.

His shoulder seemed to feel better for the movement. He started to raise himself up again but stopped short when he saw two black bare feet in front of his face.

"I knew you were too dumb to see those White men," Sam said contemptuously.

"Help me up, Son."

Sam held out his hand and Jackson gratefully accepted it. "Are you sure you can get me up?"

"I'm strong. I can do it."

The boy got Jackson up to his feet.

"How did you know I was in trouble?" Jackson put his arm around Sam.

"Mamma told me to come get you. We saw the men follow you. Mamma knew one of them. They ain't no good. She gave me this horse. He ain't much now, but you shoulda seen old Derby Doll when Mamma went to town in the old days!"

Jackson thought, through his pain, it was strange for such a young boy to be talking about the old days. He was leaning on Sam's shoulder and was close to his face.

"Don't you ever call me dumb again."

Jackson's arm went tighter around Sam's shoulder

"Do you understand me?"

"Yeah, yea... hey... I'm here to help you!"

Jackson kept the hand on Sam's shoulder hard for a while then, let up on the pressure.

"You respect your elders, Sam. We're here to help you, too, you know."

Sam started to say something but thought better of it. He helped Jackson on the horse. Jackson leaned forward to ease the pain of his shoulder. The horse was old. Jackson winced with every step Derby Doll took. Slowly they made their way to the mansion.

A summer storm was brewing in the West. Jackson was relieved when he caught sight of the white house.

"I'll wait for you here, Sam. Tell your Mamma what happened, she can tell me what to do. Ask her if I should go to the sheriff."

Sam started to run to the back stairs to his mother's room. About halfway there he thought about leaving Jackson on a horse in his condition. It bothered him. As he began to walk back to Jackson, he heard Sully call to him. "Yore mamma's not here, Boy! They took her to the hospital. I have your suitcase and some books she wanted you to have. You're s'posed to wait for someone. I don't know who. She said you'd know him."

"Sam ran to the kitchen door.

"Sully! Sully! I didn't say 'goodbye' to her!"

Sully didn't even bother to look up at the boy.

"Straighten up, Boy. Your Mamma wanted it that way. Here's your satchel."

He thumped it down on the kitchen table.

"She asked me to give you this envelope. You can stay in the barn 'til your man comes to pick you up. She said it might be a couple of days."

Sam looked down at the ground. He didn't want Sully to see his tears. As Sully turned to leave, he said, "You can eat in the kitchen. Miss Belinda doesn't want you hungry."

Sam took his suitcase and put the envelope inside one of the books. He walked back to Jackson, who was waiting just out of Sully's sight. He tucked the books under his arm and taking the reins, he walked the horse into the barn.

"Can you get down off the horse?" Jackson carefully slid down from the saddle. The boy put his arm around Jackson's waist, leading him to a pile of hay and helped him to lay down. Sam put his suitcase on a shelf. Sliding the envelope out of the book, he sat on an old trunk. Then, he just kept staring at it.

"What's the matter, son, can't you read?" Sam turned away. "I'll read it for you. That is, if you want me to."

It was a long time before Sam decided to hand the letter to Jackson. Jackson moved to a more comfortable position. Also, he needed more light from the dirty window above him. The envelope was still sealed. Jackson tore it open. A small bank book fell out as he unfolded the letter. Jackson remembered Carola telling him about some money she had saved for her son. "It starts out, 'My dearest Sam'." Sam could stand it no longer. He darted out of the barn into the drizzling rain. Jackson looked at the bank book. It read, 'Carola and Sam Bennett.' Good. No problem there. Two hundred thirteen dollars and forty-three cents. The sum total of Carola's life. Well, Sam did not need to know about the money until he was old enough to appreciate having it. Jackson felt unsettled about Sam being out in the rain. Perhaps he went to Carola's room. Little thoughts ran through Jackson's mind until finally he fell asleep to the patter of the rain.

While Jackson slept, there was much going on in the Stanton Mansion. Hilda Wren knocked at her mistress' door. She had heard Belinda's heavy stride going back and forth to vent her anger. "Anything I can do to help? What's the matter?" And she was perplexed. "Why are you so angry?"

Hilda knew she was overstepping her bounds as a maid, but she was always willing to try to keep Belinda happy.

"Shut the door, Hilda."

Belinda sat behind her desk situated in an alcove in her bedroom. "I've checked and rechecked. Something is very wrong with the bookkeeping."

She leaned forward, her robe loosening at the throat.

"Has Sully been spending a lot of money lately? Or has he been with a lot of women lately?"

Hilda thought for a moment.

"Well?"

"I don't think I saw him do nothing different. Maybe he's gotten a little more like Napoleon, though. He has been giving orders around here as if he owns the place. Does that help you?"

"Oh yes, Hilda. That helps me a lot. Sully has been stealing money. I'm sure of it!" Belinda's eyes turned to ice.

"That little runt! I'll cook his goose, but good"

She swirled her kimono around her thick waistline as she rose from her chair. She was about to give Hilda an order when there was an urgent knock at the door.

Sam had not gone to his mother's room. He went through the main house, up the main stairway and knocked on Miss Belinda's door. Hilda opened the door a crack. Miss Belinda's maid was very protective of her mistress. "What do you want, Sam?" Her alcoholic breath seeped through the door.

"I want to talk to Miss Belinda."

Sam's voice was loud and clear.

"Miss Belinda is busy. There's nothin' you have to say to her, now git!"

The door flew open. Belinda pushed Hilda out of the way. "What is it, Sam? You want to know about your Mother?"

Belinda softened her voice, "She'll be fine. We'll see to it she gets the best of care. You know my word is good, don't you? Sully told me she made arrangements for you."

"That's what I want to tell you about."

Sam started to talk fast.

"The man who was going to pick me up is in the barn. He's hurt! Three men from last night followed him early this morning. Took his wagon, horses, everything. He fell off the wagon and he hurt his should real bad."

"What? Take me to him."

Already angry about Sully and the tell-tale bookkeeping, it didn't take much to fire up Belinda's ire.

"Nobody's going to hurt one of my clients... Black or White!"

"Wait!" Hilda stopped Belinda from leaving the room. "Wait till I get your shoes."

"Get my barn boots!" Belinda commanded.

Hilda ran to the closet, picked up the boots, and scrambled back to help her on with them.

"Hilda, get Dr. Medcalf. Tell him to go straight to the barn." Belinda gave her kimono belt a tug.

"All right Sam, let's go."

From down in the kitchen, Sully could hear the commotion going on upstairs. He knew Belinda was working on the books. Could she have found out he was skimming money off the top? He realized he had gotten bolder about stealing lately but he never thought she would catch on. The mansion had been very lucrative the past few weeks and Belinda was no fool. Maybe he could get away with his chicanery by saying he lost some of the receipts from the girls. They must be stealing. No, the girls would not do such a thing and Belinda would know that. The girls didn't like him. He knew that, too.

The sound of footsteps coming down the stairs alerted Sully. Belinda was going to the barn in her kimono and she was in an awful hurry. He quickly followed along. Had he waited, he would have seen Sam and Hilda trailing after her.

As it was, Sam and Hilda were surprised to see Sully tailing Belinda. When she heard someone behind her, she stopped and turned around.

"What do you need, my Dear? I'll get it for you," he said. As Sully spoke, he laced his arm through Belinda's and led her deeper into the barn.

Hilda and Sam watched Sully's maneuverings. "I don't like this, Sam. Go into the barn by the side door and whatever you do, don't let Sully see you. See what he's up to. I'll send someone for the doctor."

Sam skillfully skirted the barn and entered close to where Jackson was sleeping. He gently nudged Jackson. When Jackson awoke, Sam put his index finger up to his mouth.

"Shush. Don't make a sound. I think Miss Belinda and Sully is going to have a fight. Miss Belinda, she's mad about something. She was comin' in the barn to see if she could help you and I think Sully did something to make her mad."

Jackson and Sam watched Sully and Belinda silhouetted in the doorway. Jackson motioned to Sam to hide in the niche between the wall and the post. As Sam pressed himself into the crevice, Jackson laid flat on the hay, keeping his head up just far enough to watch. He could just make out what Belinda and Sully were saying.

Belinda pulled her arm away from Sully's hold on her. "Something is wrong with the books, Sully. Do you know anything about it?" Sully began to sweat. His breath came a little harder. "Have you been taking money from me? Don't I pay you enough?" As Belinda spoke, she became angrier. "Tell me! Have you been stealing from me?"

"I... er..."

Sully couldn't think of anything that would exonerate him. He decided to tell the truth.

"Belinda, Dear Belinda. Yes. I've been taking money from you."

Belinda could not believe what she was hearing.

"What?"

"Not much at first," he quickly interjected.

"You see, it became apparent to me that you weren't a good businesswoman. I wanted to protect you from yourself." Belinda, who was indeed a highly successful businesswoman, drew back in astonishment.

"It's true, my dear," Sully insisted.

"Oh, dear Belinda. Do you know how much I love you?"

Belinda cocked her head in disbelief.

"Why, you little piece of vermin. You expect me to believe that?"

"Belinda, it's true!"

Sully's voice changed to gravel after she called him a piece of vermin.

"All these years I have watched you with other men. You will never know how I hated that. And you! You never even so much as looked at me. Even at business meetings, you never ever looked at me. You always treated me like dirt. I know what I looked like to you, so I didn't dare to tell you how much I love you. How much I want you."

Sully stopped talking. Belinda was laughing at him. Her beautiful musical laughter echoed through the barn. Louder and louder, she laughed until Sully couldn't stand it any longer.

"Belinda! Belinda!"

Belinda kept laughing.

Sully looked around to see if anyone could hear Belinda laughing at him. As he did so, his eye caught an old rusty knife used for cutting rope thrust into the wooden post. By now, he was in a rage, "I'll show you! You'll never laugh at me again!"

Her eyes were full of tears from laughing so Belinda caught the movement too late. Sully had wrapped his hand around the knife handle and pulled it out of the post. Sully gave one quick thrust into Belinda's stomach. She reeled back. Sully pulled the knife out, causing Belinda to scream out in pain. For a moment they just stared at one another. Belinda looked down at the wound and saw she had started to bleed. "Why, Sully? She could hardly speak.

Why?"

Sully was beginning to realize what he had done.

"Belinda! Please forgive me. My Dear Belinda, please forgive me, I didn't know what I was doing. Oh, my God!"

Sam gasped at what he had just witnessed. Jackson signaled for him to be quiet. It was too late. Sully heard the noise. Sam, his heart beating fast, squirmed further back into the crevice.

"Who's there?" Sully demanded.

"Who's there?" he repeated louder.

Jackson painfully pulled himself up and showed himself to Sully. "I'm waiting for Sam," he said as if nothing had happened. "Have you seen him?" If he could convince Sully he had not seen anything, perhaps he would be able to leave with Sam.

Sully was caught off guard and for a moment didn't know what to make of the situation. Belinda swayed, catching the barn door. Sully was too small to help her.

After all, she was twice his size.

He grabbed her arm and told her to sit down.

"I'll bring help, Belinda."

Belinda was feeling dizzy from fright. She wanted to tell Sully the doctor was already on his way to help the man who was to pick up Sam, but she just kept shaking her head. No words passed her lips.

"You'll be all right. Don't tell anybody what happened. That way, you'll help me. Don't you see, I didn't want to hurt you. It's just that you were laughing at me, and I... just go along with me. We're rich, Belinda, I've seen to that."

He let go of Belinda and stood up. Belinda never let her eyes leave his eyes. The clouds parted. The sun came out. The little summer storm was over. The whole world began to brighten for Belinda. She watched in bewilderment as Sully ran to the house screaming at the top of his lungs, "Someone stabbed Belinda! Help!"

The girls in the mansion were lounging, gossiping, and exchanging beauty secrets. Marie was the first to hear Sully. "What did he say? Was that Sully?" she asked.

The girl she spoke to said, "He said something 'bout Miss Belinda. But that can't be, she's upstairs working. She's bookkeeping. You know, she's always bookkeeping," she giggled.

Marie's friend Laura had been closest to the door and held up her hand for silence. "No, Sully said Miss Belinda was stabbed. I'm sure that's what he said."

As Hilda returned, she heard the commotion. "What's happened?

Is everything okay?"

Sully came to the vestibule. He looked up at Hilda. "Belinda's been stabbed by someone in the barn. He said he was supposed to pick up Sam. Anybody know anything about him?"

Hilda ran into the barn.

"Oh, my God! It's a good thing the doctor is on his way to come to help that poor man with the hurt shoulder. Miss Belinda said he was robbed this mornin'."

Sully interrupted her. "He must have come to rob us, too! He just stabbed Belinda. Help me, Hilda. She's in a bad way. Marie, bring a couple of the guys just sitting out back, they can help. And bring a blanket for a stretcher. We have to get her upstairs."

Hilda gave Laura the duty of watching for the doctor, then she was off to boil water. Everyone ran to do Sully's bidding. He, on the other hand, was of two feelings. He wanted to make sure Belinda didn't say anything about the crime he committed, and he wanted to bring help to her as soon as possible. Outwardly, he didn't hesitate. He ran back to Belinda confident she wouldn't tell anyone about their argument.

"Hurry!"

Sully was breathing hard when he got back to the barn and to his beloved Belinda. He saw Jackson bending over her and his skull-like face twisted in hate and fear. This man must have seen what had transpired. He would have to think fast on his feet when the authorities arrived. "What are you doing to her?"

"Get away from her," he said through clenched teeth.

Sully unceremoniously pushed Jackson away.

"Get away from her, I said. You murderer!"

Jackson had taken off his shirt, found a clean place that had been tucked into his trousers, and was putting pressure on Belinda's wound. Sully gave Jackson another push.

"Stop that!"

Jackson was getting truly angry.

"I was just trying to help her until the doctor came."

Sully knelt, took Belinda's hand, and stroked it.

"Don't worry, I won't let him hurt you anymore, Belinda."

Marie and the two men she found, followed by Hilda holding a blanket, were coming on the run. The yard was full of people who were workers at the mansion. Everyone was milling around asking each other what had happened. Jackson saw the doctor's surrey rounding the bend to the house. "Over here!" he yelled.

The doctor scrambled down from the surrey and ran to Belinda.

"My, God! What happened?"

Belinda kept looking at Sully and shaking her head. This worried Sully. Was she trying to communicate something to him? He did not know what to make of it. Doctor Medcalf didn't wait for an answer to his question. He hurriedly knelt to take care of his old friend. After a preliminary check, Medcalf helped put Belinda on the blanket. It took all of them to lift her. The struggle to take her to her bedroom began. As they started toward the house, Sully warned Jackson, "Don't you run away from here. We'll find you, you bastard."

Jackson stood transfixed. What should be his course of action? Suddenly he thought about Sam. "Sam, you can come out now." Sam ran to Jackson. They both watched as the procession to get Belinda home continued. "I couldn't tell if she was conscious, Sam."

Sam shook Jackson's arm.

"You better git while the gittin's good. Look, here comes the Sheriff!"

"I can't leave now. Don't you see? It'll look as if I'm guilty. Besides, Miss Belinda will tell them what happened, won't she?"

"If she's able. Maybe she'll die. Then what'll you do?" Sam looked eagerly into Jackson's eyes.

"They'll believe Sully."

Sam pointed a finger. "Look! The Sheriff is coming."

Jackson and Sam watched as everybody heaved to get Belinda up the porch steps. Getting her through the door was difficult. The girls who were just watching before now took a fistful of blanket and they all together finally got Belinda into her bedroom. She was rolled onto the bed so the blanket could be pulled away and again she screamed out in pain.

"Be careful," the doctor admonished.

"All right. Everybody out except Hilda. Take those boots off her, Hilda. Please. We have to get her as comfortable as we can."

Hilda hurried to do the doctor's bidding.

"Now, get me some water to wash my hands."

Before Hilda could act upon the request, Sully appeared in the doorway.

"This what you want? Where do you want it?"

"Here."

Medcalf indicated the table close to the bed.

"The sun isn't bright enough this time of day. Can you hold the kerosene lamp closer?"

It was just where Sully wanted to be in case Belinda began to talk.

"That's better."

After washing his hands, Medcalf began to examine the wound. He saw immediately the knife had cut through some intestine and punctured the stomach. There was not much he could do for his old friend. If there was any chance for her to survive, Medcalf was the one doctor who would be able to do it. "Hilda, wash your hands. I want you to put a drop of this liquid on this cloth every time I nod my head. Sully, give me the warm water now."

The doctor washed Belinda's stomach and nodded his head to Hilda to start the drops.

Doctor Medcalf worked skillfully, giving quick, sharp orders to Sully and Hilda. Then, it was over. Everybody washed their hands again. "Sully, get me a chair.

I'll sit with her for a while."

As Sully set the chair by the bed, he asked the doctor, "Well? Will she be all right? Everything went well, don't you think? She'll be good as new, right Doctor?"

There was something about Sully's manner that began to spawn suspicion in Medcalf's mind.

"I think the Sheriff has the man who did this to Belinda, don't you think so, too?"

Sully was perspiring.

"We'll show him justice, I can tell you that."

Medcalf closed his medicine case and sat down.

"Why would this man want to hurt Belinda, Sully? He's new around these parts."

"Well, ah, ah, oh, I know. It must have been because he wanted Vilma last night."

Sully snorted, "And uh, he didn't have that kind of money. He got me mad, so I had him go to Carola."

Medcalf straightened up. "Carola?"

"You bastard!"

"Oh, I know I shouldn't have done it, but he got me so mad. Maybe

Carola told him about her syphilis and he was giving Belinda an argument about it. Yeah, that could be it." Sully turned and left abruptly.

Medcalf took Belinda's pulse. She was moaning with pain. The doctor decided to give her another pill.

"Hilda, what was that man doing in the barn?"

Hilda told the doctor, "This man in the barn had come to claim Carola's boy, Sam, and the reason you had been sent for was because this man had fallen off his wagon, hurting his shoulder. Three men who had spent last night in the backyard followed him and robbed him of his wagon, horses, and the contents of the wagon. Then, just before she went to the barn, she and Sully quarreled about the books. Miss Belinda was going to accuse Sully of stealing money from her. Sam and I followed her out but when I heard her laughing, I assumed everything was all right and I went back to the house."

The doctor had heard enough. "I'm going downstairs and see what this is all about."

"Oh please, Doctor, please tell me. Is she going to be all right?"

Hilda began to cry. "You look so sad. It's bad, isn't it?"

"Brace yourself, Hilda. I don't think I can pull her out of this."

Hilda smothered a scream.

"Now, now. We don't know. If we can avoid infection and high fever, she'll pull through. As you know, that knife was rusty and the wound is deep."

Hilda sobbed softly.

"We're going to be optimistic. Belinda is a strong woman."

Hilda nodded as she dabbed at her nose with a handkerchief. Medcalf was using his best bedside manner, not on the patient but on Hilda.

"Well then, you sit by her side until I come back. I have an idea Sully did this deed and I must do something about it. I won't be long."

Long before Medcalf reached the first floor, he could hear the Sheriff interrogating Jackson.

"I'm goin' to ask you one more time, why did you pull that knife on Miss Belinda?"

Jackson held his right arm with his left hand to take some of the weight off his shoulder. He was sweating more from pain than from the Sheriff's interrogation.

"I told you, Sheriff, I didn't even know she was coming out to the barn. I had no quarrel with her."

Jackson leaned back in his chair. The kitchen began to swim around.

"Please believe me," he pleaded. "I came back here because it was closer than Stanton to get help for my shoulder. Sam Bennett brought me here. I didn't hurt anybody." Jackson was becoming faint.

"That's the truth, Sheriff." Sam had to speak up. He turned to Jackson.

"I know you didn't want me to say anything, but I just have to."

Sam walked in front of the Sheriff. "I saw the whole thing. Sully took Miss Belinda in the barn and when she asked him about stealing from her, Sully said he had. He said he did it because she wasn't a good businesswoman. And then she started to laugh because Sully said he loved her and Sully got mad at that and he grabbed the knife we use in the barn and he swung into her, like this." Sam demonstrated Sully's underhanded swing using his fist as if he held the knife. "Mr. Jackson told me to keep out of it. It was Sully. I saw the whole thing. Poor Miss Belinda

"Don't listen to him, Sheriff! He's saying that 'cause he wants a home with this no-good..."

"Hold it!"

The Sheriff beckoned to Sam, "Come closer, boy. How did you hear this?"

"Oh, Hilda told me to go into the barn through another door so we could find out what was going on," Sam nervously interjected. "I forgot to tell you that part. Sorry."

"Why, you little..." Sully tried to grab the boy.

The Sheriff took hold of Sully.

"You're not going to do anything to that boy, do you understand?"

Sully was breathing hard, but he calmed himself and gave the Sheriff a weak smile.

"I haven't finished with everybody yet. Someone give this man a drink of water," he said indicating Jackson.

Medcalf had taken in the scene before he spoke. "Sheriff, I have known this boy ever since he was born. He's a wild kid but he does not lie. Better let me see this man's shoulder." "There, that should hold you." Medcalf listened to the questions the Sheriff was asking the girls.

After Medcalf examined Jackson, he opened his case and took out a large roll of tape. Jackson felt better after he was taped up and he thanked the doctor.

"Sheriff," he called out. "Ask this man if he's right-handed."

The Sheriff looked at the doctor then, to Jackson.

"Are you?"

"Yes," Jackson replied.

"Well," the doctor said shaking his head, "with his shoulder out of place, this man could not have delivered such a hard thrust with a knife into Belinda. Also, the person who used the knife was noticeably short."

Medcalf looked straight at Sully, who kept very calm at the innuendo. Jackson wilted in his chair.

"Wait a minute. You mean Freeman couldn't use his arm?"

The Sheriff scratched his head. "I guess I'll have to ask a lot more questions around here. Sully, tell Hilda to come down here for a moment if she can leave Belinda alone. Get one of the girls to stay at Belinda's bedside."

Sully hurried up the stairs. He would see to it Miss Belinda would not live through the night. He stopped at the door. His eyes were slits of fire. He could make her bleed, he thought. Under the covers nobody would see it until it was too late. He cautiously entered the room. The lamplight cast long shadows on the wall. "Hilda," he whispered, "the Sheriff wants to see you. I'll stay with Belinda until you get one of the girls to come up."

Hilda hesitated but she was used to taking order so she patted Belinda's hand and said, "I'll be back as soon as I can, Miss Belinda." Belinda smiled. "Oh, Sully! She heard me! That's a good sign. I'll get the doctor."

Hilda rushed past Sully, leaving the door open.

Sully's heart skipped a beat. He craned his scrawny neck to see if Belinda's eyes were open. They were! Sully called to her softly at first. There was no movement on the bed. "Belinda," he called louder. Belinda slowly moved her head in his direction with glazed eyes. "It's Sully."

"Belinda."

"Sully?"

Frozen with fear, Sully watched Belinda painfully get out of bed, dragging the white sheet with her like the train of a wedding dress. Her voluptuous body made a large silhouette on the wall. She began to gracefully waltz across the room. At first Sully couldn't make out what she was saying. Then he realized she was humming a song. The song became louder until she was in full voice.

"After the ball is over…"

The sheet covering her turned red with blood.

"After the break of dawn…"

Belinda sang as she whirled faster and faster with an unseen partner.

Soon she was in good voice and sang out loud clear as a bell, entertaining her clients.

Even as she turned and swirled, she never let her eyes wander. She was always looking at Sully.

"Don't, Belinda. Please!"

Closer and closer she came to Sully, black curls bouncing with each toss of her head. Her lips were pale, making her teeth seem yellow.

"After the stars are gone..."

"Belinda, wait. Stop!"

Sully was shaking with fright.

"Many a heart is broken…"

She had never been in better voice.

The light flickered as Belinda's heavy body danced near the table. Sully could not believe the nightmare he was witnessing. He tried once more. "Please, I'll get the doctor. Don't, Belinda. Please don't!"

"If you could read them all..."

Belinda danced into Sully's arms. Putting her arms around his shoulders, she leaned on him as she made him dance with her.

"Many the hopes that have vanished..."

Belinda began to crush Sully. He twisted mightily to get out of her grip. But try as he may, Sully could not extricate himself from her clutches.

Her arms were tight around his throat so he could not scream out. She danced him out of the bedroom into the hall. They were crazily swooping and turning.

"After the ball…"

Belinda held the last note. It felt as if the world stopped. There was silence. Only the sputtering of Sully's throat against Belinda's chest could be heard. Everyone downstairs gathered in the vestibule. With all faces straining to see what was going on, they became Belinda's last audience.

Belinda fell forward, bending Sully back. He could not hold her. Her enormous weight leaned him over the railing. Everyone screamed as Sully and Belinda fell to the floor below. Still holding Sully, Belinda watched him die in her billowy arms.

She rolled off his body. Her eyes peacefully contemplated the beautiful ceiling. The sheet, now caressing her body, became her shroud. Black curls flared around her lovely face. The ceiling began to fade from her sight and she let out her last breath of life.

Hilda collapsed to her knees. No one else moved.

# XXIX

Anna felt guilty she had gone to visit Jenny. The visit could have waited until she gave Jackson his lunch and a big send-off to Stanton. After all, he was making money selling all the vegetables.

"I guess I could have been nicer," Anna said to no one in particular. What was she thinking when she started her visit so early? Well, she was guilty about ignoring Jenny lately. She and Jackson worked from Sun-up to Sun-down. No time for visits.

The potatoes were doing well. The best crop ever. What was the reason for so many potatoes? Jackson insisted the potatoes would make them rich. His promise to her. How could that be? It was true, Jackson made more money than Willie did by taking produce to the towns that had large restaurants. Anna had to give him credit for working so hard and for not being afraid to try something new. The weather had cooperated this year and all was going well. But all those potatoes...

Anna went outside for a breath of fresh air. The white flowers lining the porch were beautiful in the moonlight. It was becoming obvious to Anna that Jackson had made a big difference in her life. She felt more educated, more sure of herself, more aware of her body. She blushed at that. She remembered the Saturday night Jackson took down the round wash tub off the hook from the back porch, filled it with warm water and invited her to take a bath. "Well, I'm waiting for you to leave," she had told him. "Oh, no, you get in and wash your legs and feet, then you stoop into the water and I'll wash your back. You get out the tub, I'll put this towel around you, and I'll get in and wash up and you'll wash my back. That way, the water will still be warm for me. I'll be quick."

Anna had always wished she could have been as responsive to Jackson's lovemaking as she was the night in the barn when she thought Willie was there watching them. She had told Jackson she would allow one night a week. On Saturday, after they bathed. She never admitted to herself... would not admit... that she never knew sex could be so wonderful. Jackson was not fulfilled. Anna knew that. But she just couldn't bring herself to give in to him. Probably not to any man. Willie had done that to her. On well, that's the way it was. However, it was nice to have someone to plan with and argue about things in general with. That was part of married life, wasn't it?

Anna became aware of movement on the road. Perhaps having Jackson home with her, she had now become more uneasy about being alone. Peering into the darkness, she could make out a small figure leading a horse with a man on mount. Aware she was silhouetted against the light from the door, she ran inside and lifted the rifle from the wall.

"It's me, Anna!" Jackson was almost too tired to call out.

Anna put the rifle back on the rack and ran out to meet him. "Jackson? What's the matter? Why are you here? Where is the wagon?"

Sam stopped the horse horizontal to the porch steps so Jackson could slide off the horse one step closer to the top. Anna quickly ran to help him. Jackson leaned heavily on her. He was grateful Anna was strong enough to help him into the house. She pulled out a chair for him to sit on, but Jackson rejected it. "If you please, Anna, I have to lay down. I can't make it up the stairs to the bedroom, I'll have to use your room."

Waiting outside in the cold night, Sam didn't know what to do. So, he sat on the steps holding his arms around his body to keep warm. It seemed a long time before Anna reappeared at the door. He looked up expectantly.

"Sam?"

"Yes, Ma'am."

"And I guess that's Derby Doll?"

"Yes, Ma'am."

Anna tightened her shawl as she came toward Sam.

Sam dutifully followed Anna into the barn where they both unsaddled Derby Doll, fed her and patted her good night.

"And now you." Anna put her hands on her hips.

"Well, we'll put you up in Mr. Freeman's room. Let's go back to the house. You look cold."

She turned to go but stopped in her tracks. Sam almost bumped into her.

"I guess that means we will have to find you a jacket or something." He looked up at her.

"Well, c'mon."

Sam was more hungry than tired and cold. He didn't have to worry. Anna knew he needed food. She showed Sam where to wash up and while he was getting clean, she tiptoed into her room and got the nightshirt she brought for Jackson to put on but was too much in pain to wear. He went to bed in his underwear. Sam hid behind the pantry door to undress. After putting on the nightshirt, he hung his clothes on one of the kitchen chairs. No one had ever treated him so kindly before. Surely, this bubble would burst. This would all be a dream. A dream.

Anna warmed a plate of leftovers from her dinner and offered it to Sam. He began to wolf down his meal until he noticed Anna watching him. She filled a tray for Jackson. As she took the food to the bedroom, she said, "Finish your supper and I'll be right back." Quietly she entered the bedroom.

Again, Sam was left alone to ponder his fate. Why did Mister Freeman come to this White woman? Why is she taking such good care of him? Sam became frightened. Did Freeman kidnap young boys to work on farms? He decided to make a run for it. Quickly finishing his supper, he looked around for more food. He was not successful. There was only a piece of bread on the counter. Did he dare to open any of the cupboards? He thought not. He rammed the bread into his coat pocket still hanging from the chair. While putting on his shoes without his socks, he hurriedly started to pull the nightshirt over his head when there was a knock on the door. Anna rushed out of the bedroom. The look on her face told Sam she did not expect anyone. "Who's there?" Anna's heart was pounding. Was it the Sheriff about the murder?

"It's me. Dutch. Don't be afraid, Anna."

Anna opened the door with a sigh of relief when the light confirmed who the large figure was.

"I heard there was a murder at the Stanton Mansion and that Jackson was held for interrogation. I came to help if I could." Dutch stood in the doorway not sure whether to enter the house. Anna threw open the door.

"I wasn't sure if I should come but I just couldn't stay away, Anna. The whole town is talking about this terrible murder. Some of the women are laughing about Belinda Resnick. You know, saying how she deserved it and all, but it still is a terrible thing."

"Oh, how good of you, Dutch!"

Anna embraced him. He put his arm around her shoulder and came into the room. Then he let her step back and close the door.

"Jackson is hurt and it's a good thing he couldn't use his right arm. The Sheriff knew Jackson was unable to raise his arm to kill that woman."

"How did he get hurt?"

Anna told Dutch about the Norton brothers and Villon Wreak following Jackson at breakneck speed until the wagon rolled out of control.

"Jackson landed on his right shoulder and of course he is bruised."

Anna sighed. "Those rotten men saved Jackson's life. Just the same, I wish we hadn't lost our wagon and our horses. We'll have to do something about that soon."

Anna turned away so Dutch wouldn't see eyes well up with tears. Anna was too proud to have anybody see her cry. She turned back to him, "It's good of you to come to help us, Dutch."

Dutch's eyes widened, "I know who they are. They were caught in Stanton. Why, they're in prison right now! They got drunk and tried to sell the horses without proper papers... Everybody knows your horses, Anna. I'll get them for you since Jackson won't be able to do much for a while."

Dutch and Anna began to laugh. "I know you must be relieved, Anna." Anna nodded.

"Oh, you don't know how happy I am you came with such good news."

Anna noticed Dutch looking at Sam.

"This is Sam Bennett. He's... uh... staying...uh, his mother is ill and uh... Jackson thought that he would be better off here than... at... or where he was staying. I agreed."

She made an offhand gesture as if to say, 'what else could I do?' She bent down to Sam.

"When your mother gets better, we'll see to it you can be with her again."

Anna looked at Dutch for support. He smiled at Sam as if to say he thought that was a good idea.

Sam felt a lump in his throat, "It's all right," he said. He held his head up high, not unlike the gesture Jackson made when he was ready for a fight.

"I know all about it."

Anna's heart went out to the boy. Still, she didn't want him to stay at the farm. She wasn't ready to be a mother to a Colored boy. Jackson had better know that as soon as possible. Anna smiled at Sam.

"I'm sure she will be better in a few weeks and you'll be able to be with her again."

Sam narrowed his eyes. "Mamma's going to die," he said very calmly.

"She told me Mr. Freeman was going to take care of me. He promised."

"If Mr. Freeman said he was going to take care of you, then that is what he'll do," Anna said in a kindly voice.

"That doesn't mean you'll be staying here. Mr. Freeman knows some genuinely nice people at the church he attends. Perhaps there..."

"No! No! Mr. Freeman asked Mamma for me! He told her I would become his son!" Sam was determined to make clear what his mother told him. His hands became fists at his side. "Mamma said..."

"All right," Anna interrupted. "That'll be quite enough for tonight. Now go upstairs and go to bed. I'm sure it'll be hard for you to go to sleep right away, but at least lay down and rest. We'll talk about your future in the morning."

"Mrs. Freeman is right, young man, it's getting late," Dutch chimed in. "Better do as she says."

"Missus Freeman?"

Sam became frightened. If she was Mister Freeman's wife, she would have her way and he would have to leave since that was what she wanted.

"But he promised!" Sam insisted.

"Mister Freeman said I would be his son and he would learn me readin' and writin'. He said he would buy me new clothes. Mamma told me so. She wouldn't lie!"

"Sam, please. I'm weary of the whole thing. I'm tired. Dutch is tired. Now go upstairs, Mister Freeman will talk to you in the morning and he'll make everything right for you."

Sam stood his ground for a while. Then, taking the kerosene lamp Anna held out to him, he slowly climbed the stairs. Stopping midway, he looked down at Anna and Dutch. The kitchen was so warm and cozy even with the fire almost out. Sam had never felt like this before. Wanting to stay here, belonging to someone who would give him a good home. Now what would become of him? Suddenly he wanted his mother so much his stomach ached. Where was she tonight? Was she in pain? Could she be helped? She said she would be all right. That Miss Belinda took care of all her girls. He began to feel sick to his stomach.

"Missus Freeman...?"

"What is it Sam? Are you all right?"

"No Ma'am. I feel funny."

"Well. come back down and I'll give you some peppermint."

Sam did as he was told. Anna took the lamp from Sam and turned to Dutch.

"Jackson made quite a nice room in the barn, perhaps you better sleep there tonight. Things will be settled tomorrow morning."

"I am tired, Anna. Thanks for the offer. I'll see you in the morning, that is if you think everything is all right here. If you need me, just call out."

Dutch took the lamp.

"I'll find the room. Don't come out in the cold." Anna opened the door for him. They looked into each other's eyes. Softly Dutch said, "Good night, Anna."

Anna's face lit up as she smiled her good night.

Sam and Anna watched Dutch lope across the road to the barn. The moon was high and bright enough to make the sky a deep, dark blue. It was the first time Sam looked at the world around him. He felt strange. One thing he knew for sure, he was home. How could he make Anna Freeman know that he intended to stay here? It would be all right. Mr. Freeman wanted a son. The night air made him feel better or it could be that he had made up his mind to fight to be with this man his mother trusted, he didn't know which. Looking up at Anna, Sam gave her a big grin, "I don't feel bad now."

He was hoping to show he would be no trouble to her.

"Well, you had better have some peppermint anyhow." Anna gave him the medicine which was always handy in the cupboard. Sam held his nose and drank it all down without comment.

"Do you think you can go upstairs and into bed now?" Anna asked with feigned sarcasm.

"We won't need a lamp, that room will be lit by the moon tonight."

As Sam started up the stairs, Anna caught sight of his thin legs from under Jackson's nightshirt. She followed him into Willie's bedroom, and turning down the covers, commanded him to hop in.

Sam got into the bed and only then did he realize how tired he was.

"If this blanket isn't enough, there is an afghan on the chair, you can use that."

Anna covered him up to his chin, the way his mother did.

"I remember when I lost my mother, Sam. I know how you feel."

Anna sat on the edge of the bed.

"Tell you what. In a couple of days, when Jackson is feeling better, we'll try to find out how your mother is doing. You'll feel better about her. It'll ease your mind to know she is all right. Anna walked to the window. Sam watched her face turn a light bluish color as she pulled the curtains aside.

"It's a beautiful night," Anna said, her eyes scanning the area around the barn. She quickly recovered and let the curtains out of her hands.

"Try to get some sleep."

As she started to leave the room, Sam lifted himself on one elbow.

"Thank you, ma'am... for everything."

He blinked his eyes to stop the tears. Perhaps it was the unexpected courteous manner of the boy, but somehow Anna had an urge to blow him a kiss. She did not want to give the impression she wanted him to stay at the farm though, so she merely said, "Good night."

For a moment, Anna's body shut out the light coming up from the stairs. As she descended the yellow rays came back and spread like a fan on the ceiling. Sam shivered. Not from the cold but the feeling of being alone again. He listened as Anna moved in the kitchen. Then the door to her bedroom closed and the night became very still. The boy's thoughts wandered. Where would he be tomorrow night? Who could he turn to? "Mister Jackson, he'll take care of me!" Sam hoped he was right as he turned to hide his face in the pillow.

"Mamma! Oh, Mamma. I'm sorry for all the bad things I did to you."

Sam slid out of bed and knelt to pray. "Sweet Jesus, please help me to find a home here with Mister Jackson and his wife. Please forgive my sins and please let Missus Jackson like me. Amen."

He quickly jumped back into bed and this time he shivered from the cold. There was one other thing. Sam decided to pray while he was in bed covered up and warm. "Thank you, Lord for all the blessings you have bestowed on me this night."

Eventually the light climbing the stairs from the kitchen grew dim. Sam wiped his eyes with the sheet and got into a better position on the bed. He tried to make plans in his head as to what he would say to Mr. Jackson in the morning, but he couldn't keep his mind on it. He was so tired. For a boy so young, he surely had one hell of a day. As his eyes closed, his thoughts became a jumbled mess of Miss Belinda, Sully, the sheriff, and Anna. Sam did not know what tomorrow would bring. Gradually his body gave way to a deep sleep.

Anna pulled the old armchair close to the bed without waking Jackson. She undressed in the dark, making as little noise as possible as she tiptoed around the bed to get her pillow. After puffing it up in one corner of the chair, she closed the bedroom door. She didn't need the fire light from the kitchen now. Anna sat at an angle on the chair, slowly putting her legs under the blanket and using her robe as a blanket, she snuggled into a comfortable position.

Anna's steady breathing told Jackson she was asleep. He stared up not seeing the ceiling. He had heard all the unspoken words between Anna and Dutch. The time he had spent in town with Dutch came rushing back to him. It was true, Anna had become quite pretty in the last couple of months, mostly because of his quietly pointing out how she could improve herself. This winter had been a big turning point for Anna and Jackson. It never occurred to him that Anna would look at another man. They were so isolated on the farm. Jackson never gave a thought to Anna's making herself more attractive for somebody else. Besides, she was the wife of a Colored man. She was too smart to think a White man would want her now.

Where would he fit into Anna's life if she suddenly became interested in Dutch? Dutch certainly was still interested in Anna. Jackson became angry thinking of these possibilities. He closed his eyes against these thoughts. Anna would keep her vows; he was sure of it. Or would she? He couldn't keep the soft voice she used as she spoke to Dutch out of his mind. Well, there would be hell to pay if Dutch would make a move toward her. She was his wife. Dutch had better not try anything! It would be a great mistake to think Jackson would not do something about it. He would have to watch him closely.

One of the things Jackson would do is start putting his plan into place. Anna was always scornful of his planting all those potatoes. Always chiding him about his idea of getting rich selling them.

"If I tell her about what I have in mind, she'll be willing to work toward the plan. That will occupy her time and if Dutch works with us, I can watch them every day," Jackson thought. He turned on his good side. Now that he had made up his mind to tell her what he was doing with the potatoes, he could rest easier. He buried his head in the pillow, and with his mind clear of these worries, he fell into a deep sleep.

Dutch, in the meantime, was twisting and turning. The bed was a good one. The room Jackson turned into his bedroom was quite nice. Why was he unable to sleep? He kept picturing Anna with Jackson. How could that be? He could no longer see her as she used to be. Now, she was the wife of a Colored man. It was repugnant to him. Still, he kept thinking of her. She was not like any woman he had ever known.

# XXX

Jackson awoke feeling worse than he did the night before. His head ached from the deep sleep he had been in. It took a little time before he could focus his eyes. Feeling swollen all over, he carefully moved to get up. However, hearing soft conversation coming from the kitchen, he stopped in his attempt to get off the bed. Anna was saying, "You know what it's like to be alone, too. Please feel free to spend some time with us. We must get together at holidays and you can bring a friend. Whomever you wish."

"No, Anna, I'm quite alone. Come to think of it, I do have a distant cousin who is thinking of coming to live here in Stanton. I told her I would help her get acquainted... you know, church and all. But come here? I don't think so. Frankly, Anna, I don't know of anybody who approves of your marriage to a Negro. I don't think Phyllis would like what you have done."

Anna's voice was cold.

"What have I done, Dutch?"

Anna waited for a response. Dutch looked away from Anna's penetrating stare. In the bedroom, Jackson waited for the response also. He stiffened, trying to get every word. Anna felt hot with anger, her blood temperature rising in her veins. Her voice came through the door a little louder.

"I have a man who is educating me. Oh, sure, I used to read a little with help from my lawyer. But now I can read and write without running for a dictionary and not finding the word I want because I couldn't spell it! Is this the man who is so inferior to me? No! I was the stupid one. Besides, what Keith and his bunch of so-called friends did to me was terrible. Telling everyone I had a Negro lover! Did anyone come to help me? No! They loved making fun of me. Why, I had to run in and out of Stanton when I came to shop. Did you come to my rescue?"

"You don't understand, Anna. I was the one who made Jackson come back to the farm. I feel responsible that you married him."

"Well, you needn't. Jackson and I have an understanding. We were both maligned. Jackson made it right."

Anna felt she had proven that right to be on her side.

Jackson had to break up this conversation. Besides, he had the urgent need to use the bedpan.

"Anna! Anna!"

There was silence in the kitchen, then a scuffling of feet and Dutch and Anna filed into the bedroom. Sam, who was washing up for lunch, entered the kitchen just as they were leaving and followed after them.

Jackson felt a little embarrassed as they gathered around him. Dutch patted his knee.

"How are you, old man?"

"Oh, I guess I'm all right. Uh... can I see you alone, Anna?"

Dutch put a big hand on Sam's shoulder.

"We'll be waiting outside."

To Anna he said, "If you need me to help Jackson move..." Anna thanked him with a smile. Sam thought Anna was smiling at Dutch a lot. He would watch if anything looked suspicious between the two of them.

Dutch closed the door and followed Sam into the kitchen. He tried to think of something to make conversation.

"Ah, we could set the table for lunch. My mother always made me set the table. Bet Jackson will be hungry now."

Sam made no response.

"Say, it was very brave of you to tell the sheriff what happened there in the barn."

Sam was afraid he might say the wrong thing, so he just nodded his head and gave Dutch a weak smile, "Oh, I forgot. you're just as much a stranger here as I am."

Sam started to take dishes from the cupboard. "I heard how you told the sheriff about how that man killed Belinda Resnick. That must have been a scary time for you."

"Yes sir."

Sam was beginning to feel good about what he had done.

"Well, it just goes to show you things will turn out all right if you tell the truth."

Dutch was aware he was preaching, so he was relieved to hear Anna coming out of the bedroom with a bowl of water Jackson used to wash up with.

Sam opened the door. He took the bowl from a surprised Anna. He kept the door open with his back as he went through it and then with a flick of his foot, closed it. He swung the bowl to the left and as he turned on his feet, he whipped the bowl to the right, making the water clear the rail. Anna opened the door just in time to see the sheet of water spill out of the bowl. She could not help but smile.

"All right, come on in now."

Proudly, Sam held out the bowl to Anna who took it to the sink and cleaned it.

"Here, take it back to the bedroom and help Mr. Freeman to dress."

As Sam entered the bedroom, Anna looked at Dutch. Dutch watched Anna open the bedroom door. "Sam, bring the pitcher out when you're through.

The boy can help him with his shoes and socks."

Jackson, we're having sausage and gravy, is that all right with you?"

"Anything Anna, I'm very hungry. I guess that's a good sign, right?"

Sam came out with the pitcher and followed Anna back to the kitchen.

"He likes that on toast. Does that sound like a good lunch, Dutch?"

Dutch was glad the gloom of the conversation with Anna had lifted.

"Sound good to you, too, Sam?"

Anna was enjoying the company.

"All right! Sounds very good!"

"All right! Sounds very good, " Sam imitated Dutch.

"I'll help Mister Freeman to the kitchen."

Sam ran to the bedroom.

Dutch and Anna laughed.

"The boy is engaging."

"Yes, he is," Dutch agreed.

Dutch wanted to clear the air.

"Anna, don't be mad at me. You see, I didn't think you would like to go out with a hulk of a son of a blacksmith like me. You lived on the best farm in the area and you were so pretty. I didn't think you would even look at the likes of me."

Anna's face softened, "Oh, Dutch. I would have liked that." She blushed. "I was so lonely all those years. My marriage to Willie was a farce. Now I have no children. Nobody to call family."

She began to get angry again. Not so much because she felt the pain of her circumstances, but because she was feeling sorry for herself. This she could not abide in anyone.

Dutch watched Anna at the stove. Her fingers were thick from hard work. She was what was referred to as 'pleasantly plump.' Her hair was her crowning glory. The streaks of white melting through the dark reddish-brown gave her hair a soft, silvery, sandy look. She worked with precision in the kitchen. Dutch admired her gracefulness.

He began to take in the rest of the room. It was more of a sitting room than a kitchen. A carpet under the table. Now who would have thought of that? The wall sconces with silver backs gave the kitchen the look of a living room. Anna had sewn lovely curtains and braided pads were on the chairs. Dutch had to admit to himself that he would not have been able to give Anna such a nice house.

Jackson tried to hear what they were saying in the kitchen. As Sam helped him with his socks he said, "I don't think I can wear my shoes, Sam, my feet feel so swollen. Help me put on my slippers."

Jackson held out his feet and Sam hooked the slippers on his toes and waited for Jackson to scold him. Instead, Jackson sang out, "Smarty, Smarty, thought you'd have a party!"

Jackson laughed. Sam's eyes twinkled with delight.

"Mister Freeman?" Sam looked straight into Jackson's eyes. "Am I going to be your son?"

Jackson carefully rose from the bed. "Help me to the..."

"Mamma told me you were going to take care of me. Missus Freeman likes me, I know she does."

Sam's eyes welled up with tears. "She even said you would take me to see Mamma when you got better and..."

"You don't understand. I must go easy with her. I'll just keep you busy and after a little while, she'll forget all about whether you should be here or not. You'll become part of the family. That's how it'll have to happen."

Jackson looked at Sam with great affection, "To answer your question, Yes! You will be my son. About your mother. She will be too far away for you to visit."

Sam lowered his head. This was the last blow to his bravado. He began to weep openly.

Jackson let the boy cry. So much of his life had changed in the last twenty-four hours. And he still had a hearing to go through but of course, he didn't know about all that at this time. Jackson gave Sam a handkerchief and sat down beside him. "Just let one day's trouble be a trouble to you, Sam." Sam wiped his eyes. "Now, get me to the kitchen and you and I will both feel better after we have some breakfast. We'll write your mother a letter and then we'll wait for the answer. Something to look for in the mail." Jackson rose. Sam put his thin arm around Jackson's waist and just as Jackson got to the door, Dutch and Anna began to laugh. Jackson cocked his head.

Sam looked up at Jackson, "I been watching her, Mister Freeman. She don't like him all that much," he said scornfully.

"What are you talking about? I just wondered if he had left yet, that's all."

Sam made a move to open the door. Jackson stopped him. "You know I'll need someone to help me and I think I've found the man. Now help me to the kitchen."

Nevertheless, Jackson was flustered.

Anna and Dutch stood up as they entered.

"Are you boys ready to have your breakfast?" Her voice was lilting.

"Yes!" They all answered in unison.

Dutch pulled out a chair for Jackson.

"Thank you, Dutch," Jackson said, never thinking Dutch would be so kind to him.

"You look better already, Jackson. I think you'll knit sooner than you thought. You look like you could start things moving."

Anna gave everybody their share of food and sat down close to Jackson

"You don't know how right you are, Dutch," Jackson, said. "We all have some planning to do. Anna, would you please cut my toast?" Anna stood up to help him. "And some coffee?"

"You look serious, Jackson," Dutch said. He pulled up his chair closer to Jackson.

"What do you have in mind? What do you mean we have some planning to do?"

"Coffee is good, Anna." Jackson put his cup down. Anna remembered the first time he said that to her. Little did she know, she would become his wife.

"Well, Anna, you always wanted to know why we planted so many fields of potatoes. I wasn't sure how I was going to go about my plan but with Dutch here, it all came to me in a flash. Now I can tell you what we're going to do. But first, I must tell you how I found out about the way we're going to use the potatoes."

Jackson told them about how he went to the little town out of the county to find Vivian. How her doctor, Doc Straw-Hat, showed him how he fried potatoes.

"He invited me to his cottage and made these thinly sliced potatoes into the most delicious potatoes I have ever eaten." Jackson went into detail about the process of putting the slivers into the oil and being careful not to let the oil spill so as to prevent a fire and then placing them on paper to drain the oil off.

"Just a little bit of salt made the most delicious tidbit you've ever eaten."

Anna had enjoyed the story about Vivian, but when she heard Jackson talk about the potato tidbits she grew angry. She put her hands on her hips, "This is why you planted all those potatoes? For tidbits? This is your big plan?"

"Wait Anna," Jackson was irritated by her remark. "Let me explain everything.

"In Saratoga Springs there was a chef," Jackson leaned forward, "Who had five wives, mind you. He was an Indian named George Crum who worked in a restaurant in the Moon Lake House Hotel."

Anna sat down to hear the story.

"One day a French patron came into the restaurant and told the waiter he was in a great hurry. There would be a nice tip in it for him if he could get a meal on the table quickly. Well Crum, the chef, had a bad temper. But he had pride in his work, so he put a meal together. But when it came to the potatoes, he had to think hard about what to do to make them edible fast. He got the idea of cutting them into strips and since the oil was hot, but the water was not, he put them in the oil. They were done in no time.

"So?" Anna interrupted.

"I cut potatoes in small cubes and they boil quickly in hot water. What is so..."

"Anna! Please let me finish. Those potatoes were called French fries. Later, Crum made the slices so thin you could almost see through them. Now, when they were put in hot oil, they were crisp. He drained them and put a little salt on them, and they were extraordinary! The restaurant put them on the tables with a sign that read, 'Help yourself', or something like that. The patrons loved them!"

Dutch shifted his weight on his chair, "But what has that to do with your crop of potatoes?"

"Don't you see? There is a market for them. If we sell potatoes to people who will make these po... let's call 'em sliced potatoes... we'll sell all the potatoes, we can harvest!"

"Why wouldn't people just make them themselves?" Dutch insisted.

"Because to make a lot of them takes a lot of time. Did you ever peel, wash, and chip a great amount of potatoes? No, I'll bet you haven't. Now, if we can get a group of people, who will be monitored for cleanliness, and put them in business for themselves, that'll be a lot of our crop sold already. The thing is, to make the restaurants and grocery stores see that they will make money selling these chips. Chips. I keep saying chips."

"Potato chips!" Sam cried out, "…or maybe 'chippeys.'"

"No, I like 'potato chips' better," Anna said thoughtfully.

Dutch looked astonished.

"Is there a lot of money doing this? Because the money will be split up many ways, you know."

"If you get two cents from the price of something you sell thousands of...well, you figure it up. It adds up to a lot."

Jackson flashed that smile that could light up the sky at midnight.

Dutch was still not convinced.

"How do you know people will buy the, ah, chips? Won't that be a luxury?"

"They'll be cheap. It won't pay for people to make chips for themselves. And I guarantee that they won't be able to eat just a couple of these tidbits. They're THAT good."

Jackson finished his meal and leaned back in his chair.

"The people who make the chips will be subject to having their kitchens checked at odd times so they won't know when someone will come to see that they're clean and that every package contains the same amount. And quality is important."

"Now, I know many Coloreds will be ready to go into business for themselves. These are good people who would never have a chance like this in a million years. You've been close to Colored people, Dutch. If you would be an inspector, they would trust you. It'll be hard at first. I know that."

Jackson put his elbows on the table and rubbed his hands together. "Another thing. We must not let it be known Negroes are making our product. We'll distribute their chips among Negro stores, night clubs and bars. I can monitor that because I'll be the one who picks up and delivers. When I pick up and deliver in the White districts, they'll think I'm the delivery boy. So, you can see why I need someone who is White to try to sell these chips to the White businesses." Jackson looked at Dutch long and hard." Dutch slowly began to realize what Jackson was saying. Will you do it?"

Dutch looked at Anna for help in making his decision. Anna's eyes were sparkling with greed. This was what she was waiting for. She would show the whole town how successful she could be. Keith and everyone who maligned her would have to admire her now. Dutch wanted her to like him, but he just couldn't accept the idea. Dutch turned his head away from Jackson's gaze.

"Yes, perhaps it could work that way. But I'm a little skeptical, Jackson."

"Well, this has to be your decision, of course."

Jackson didn't push. He was a Colored person. In all probability, there would be no White man who would want to work for him, thinking he was working for a Colored man. "Perhaps, if I play my cards right, I'll interest the White community when they find out the Colored people have something really good here."

Sam could stand it no longer.

"What can I do, Mr. Freeman?" Sam's eyes sparkled at the thought of getting out of doing farm chores.

There was silence. Everyone was thinking their thoughts about "the Plan" and what their part would be. Jackson got up from the table. "Sam, maybe you should call me Jackson."

Sam was crushed.

"But Mamma said I was going to be your son!"

Jackson's cheeks turned orange under his dark skin. 'You want to call me Dad?" Jackson asked, remembering a wild boy running out of Carola's door just a few days ago. He never dreamed the boy would become attached to him so quickly. "Well, yes, that would be fine, Sam. Just fine." He had a son!

That smile again. Anna stiffened her back a little.

"I haven't made up my mind, yet. We have not decided whether you're going to stay, Sam. Go on, Jackson. I want to hear more."

Anna could not get enough of the plan.

Jackson rocked his chair back.

"You, Son, will be with me up on the buckboard. You can get up and down that wagon quicker'n I can. We'll be a good team.".

Sam nodded, picturing himself being a young businessman. Er, boy. The other fellows would be jealous of him.

"Potato chips are very lightweight. You'll handle it easily." Jackson smiled at the thought of working with his son.

Anna abruptly came out of her reverie.

"Wait a minute!" she interrupted Jackson's dreamlike state. "Sam will go to school. He will...," and she emphasized the word 'will,' "...help in the fields. The fruit trees will be his responsibility. The money from the fruit we can put aside for his schooling, that is if he's smart enough to go to the higher grades." She gave Sam a sideways glance as if to say she was skeptical of him making a good student. Anna stopped speaking. She was making plans for the boy whom she did not want.

"Anyway, I don't think there is a school for young Colored boys here. Is there, Dutch?"

Dutch looked helpless. He didn't want to get involved in the family affairs of Jackson Freeman.

"Besides, Sam may not want to stay at the farm," she said dismissing the subject.

It was happening just as Jackson had thought. Anna liked the boy. It would take a little time and she would accept him just as she had accepted Jackson to her bed. He stood up abruptly.

"Well, we'll have time to make all kinds of plans once we get the business going."

He leaned over the table.

"Dutch, you don't have to make a decision right this minute. I don't mind telling you I need your help desperately, but I'll understand if you don't want to work with a Colored man." Dutch flinched a little at that. He had not thought about that at all. He began to understand how Anna could have gotten used to being with Jackson.

"Aside from all that, what do you think about my plan?"

Dutch thought for a while. He was aware of Jackson's penetrating eyes on him.

"I guess, Jackson, I don't have the visions you have. I'm just a smithy, uneducated as Anna was and I'm not able to see how this'll work. It isn't you. I want you to know that. You're big city and used to thinking in a different way. I guess I'll go back home. I wish you the best. The only thing I can contribute is my work. I'll take care of your horses for free until you get going in this potato chip thing."

"Oh, how nice of you, Dutch. We appreciate your doing this for us."

Dutch caught the disappointment in Anna's voice. He gave her a look of one who was forlorn and alone.

"Jackson told you not to make a decision now. Think about it."

Dutch shook his head and began to get ready to leave.

"If there is something I can do for you before I go home, tell me now, and I'll do it."

He slowly walked to the door.

Anna tried to think of something for Dutch to do just to keep him from going, but there was nothing she could think of that she or Sam couldn't handle. As Dutch walked through the door, Jackson stood up.

"Thank you for everything, Dutch. If ever you should change your mind..."

Dutch turned and smiled at the three people he had come to like very much. He would go home to a dingy room and wait for his distant relative. That is if she was serious about coming to Stanton. Dutch lowered his head and putting his hat on, he made for the barn. Anna slowly closed the door.

Verbalizing his plan to get rich gave Jackson new energy. He looked at Anna, who had sat down across from him.

"Do you trust your lawyer?"

"Henry Fenton has helped me ever since Willie died. Of course I trust him. I don't think he liked Willie. Perhaps that's why he was so good to me. Almost like a father you might say. Why?"

"We'll need a lawyer, Anna. Can you afford all the things we have to have?"

Jackson saw Anna's back stiffen.

"Now, don't tell me you didn't know we'd have to spend some money?"

"How much money?"

"Oh, I don't know. We wouldn't need a lot to begin with. There'll be ingredients like oil, salt, paper for draining the oil, large pots, large ladles. Things like that. Don't forget, the people who will go into the business of making the chips will buy these things from us. There will be some profit there. However, I don't think we should take too much money from them. It would be to compensate our time for getting the stuff for them."

There was a timid knock on the kitchen door. Sam looked out the window before running to open it. Dutch filled the doorway. He was standing straight and tall.

"I have changed my mind."

Anna gave an emotional, "Oh, I'm glad!"

Jackson waved with his good arm.

"Come in! Come in!"

Sam leaned on his elbows and listened intently to all the planning. Jackson and Dutch began to put things down on the paper that Anna supplied. At times, everyone was talking at once. There was electricity in the air. "I'll keep my promise to you, Anna. You will be rich!"

Jackson, Anna, Sam, and Dutch fairly bumped into each other during the next few days. Because of Jackson's shoulder being taped up, Sam literally became his right hand. There were many trips to the church. Reverend Williams was helpful, bringing people to the meetings that Jackson was setting up to try to sell this idea of going into business for themselves. The men all were skeptical, but it was the women who made the final decision to give it a try. Jackson used all his charm and it worked.

It was a good thing for Sam. He got to know some of the other children his own age. Jackson did not have to convince Sam to go to Sunday school. He willingly went. Then there was the singing. While Jackson helped set up kitchens and gave many lectures on keeping utensils clean, Sam took care of the horses, the wagons, and started to pick up potato bags for the grocery stores in the Negro community. Everyone admired Sam. He knew it. He basked in it.

Dutch became a good inspector. Coming at odd times to see that all was clean and that the chips were of good quality. He too, felt good about himself. He was in business. Not bad for an uneducated man. He did his job well.

Anna complained as she usually did about the work, as she was always cooking more food than she was used to. She hardly ever saw Jackson. There was more work to Jackson's plan than any of them anticipated. Their Saturday night bathing in the large tub gave way to an outside shower Dutch built near the side door that opened into the pantry. It was just as well since Sam was upstairs now. Anna had to be content to let Jackson sleep in her bedroom. She was annoyed about that, too. Instead of being too tired for sex, Jackson would tease her until she would give in to his amorous lovemaking. She told herself she allowed him more leniency because he seemed to need it. She would never admit, even to herself, that she relied on him for everything now. If he was depressed about something, which was not often, she would make a dessert he liked or tried to make light of the problem. However, she didn't let him have his way with her too often. That would let him know she was dependent on him. And that he should never know. They never spoke of loving one another.

When Jackson and Sam made their rounds, which took about three days, she was very lonely. She, of course, could not know that Jackson hated to be without her, too. He wanted to know she was within reach for comfort. He even enjoyed the arguing. They were both the same, two of a kind. Jackson had to admit he liked watching her move. Her hips moved slowly from side to side when she walked. For all her plumpness, she was a very graceful woman. He was not thinking of Clarabelle so much lately. There was one thing he did do, however. He now had Sam to tell about the loss of his children. Sam tried to be sympathetic.

Secretly, Sam was glad things turned out the way they did. Not that he didn't understand what it meant to lose a loved one, he thought about his mother all the time. Very soon, he would ask his "dad" if they could go to see her. It was just that everybody was so busy, he didn't know when to mention it. He felt sad that they all seemed to forget her. As it turned out, he was wrong.

Anna never forgot a promise. Through her lawyer, Anna had contacted the hospital where Carola Bennett was now laying in a stupor. Her disease had progressed very rapidly soon after she was committed. Anna knew that for Sam to see her in such a condition would be hard on the boy. Never-the-less, she had made a promise. She would prepare him.

One of the nice things about coming home after a hard three days of deliveries was sitting down to one of Anna's wonderful meals. Working together made Jackson, Sam, and Anna a closer-knit family. Anna always insisted on cleaning the dishes before they sat down to their desert. That way, they could talk about how the chips were selling, what to do to make things easier for the people who were participating in the business and now, it seems, the product was selling so well, they had to put a name to it.

"There is one thing I have to discuss with you and Dutch," Jackson said seriously. Sam and Anna stopped eating and waited for Jackson to continue. "Oh, it's nothing real bad, so don't look like that. It's just that we are now having competition. It seems that chips have caught on and other people are starting to make them. What we must do is make people aware that our product is the best and that they should buy our chips. You know, uh... say something like 'In business longer than any other potato chip company'. Or 'We are the best,' something like that."

"What do you mean 'or something like that'? Who'll we say that to?" Anna was puzzled.

"We'll have to advertise in the daily papers. Oh, and a big ad on Sundays. In store windows, too. We must have a name to go by so people will know the product is ours. I'll see Dutch tomorrow and we'll choose a name. I've been thinking about some. I'll write 'em down and in the meantime, you, both of you, write down something you think would be a good name for the potato chips.

"I have a good name, Dad!" Sam cried out.

"Chum's? Why Chum's?" Jackson chuckled.

"Because we're all chums. Say it. Chum's Potato Chips. Chum's Potato Chips. Doesn't it go together?"

"I have to admit it does go together, Sam. What do you think, Jackson?"

"I think it sounds great! We better ask Dutch what he thinks. He has been such a hard worker. We don't want to keep him out of anything we plan. Things have been going well so we'll have to be careful we keep him informed about everything we talk about when he's not here. We must all get along."

"Since you're going to be in Stanton, Sam and I will go with you."

Anna watched Sam to see if he knew what she meant. She could tell he only thought about getting out of doing farm chores. She put her hand on his shoulder.

"I know you have been very patient, Sam, so you won't have to wait any longer. We'll see your mother in two days. I have made arrangements at the hospital."

Sam could not believe his ears. He gulped a couple of times holding back tears.

"I know the way, Jackson, so don't worry about us. We'll be just fine. My father was there when he drank so much we didn't think he would live. But he was strong. He made it." Anna patted Sam's hand.

"You'll have to be strong, too."

She turned to Jackson and smiled, "I'm sure Dutch can put up with you for that length of time. And you can do some shopping. Remember, Sam will need new clothes and there are some things I need. I'll make a list. If that's all right with you?"

"It seems you've made a lot of plans."

Jackson thought for a while.

"Sure, it's all right with me. Besides, Sam should see his Mamma as soon as possible. Yes, you have the right idea and yes, I do need to buy some things in town."

It was settled.

# XXXI

The Freeman family woke up to a promising day. The sun was not up yet as it was about four-thirty in the morning, but farmers know the weather. And this was going to be a beautiful day. Jackson and Anna were not looking forward to taking Sam to his mother. When Anna had spoken to Henry Fenton, he made it clear that she should take the boy as soon as possible. He said Carola was failing fast and her mind was almost gone. Anna prayed she would at least recognize her son. Sam, of course, did not know any of this. He sat upright in the surrey holding a gift for his mother, a lap robe that Anna had made. Sam had been grateful and proud that he could bring his Mamma a pretty gift.

All too soon they crossed the wooden bridge into Stanton. Jackson gave Anna the reins. Before getting out of the surrey, he patted Sam's knee, "Your Mamma may be extremely sick, Sam. You'll have to be ready for that."

"Yes sir." Sam gulped. "I'll be all right." Sam tightened his hold on the gift.

"She'll be better after she sees me in my new clothes and after she sees the fine gift Mrs. Freeman made her. She'll be better... you'll see."

"Of course she will," Anna reassured him.

Jackson was filled with gratitude to Anna. She was so kind to Sam. Noticing the streets were empty of people, Jackson, on a whim, quickly gave Anna a kiss on the cheek. Anna stiffened as she usually did when someone was especially kind to her.

"Be careful, Anna. I'll be anxiously waiting for you and Sam to return to the blacksmith shop."

He looked deep into her eyes. "I care for you, Anna." Anna blushed. Jackson quickly jumped off the surrey.

"'Bye!"

Anna brushed Jocko with the reins and he trotted toward Cemetery Hill, where the asylum sat brooding as it loomed over the city.

The asylum served as a hospital after the family who owned it moved to the other side of the river. It was in need of repair but there was no money to renovate the aging building. Every incoming politician promised to fix the old home to better the needs of the afflicted, but the promised repairs never came about. The insane didn't know anything anyway, did they? And besides, didn't the new hospital, halfway up the hill, deserve money to keep it up to date with the latest equipment?

Anna watched Sam from the corner of her eye to see if he noticed how decrepit the building was. No. He was too excited to notice anything except that they were coming closer to seeing his mother. He fairly flew off the surrey.

"Sam! Please, wait for me."

Sam, already on the porch, waited as he was told. Anna rang the bell and gave Sam a weak smile. The large door opened. Anna and Sam stepped into a vestibule which was dark and dingy. The room had a peculiar smell.

"I'm Anna Freeman and This is Sam Bennett."

"I'm Matilda Bonflere. Oh, I know it's a strange name. I think my people came from France, ya know. And when they got here, no one could pronounce their name so, they changed it to this odd --" Matilda giggled, "but of course, you don't want to hear all that."

She gracefully gestured with her whole arm. "Please come in and have some tea. I'm sure you would like some refreshments after your trip."

Matilda led Anna and Sam into the living room. "Please make yourselves comfortable." She fairly danced out of the room, then poked her head back in and said, "I'll be right back," and then with a wave of her lovely ruffled sleeve, she disappeared.

Sam and Anna looked at each other.

"I didn't expect anyone so pretty to meet us," Anna said. "The young lady doesn't look as if she belongs in this old broken-down house."

"Yeah," Sam agreed, "look at this place."

Anna and Sam stood in the middle of the room. The sun was

completely up and igniting the little dust particles wafting in the air. Anna picked up a straight-backed chair to sit on.

"Sit on the other chair just like this one Sam. It doesn't look as dirty as the over-stuffed furniture."

They waited for quite a while. Sam got fidgety and began to whine, "Mrs. Freeman...."

"Yes, I know. I feel the same way."

Anna got up from her chair. Her back was stiff. Something had to be wrong. Sam watched Anna walk to the archway, "Is anybody here?" No answer.

"Stay here Sam. I'll get to the bottom of this."

"I want to go with you."

"I won't be long. If I can't find anyone, well, then we'll just go upstairs and find her ourselves. Now, be patient."

Anna turned around to leave and walked into a large woman wearing a dark iridescent dress.

"Are you Mrs. Freeman?"

Her voice was soft but carried the authority of proprietorship. "I'm sorry about Matilda, she often thinks she is the owner of the house. She's harmless and a big help to me in the kitchen." Anna stepped aside to let her pass.

"I guess you're Sam?" Sam nodded, his eyes never leaving the woman's face.

"There are breakfast muffins on the table in the kitchen down the hall. Matilda will pour you some milk."

Sam looked at Anna. Anna, realizing the woman wanted to speak to her alone, gave a nod of approval to Sam.

Hoping Anna would say it was all right for him to stay, Sam was slow to obey. Anna gestured for him to leave. He stood in front of her, his face clearly pleading to stay.

"Ma'am, I'm afraid of that girl."

"I'm Margaret Stanton, Mrs. Freeman. I am a second cousin to Mary Stanton, who grew up in this house."

Miss Stanton and Anna shook hands. Margaret turned to Sam, "There is no reason for you to fear Matilda. She is not a mean person. It's just that she has never grown up in her mind." She addressed Anna, "She'll be thirty next month. However, she has the mind of a twelve-year-old. It's pitiful to see the progress of the body and not the brain. The poor child. At least she's a happy soul."

Margaret put her hand on Sam's shoulder and turned him toward the kitchen.

"Down the hall, now."

Sam gave Anna a mean look as he walked around Miss Stanton. Anna had never seen Sam do that before. He had no alternative but to leave the two women alone - probably to talk about him. Sam resigned himself to find the kitchen. That girl better not do anything funny, he thought.

Margaret Stanton waited until Sam was out of sight.

"Please sit down, Mrs. Freeman. I take it you did not receive my letter in time."

"Letter? In time? Mrs. Bennett is still alive, isn't she?"

"Yes. I wrote to you because Carola is in an awfully bad way. She has only a few weeks to go before... well, you know what I mean. Frankly, if she weren't one of Belinda's 'girls' I wouldn't have taken her in. Miss Belinda had been very generous to our hospital, so I felt obligated to do as she asked. It's a shame the community doesn't support us."

"Yes, it is."

Anna nervously shifted in her chair.

"What you are saying then, is that Sam won't be able to see his mother? I promised him this visit. It would be a shame to disappoint him when he's so close to her now."

"I have Carola in a darkened room. Matilda has dressed her and put on her make-up. Carola has good days and she has bad ones. Let's hope this is one of her good days."

Anna said "yes" under her breath.

Margaret continued, "It's just that we must prepare the boy. Now, while Matilda gets Sam his refreshments, let's have a cup of tea and some scones."

"Thank you," Anna said softly, accepting the cup of tea.

Sam entered the kitchen expecting to see Matilda. No one was there. He was relieved. On the table by the sunny window was some fruit in a small bowl and a platter of scones next to it. The lady had said he was to have something to eat, what would be the harm in taking an apple? Sam helped himself to a scone, too. He looked for jelly in the cupboard, which was very bold for him, but he felt he should be with Mrs. Freeman, so he didn't care if they caught him making himself at home. He had a right to hear their conversation. After all, it was his mother they were discussing. He was finally successful finding jelly right in front of him on the table. Just as he was about to begin his snack, he heard a soft giggle coming from the back door.

Sam was glad for the company of the little Black boy standing there.

"Hello! I was told to come in here for a snack," Sam said being careful to emphasize the word "told." The small boy in dirty, wet clothes just smiled. "Hey, you're a Colored boy. You allowed in here?" There was something strange about this boy. He just kept smiling at Sam. Then, Sam remembered Matilda was not who he thought she was, perhaps this boy was not right in his head either. When Sam sat down to his snack, he spotted marmalade on the table.

"You want to eat something? No one'll know. That Matilda, she don't know anything anyhow. Here, sit down." Sam pushed a chair away from the table for the boy to sit down. "I'm glad you're here. I'm kinda scared to be alone." The boy just kept smiling. If this fellow was not "all there," Sam felt he could handle him. This guy was small and thin, and his eyes were hollow with dark circles under them. Where Sam was sitting, he couldn't see if the boy had on any shoes.

Sam ate in silence watching this boy. He judged him to be about six or seven years old. Sure, he could take care of himself if he started something. As Sam was licking his sticky fingers, the boy suddenly was sitting at the table. "You want an apple?" But the boy just smiled. Sam wiped his hands on the edge of the tablecloth and leaned forward to talk to this fellow. "What's your name?" Now that Sam was closer to him, he noticed the boy was not smiling. He looked as if he was trying to breathe through his teeth. It was then that Sam began to realize the child was all wet, as if he had come in from out of the rain. His blood ran cold. "Who... who are you?"

"Wilton Perry Stanton." The boy spoke but his lips didn't seem to move. Sam's heart began to pound. "Don't call out. I won't hurt you... here!" Wilton Perry Stanton dropped a military button on the table. "Give this to Miss Stanton and tell her to look in the old dried-up well. She'll understand." Sam watched the boy stand up and drift to the back door. "Tell her I won't have to go alone."

Sam picked up the button. He looked up, "Go where?" But the boy was gone. Sam was so frightened, he couldn't move.

"Well, here I am!" Matilda sang out.

Sam looked at her and forced his shaking knees to work, he ran out the door and into the living room.

Before he could tell Miss Stanton what had just happened, Anna stood up and took him by the arm into a corner of the room. She whispered, "Sam, your mother is extremely ill. We cannot stay too long. Miss Stanton says your mother is under a lot of medication so don't be surprised if she seems sort of sleepy." Anna turned to Miss Stanton, "I think we better see Missus Bennett now."

Margaret touched the knob of her hair. "Yes, of course. I'll lead the way. If you see anyone acting strangely, pay them no mind. They're all in their own worlds, they won't know you're around."

Sam was so happy to finally go to his mother, he forgot his adventure in the kitchen. Margaret climbed the creaky stairs followed by Anna and Sam. When they reached the top of the stairs, Margaret whispered, "Remember not to disturb her too much." She opened the door to Carola's room. Sam tiptoed in.

The drapes were drawn against the sun. Carola lay on high pillows in the darkest corner of the room. Margaret stooped close to Sam's face, "I have told her you are coming. With so much medication in her, I don't know if she'll remember anything. Just don't move too fast."

Sam slowly approached the bed. "Mamma?" he whispered. "Mamma," he said a little louder.

"Is that you Sam?" Carola sounded as if she didn't believe her ears.

Anna closed her eyes. It was a good day!

"Miss Stanton, can I hug her?"

"No, Sam," Miss Stanton said quickly. Do not touch her.

"It's just because I hurt, Baby. It's all right, we can talk. How are you? Are you happy on the farm?"

"Oh Mamma, it's nice. Mister Freeman lets me call him 'Dad.' And... and... Missus Freeman is good to me. And... can you see my new clothes?"

Margaret Stanton looked at Anna.

"She is blind," she whispered to Anna so Sam couldn't hear.

"My, how handsome you are," Carola said in a lilting voice with all the strength she had.

"When I feel better, maybe you can stay for a full day and tell me more. It's good of Missus Freeman to bring you like this. Oh Sam, why didn't we get along?"

"I don't know, Mamma. I guess I hated that place. The boys used to make fun of me."

"What! I didn't know that. You never told me... is that why you wouldn't go to school?"

"It's all right, Mamma. It's all right." Sam tried not to cry. "It's all right now."

Carola was exhausted. She grew quiet. "Guess what?" Sam's voice brightened. "I brought you something." Sam proudly displayed his gift. "It's a lap robe. Missus Freeman made it for you." He put the robe gently on his mother's lap. Carola patted it, then brought it up to her breast and caressed the edge.

"Thank you, Baby."

The words fairly choked in her throat.

Margaret, seeing things were getting too hard on both of them said in a soft voice, "I think we had better let your Mamma rest now." She opened the door.

"Mamma!" Sam cried out. He hugged the thin body that was his mother.

Carola cringed with pain. She steadied herself, "Sam, my darlin' Sam. Come back soon."

Anna touched his shoulder. Sam allowed her to take him to the door. He turned to have one last look at his mother.

"Yes, Mamma. I'll be back." He started to leave but turned back one more time. "Goodbye, Mamma." He said with no emotion in his voice. "Goodbye."

Carola did not hear. She had wandered into that realm where people who are ill go when they seem comatose. The women watched Sam start down the stairs. Miss Stanton, with a wave of her hand, indicated for Anna to follow. She slowly closed the door of the room and was the last to descend the stairs. She opened the front door. They all stepped out on the porch to a late, bright, sunny afternoon.

"It was nice meeting you," Miss Stanton said with a coolness that was not there before. Anna guessed Miss Stanton was reminded of Carola's past. She must know about her own situation. In a small town, everybody knows about the scandals. Miss Stanton had been kind and Anna was relieved the visit was over.

"Thank you, Miss Stanton. Sam, don't you want to say something to Miss Stanton?"

"Oh, oh, yea, I forgot." He stood in front of Margaret. "When I was in the kitchen, a little Colored boy came in. He told me to give you this." He held out his open hand showing Miss Stanton the military button now gleaming in the sun.

"What is it?" Margaret was about to pick up the object when she realized what it was. "Oh, my God!" She pulled away from Sam's hand.

"The boy said to look in the dried-up well. If it's dried up, how come he was all wet? He was soaked form head to toe."

Margaret could hardly catch her breath. "Where did you really get this button?" she demanded.

"From the..."

"Never mind. I'll take it." Margaret snatched the button. "Uh, ah, it's nothing Sam. The boy was playing a trick on you." Anna gave her a look of disapproval.

"I am sorry, Mrs. Freeman, I'll say goodbye to you now."

Anna blocked Margaret from the door.

"Something is wrong here. What is this all about?"

"Go sit yourself in the surrey, young man. Mrs. Freeman will be with you in a minute." She gave Anna a cool look. "Well, you of all people would understand. One of Mr. Stanton's daughters had an affair with a Colored man. She died having his child. Her lover disappeared, so the family raised the boy. Of course, they never let on what happened and as far as I know, the boy never knew who his mother was. When the boy disappeared too, the family simply figured his father came back for him."

Margaret leaned on the porch railing.

"Lately, Matilda has been telling me about a child following her around the house. Naturally I had pretty much dismissed what she was saying. But if Sam saw him, too...well, now I don't know. Perhaps I have a problem."

"You don't believe in ghosts, do you?"

Margaret touched the bun at the nape of her neck. It was a nervous habit.

"Mr. Stanton had been in the army and he wore an army uniform on patriotic holidays. What would you think, Missus Freeman?"

"Well, I don't know." Anna thought for a while. "Perhaps we should look into that well."

Margaret closed her eyes, "What difference would that make now?"

"If someone killed that little boy, the least we can do is to give him a Christian burial." Anna touched her arm. "It can be private." As usual, Anna took charge. She went to the top of the porch steps and waved at Sam. "I'll be with you in a minute," she called out to the forlorn figure in the surrey.

Sam waved back. He was relieved. He wanted to be alone. Feeling stoical was strange to him but that is what he felt. No crying. No thoughts. Just an empty feeling. There was no use looking up at the second story windows, Mamma was in the back room. When he left, Mamma didn't seem to be in pain. Perhaps Missus Freeman would bring him back to see her again. Sam was about to lean back when a thought struck him. The boy had said, "Tell her I won't have to go alone." Sam's blood ran cold.

"Mamma's dead." he said. He leaned back in the seat and waited for Missus Freeman.

Anna and Miss Stanton entered the kitchen on the run. Margaret was white as a sheet. "Here, sit down, Miss Stanton." As she began to sit, Anna noticed a glint of water and quickly said, "Oh, no, not in that chair. Why, it's all wet!" Margaret stared at the chair.

"I can't stand it anymore!"

Anna pulled out another chair.

"I'll get you some water."

Anna drew some water and handed it to Miss Stanton. As Margaret began to drink, Matilda came running into the room. Her eyes were wide with terror but before she could speak, Margaret addressed her sharply, "Get out of here! Go upstairs and tend to Carola. And don't leave her again."

"But that's what I want to tell you. That dirty little Colored boy was standing at her bed. He was stroking her hand. I ran out of there fast! At least he wasn't smiling that silly smile of his anymore."

The two women stared at her. Matilda started to cry. "Well, I didn't know what I should do. Missus Bennett looked at the boy and then she started to smile. It was awful!" Matilda blew her nose into a pretty handkerchief. "Missus Bennett heaved a big sigh, she did. Oh, Miss Stanton, I think she's dead. I was scared so I came down here."

"Stay here, Missus Freeman."

Margaret ran out of the kitchen. She fairly flew up the steps. Anna stood at the bottom of the steps and waited for her. Margaret came down the stairs almost immediately. The two women just looked at one another. "It is a blessing. She was in so much pain. I did think she would hold on a few more weeks but this is for the best." As they walked out into the sunshine again, Margaret said, "We've had a terrible afternoon, haven't we, Missus Freeman?"

"Call me Anna., Margaret. No, just think about it. In just a few hours, we have found out something important. You and Sam and I will never forget this day. Now we know for sure there is a power above us."

Margaret raised her eyebrows, "I wasn't thinking about anything except that I was frightened. Oh, Missus. ...Anna! I'll never be frightened again."

Matilda appeared in the doorway.

"It's all right, Matilda, I'll be in right away, dear. We don't need to be frightened anymore." Margaret put her arms around Anna's shoulder. Walking to the surrey, she said, "You'll have to tell him". She stopped. Turning Anna around to look at her she whispered, "After meeting you, I can't believe all the terrible things people have been saying about you. Why did you marry a Colored man? It might help me understand the young girl in my family."

"It's a long story. Believe me, I have not been sorry. There were men in this town who wanted to buy my farm. They were fooled. Mister Freeman has been remarkably successful, and we are proud of our lives. These men went to great pains to tarnish my reputation. I am grateful to my husband. He is a good man."

"Anna, do you really think the little boy took Carola with him?"

Anna answered slowly, "I don't know, but it would seem so. They will be at rest now."

"Yes, I'll give the child a Christian burial. Carola's interment has been taken care of, too."

"Goodbye, Margaret. We'll see each other again. Thank you for taking such good care of Sam's mother. Perhaps we can do something about renovating your house. We'll see what we can do."

"Oh, that would be wonderful. How we would appreciate any help. Well...,"

There was an awkward pause.

"Well, goodbye, Anna. Be kind to Sam. He seems like such a nice little boy."

As Anna reached the surrey, she smiled. Sam wouldn't take kindly to being called "little." She turned and waved, "Yes, I will."

Anna seated herself and reached for the reins. She looked at Sam. He was so dejected.

"Sam, you're old enough to drive the surrey, you take the reins. I'm tired."

Sam sat up straight. "Yes, Ma'am!" He took up the reins but before he gave Jocko a slap to go, he looked up at Anna. "The Colored boy took Mamma, didn't he?"

Anna's eyes welled up with tears.

"It's all right, ma'am. I couldn't go so, she went with Wilton Perry Stanton," he said proudly.

# XXXII

Jackson sat at the table where he and Dutch had lunch the day they met. Dutch had spruced up the small area he called his 'back-dirt.' It looked nice. The afternoon was waning and Jackson was becoming anxious for Anna and Sam to arrive. He watched Dutch taking care of his customers. Things were a little different when he came into town that night... how long ago?

There it was again! Jackson heard a noise. He heard it earlier this evening after getting to town. He could not figure out where it was coming from. At first he dismissed it but now it was beginning to annoy him. The noise sounded like someone snickering.

Dutch came out to join Jackson. "Well, that ought to be the last of it today." He plunked down heavily across the table from Jackson. "We have had a good meeting, my friend. Even with the interruptions."

"So, we are agreed?" Jackson was pleased that Dutch was easy to get along with. "We'll advertise. The chips will have a new package and we'll eventually build a factory. Sammy's Chips was good for you, right?" Jackson heard the noise again. It sounded closer this time. He turned to see where it was coming from.

"I heard it too," Dutch said. "Sounds like someone sneaking around." Both men got up ready for... what? The feeling was there... someone lurking in the bushes.

"Hey! I can get you now." The voice came from the left.

"Over here!" That time a voice came from the right. Then nothing.

Jackson and Dutch waited. Suddenly, Keith Cailern rushed out of the bushes followed by Beany and Lem. Keith obviously had been drinking. "I watched you and your woman come into town, you son of a bitch. I'll teach you to kick me around!"

"What are you talking about, Keith? I haven't seen you for almost a whole year."

"You took the farm away from me," Keith slobbered. Jackson's eyes widened. "You stole that farm by getting Anna to marry you, you bastard. If we hadn't picked you up in that little town, I would have had that farm and I would have had Anna." Keith started to stalk Jackson by the sheer weight of his body. He staggered into Lem, who backed out of his way but steered him toward Jackson's direction.

"Get 'em, Keith. Get 'em," Beany kept repeating over and over.

Jackson looked helplessly at Dutch. A calm fell over him. "It's all right, Dutch. I just realized I have unfinished business with Keith here. Jackson, palms up, indicated with all his fingers waiving for Keith to come forward and fight. Through the corner of his eye, Jackson saw movement. He didn't need to worry. Dutch noticed Lem and Beany were going to help Keith and grabbed them by the scruff of their necks. Pulling them toward him, he tucked them under each armpit rendering them helpless.

Jackson waited for Keith to make his move. Since he had rested all afternoon, he now felt the need to move around after his lethargy. He surely had the advantage of being sober. That should be somewhat of an equalizer.

Keith threw a hard punch, just missing Jackson's cheek. Jackson felt the breeze of that one. He had moved his head just enough to miss getting hit. Keith followed with a left hook that caught Jackson on the chin. This threw his head back. It was sheer good luck that Jackson was moving away or that would have ended the fight right there. Jackson danced around Keith, making Keith turn and turn in order to keep Jackson in focus. Keith began to feel dizzy. Keith caught Jackson with a swift left and a right to the body. Stepping back, he still had to keep turning around as Jackson kept dancing in a wide circle.

Dutch became anxious for Jackson, who had yet to throw a single punch.

"Git 'im, git 'im!," Beany called out, his face red from the effort. He could hardly talk with the hold Dutch still had on him.

Jackson, remembering Joe Gans, began his strategy. He danced in, gave Keith three hard punches to the chest, danced back, and began circling again. Keith staggered back. The hard punches were unexpected.

How could Jackson be that strong? It sobered him up. Keith flailed at Jackson. One punch, then another, all missing their marks.

Jackson managed to keep Keith in the center while he danced around him. First to the left, then to the right, keeping Keith off balance, not knowing where Jackson was going to be from one minute to another. "Stand still and fight like a man, you Black bastard!"

That angered Jackson but he kept his cool and tapped Keith with a left to the cheek then, gave him a hard right to the solar plexus sending Keith backward. "Now, you've got me mad," Keith spit out. Gathering all his strength, he made a lunge for Jackson, contacting with a hard punch to the stomach. Jackson doubled over. Keith, seeing his chance, hit Jackson with an upper-cut throwing Jackson clear across the room. Jackson landed under a frightened horse giving him a little time for his head to clear before resuming the fight.

Keith, thinking Jackson was out cold, straightened up. Heaving a big sigh of relief, he turned to Dutch, still holding his two friends under his arms. "Well, that ought to learn him a thing or two. I just gave him a lesson he'll never forget." Then, he squatted, shouted to the horse's underbelly, "Don't start with me!"

Dutch became furious. He threw both of Keith's friends to the ground as if they were rag dolls. "Who started this fight, you addle-headed dummy? You had better keep on fighting Keith, I'll be takin' you on next... and I'm your size."

"Wait, Dutch." Jackson staggered out of the stall. "I'm going to finish this fight. Jackson began dancing again. Keith threw his head back and laughed. Jackson took advantage of that and stepped in, punching Keith in his open mouth and causing blood to flow. It hurt his hand, but now he was in command.

Keith began fighting with all his might. Jackson stepped into him. Keith threw punches which Jackson neatly dodged, dancing in and out of Keith's reach, rattling him and making him lose his temper. When Jackson realized his strategy was working, he began to enjoy the fight. Dance in, dodge a punch, dance out. Over and over again. Keith was beginning to tire. His arms felt like lead and he was starting to see double.

Jackson got his second wind and felt light, ready for anything. Dutch, Beany, and Lem watched, not believing Jackson could fight so well. Finally,

Jackson gave Keith an upper-cut that shook him up. Keith stood still for a minute then fell face forward to the ground. He lay there, motionless. Jackson had won the day.

Lem and Beany rushed to Keith. Lem found a bucket of water and started to wipe his fallen friend with a wet kerchief. Keith did not respond for a while. Beany was whimpering at his side. Slowly, Keith came around. The two bumbling dolts tried to pick him up. Dutch was anxious to get rid of the three of them, so he picked up Keith and threw him over his shoulder. "Where's his horse?" Lem pointed to the bushes. As they left, Beany turned to Jackson. He put his thumb up to his nose and rippled his fingers at him. Jackson moved to wash his wounds and merely shook his head.

"You son of a gun!" Dutch said as he brushed off his clothes from the dust Keith left on his shoulder. "I didn't know you had that much fight in you!"

Jackson pulled his kerchief out of his back pocket. Wiping his face and the back of his neck, he looked up at Dutch through his eyebrows, "I didn't either." Dutch lit a lantern and brought it close to Jackson's face.

"Well, you're not too badly hurt on your face, but your hands'll be swollen up for a while."

Jackson grinned from ear to ear. He lit up the sky at midnight. They both turned to the sound of the surrey coming down the street. When Jackson realized Anna and Sam were coming, he became a little bit nervous. "Dutch, don't tell the Mrs. about the fight. I'll think of something to tell her. No use getting her upset now. Besides, I've settled the difference with Keith. What d'ya say?"

"I think she'll notice a few bruises on you, Jackson. But... I won't say a word."

"Thanks. Come for supper soon." With a jaunty wave of his hand, Jackson met the surrey and jumped on. All three passengers waved. Dutch waved back. He took a long look at Anna. Dutch shook his head in disbelief at the outcome of the day and watched his friends turn the surrey toward home.

# XXXIII

Jackson stood on the porch feeling like a baron surveying his land. Everything was done all the way up to the row of evergreens. Anna had finally put his name to the property. It was theirs! His and Anna's. He had fulfilled his promise. They were rich. Anna should be happy; she could now do what she always threatened to do. Leave the farm in his hands and travel. Jackson tried to picture himself without her. He would have Sam, of course. Somehow, that did not make it right. A man should have his woman. Come to think of it, Anna did not mention going on trips lately. Maybe she was not so ready to leave now that they seemed to get along so well. Not that they did not have a lot of differences, especially about sex. She still made him feel she was doing him a favor, even though he knew he made her happy. Only on Saturdays. That was her stipulation. And so only on Saturdays it was.

Jackson looked up to read the sky. There was still time to get those pesky weeds out of the last patch of potato plants and pick off the potato bugs. He walked through the field fondly touching the leaves. Already the plants were waist high and the potatoes he had dug up to test were the best he had ever grown. It was not as easy to read Sam. He was still too young to know if farming was what he wanted to do the rest of his life. That was all right. Jackson remembered how he yearned to be free from employers who gave Negroes the jobs White men did not want. If he could instill the desire for freedom in the boy, then he would feel he had been a successful father.

Anna did not protest when Jackson broached the subject of leaving the farm to Sam. She had said if the boy applied himself, she was willing to have Sam inherit the property and all the money they had acquired. It was obvious she had come to love him, too. There was something spiritual about him. Sam and he would often sing together in the evening. Anna did not join them. "It's good to sing," Sam would tell her. Anna was not the motherly type but that was to the good. Sam knew he had the best friend he would ever have in Anna and he let her know he loved her very much.

Jackson stopped his musings and started to roll up his sleeves but before he could begin to work, he heard a rattling sound coming from the road. "Somebody's lost," he mumbled to himself. Sure enough it was a car coming in off the road into the fenced in area of the yard. Jackson waited but there was no move from inside the car. He began to walk toward the vehicle when suddenly the door burst open and Jackson heard a familiar voice.

"Son of a gun! I find you! Jackson, it's me, Carl."

Jackson stopped in his tracks.

"Carl!"

The two men moved to each other but stopped short when they came close. Carl cocked his head, his face beamed with happiness, "Son of a gun," he said quietly. "I find you."

He extended his right hand, Jackson ignored it. Instead, he gave Carl a big hug. Carl stiffened. Jackson backed away not knowing what the problem was. It was then he noticed it. His friend was missing his left arm just below the shoulder. "I... ugh... you see I had accident... you know... oh, Jackson." Jackson could tell he felt very awkward about it.

All the friendship Jackson felt for Carl came back in a warm rush. Carl threw open his right arm and Jackson hugged his old friend. The men drew back, both talking at once.

"You look good!"

"So do you."

"How are you?"

"It's so good to see you."

Then, remembering their last meeting, they fell silent.

Jackson broke the silence. With a wry smile he asked, "How is Hans?" Both men looked at each other. Suddenly they started to laugh.

"You had to remind me," Carl said wagging his finger at Jackson.

From the porch, Anna was straining to hear what was going on. Her imagination was piqued. Jackson was laughing with a stranger and she was not in on the conversation. Sam was cleaning out the chicken coop so, she did not have him to go out to see who had some to see Jackson. She slammed the screen door.

"Come in, Carl, come into the house and meet my wife."

"Yes, I hear you married again."

Jackson was proud as he led Carl to his home. He pointed to the end of the evergreens. "It's all ours, Carl. And I'm a damn good farmer!"

Carl stopped and looked at the expanse of the farm. He shrugged his shoulders, 'You see, maybe you were right. I should haf gone into farming vith you." He patted his left sleeve tucked in his suit pocket.

"What happened, Carl? How did you lose your arm?" Noticing Carl turning red with embarrassment, he put his arm around Carl's shoulder and marched him up the porch steps. "Oh, what does it matter. Come on in. It's so good to see you. Have you seen Thomas and Sarah? My last letter from them sounded as if everything was going well with them. How is the old neighborhood?"

"Vhoa, Jackson. I came for a little vhile. Not to make long speeches about everyone. I..." Carl looked up and saw Anna at the door. "...going to Cleveland. I haf business there. It vill take couple of days but I stop to see you. I knew you vere living on my vay vest." He lowered his voice. "I don't vant you should get in trouble with 'ball and chain' for entertaining me." He said with a smile.

Jackson grinned. "This is our farm, Anna's and mine. I married rich, Carl, but the union is a good one. Come in, Anna's a good cook." Carl reached the top of the steps. He entered the house trying not to look at Anna. He could not make out if she was a light Negress, Mexican or white. Carl hesitated then, walked to the middle of the room. "Oh, Jackson! So nice! I got lots of money, but my house is not so nice."

Jackson beamed. "Annabelle, we have a guest." Anna had been cooking and the heat of the stove made her face pink. She tucked a stray strand of hair away from her face. She didn't hide the fact she was taken aback when she saw Carl. "Anna, this is Carl." Anna nodded her head slightly. "I told you about him. He was going to be my partner. We were going to have the best farm in Baltimore." Jackson noticed Carl was staring at Anna. He moved to her side as if to protect her.

"He can stay for dinner, can't he, Anna?"

Anna nodded her approval and held out her hand. Carl quickly shook it.

"Tank you, Missus Freeman. You are kind."

Jackson pulled up a chair and motioned to Carl, "I'll clean up a little. Here, sit down. Anna, bring Carl a drink. I'll be right back. Now, don't talk too much, I want to hear all about what had happened to you since the last time I saw you." Jackson left with a flourish. He felt he was walking on air. He was the success he always wanted to be.

Jackson went to the side of the porch, quickly pulled his shirt off and washed in the pan that always held clean water for him. He dried himself off as he went to the back door that opened to the hall from which he could get to the bedroom. As he started to dress, he could not help but compare himself to his friend. Jackson looked in the mirror. His arms were muscular, his back straight, and he had not an ounce of fat extra on his body. Fresh air, hard work and Anna's good cooking looked good on him. He finished dressing, went to the back door, and found Sam playing with his baseball instead of cleaning the hen house. Sam tried to think of an excuse for shirking his duties and was pleasantly surprised when Jackson said, "It's all right Son, come in for dinner, now. It's just as well you're not dirty because we have company. Carl Miller is from my old hometown and I want you to make a good impression. I don't have time to go into it now so, come with me." Sam was not happy about the situation, but he was not chastised for his laziness so, he decided to be cooperative.

Jackson found Carl and Anna at the stove. Carl was tasting the new recipe Anna had made. "Very goot," he said approvingly.

"It's a new recipe." And by way of bragging about her reading skills she added, "Jackson bought me a new recipe book." They both looked up when Jackson and Sam entered the kitchen.

"Did you get Carl that drink, Anna? Well, never mind. I'll get it. First, Carl, I'd like you to meet Sam. He is going to be with us now." It was the only way he could let Carl know Sam was not his son. Carl smiled and nodded to Sam. Sam immediately liked Carl and gave him a big smile. It was an awkward moment. Anna saved the day.

For the first time, Anna took charge as Jackson's wife. "Please sit down, Carl. Jackson, the glasses you want are on the new shelf and you know where the whiskey is. Sam,"

Sam stood at the ready.

"Please get another table setting. Supper will be ready in a few minutes." She went to the bedroom. Anna turned to the men, "I'll be ready in a few minutes, too. You gentlemen will have a chance to talk over old times."

"Here you are, Carl. The best whiskey from around these parts."

"To you, Jackson, my very goot friend. I never forget you." Carl lifted his glass and took a sip.

Jackson lifted his glass, "And to you, Carl, my very good friend."

Carl smacked his lips.

"Is goot. Now, tell me. How did all this happen? Anna. She is vhite, yes? I always know you are not ordinary man but how did you get so rich to have all this?"

He waved a large hand around the room.

"You did not make all this money farming. I know farming is goot living but not to get rich like this. For heaven's sakes, vhy did you marry a vhite voman? She is a handsome voman. Why did she marry you?"

Jackson laughed. His eyes were bright and his teeth gleamed. Carl noticed his good looks. Well, after all, Jackson was not a rube. He was born and raised in Baltimore and lived there most of his life.

"Carl, I'm a happy man. No matter what happens, I'll be all right. You were always happy, Carl. I learned to be a happy man from you. Look at you. You're doing all right. Automobile business must be lucrative, too."

"Vell, yes but I lost an arm."

Carl patted his empty sleeve.

"You were right not to like Hans. He is such a dummy. You see, I have car upon wood planks. On an angle. This is how I work on tires. That stupid Hans lets one plank go crooked and boom, car lands on my arm."

Carl leaned forward, "If vas not for your vonderful brother Thomas, I would be dead. He came in his car on the run. He knew just vhat to do but he explain everything before he do. I tell you, Jackson, you have good brother."

"I'm sorry, Carl. Such a terrible accident. How are Thomas and Sarah? They don't write me enough, no matter how much I complain. I write to them once every two or three weeks."

"Oh my goodness, they are vonderful! I'm supposed to tell you. Sarah vill haf baby in November."

"Carl," shouted Jackson, "What great news!"

Jackson leaned back.

"I explained to Thomas I make good money producing potato chips. I don't think he understands how lucrative making chips is."

Carl cocked his head questioningly.

"I produce chips."

Jackson went to the sideboard and picked up a bowl of potato chips.

"Here, taste 'em."

Carl seemed skeptical but took a few and cautiously took a bite.

His eyes grew wide and he grabbed a few more.

"Oh, my goodness, they are vonderful. These chips should be in Baltimore."

"I'll give you a carton to take with you. They stay fresh a long time. We sell so many boxes here and around the area that my partners and I have decided to build a factory. Soon we'll be shipping them to Baltimore and New York and all the big towns in between."

Anna came out of the bedroom into the kitchen. Her hair was beautifully combed and coifed. Her face, carefully powdered, made her skin look like alabaster. She adorned herself with earrings and the only gift her father ever gave her, a pearl choker with a cameo pendant that drew attention to the chiseled contours of her face.

Both men instinctively stood up. Sam jumped up and pulled out a chair for Anna. She gave him a smile, "I'll have a drink, too, Jackson."

Jackson took in her beauty. His eyes caressed her. When had she become so lovely? Try as he might, he could not control the bronze color his face took on as it always did when he blushed. He quickly brought another glass from the sideboard, filled it, and set it in from of her.

"I heard you toast one another and now, I want to make a toast."

The men waited with their glasses raised.

"To friendship." The glasses were drained.

"Sit down, Sam, I'll serve the food."

Anna was a gracious hostess. She did Jackson proud, as did Sam, who was really taken with Carl, the ever-happy friend. It was an evening they all would remember, an evening of fun.

First Carl, then Jackson, reminiscing about old times. Anna began to get a glimmer of what Jackson's life was like before he left Baltimore. His family were hard-working, respected citizens. It was no wonder people here looked up to him in such a short time.

All good things come to an end. As Anna walked Carl to the door, she further promoted Jackson's race by saying, "You know, Carl, we now have a Colored architect in Stanton, and his work is unbelievably beautiful. Jackson says we need more schools for our Colored children, all they need is a chance."

Carl nodded his approval for more schools. "Vell, vee'll have that when the people think they have enough saloons!" They all laughed at that. Carl turned and extended a hand to Anna. "Tank you for a vonderful supper. Such good company. Goodbye, Sam." Sam gave Carl a big smile and waved. He then turned to Jackson. "A voman makes a house a home. I know people laugh at my saying all the sayings but damn it, it's true. I still miss my Fredricka. Life is so short. I'm glad for your success." Carl stopped talking for fear he was getting too maudlin. He took in Jackson, Anna, and Sam, who was going to the orchard to pick apples to make up for not cleaning the hen house. Anna went back into the house so the men would be alone to say their goodbyes.

Carl patted the car, "You should have von of theez," he laughed.

"Also, you should have a tractor vith a gasoline engine. I hate to say," Carl laughed again, "but I told you so." Both men chuckled. "Jackson, vhat I'm doing is making vhat ve call 'car dealership.' That means men can come to your yard and you have cars for them to look at and buy." Carl straightened up, winked, and put his heavy hand on Jackson's shoulder. "I gif you good deal." He stiffly seated himself behind the wheel. "You gif a tug and I'll be off."

Jackson cranked a couple of times and the car sputtered to a start. He backed away to make room for Carl to swing the car around him. As Carl slowly passed Jackson he said, "You know, I tink you should tink about selling cars, too! I'll teach you how to make your money vork for you. Vith a dealership here, ve can both make more money. Tink about it."

"I will," Jackson shouted. "See you soon!"

Then, as though it never happened, Carl was gone. Jackson felt an emptiness for his family and the city. He decided to finish the last row of weeding. Work was his salvation.

Anna watched Jackson surveying the land. She knew how much he loved owning such a beautiful farm and now she was glad for all the decisions she made that kept Jackson here with her. He stood tall in the community. She had a right to admire the tenacity he had when things went wrong. For Jackson to become the most successful farmer in Stanton when he knew nothing about farming was quite an achievement.

Jackson took off his good shirt. That meant he was going to finish the last row of potatoes. He artfully hung the shirt on a bush. Anna pushed the screen door and went out on the porch. There was something about the way he walked that touched her. "Jackson!"

Jackson picked up a hoe he had left in the field before turning to see what Anna wanted. "What is it?" Anna was out of breath when she reached him. Her hair became loose from the running and now reached her shoulders. She had an odd look on her face.

"What is it? What's the matter?" Jackson grew impatient. They stood looking at one another in the dim light. Jackson slowly took in her voluptuous, mature body. She took a step closer to him. Thinking she was unsettled about something, Jackson lifted his chin.

Anna took a step back, took her pretty blouse off, hung if over Jackson's shirt, picked up the end of her skirt and tucked it in her waistband. She looked for a starting place in the row. "What are you going to do?" Jackson asked perplexed at her nervousness. "What are you going to do?" he asked again. 'You don't even have a hoe."

Anna blushed, "Oh, no I don't. Ah... I'll get one. I'll go to the barn and get one." But she did not move.

"I don't need any help, Annabelle," he said sarcastically. Her face fell and Jackson was immediately sorry he made that remark. Anna started to pick up her blouse. Almost to himself but loud enough for her to hear, Jackson tenderly called out to her. "Annabelle." For a moment Anna stood still then, she turned around. A slight breeze moved her silver-brown hair revealing the platinum tendrils at her temples which made her face radiant. Anna let a little arrogance show when she noticed Jackson admiring her. She took two steps toward him. Jackson did not move. She came closer. He waited, anticipating... he did not know for what. She came very close to him. Still, he was cautious. Throwing the hoe away, he opened his arms inviting her to make that last step.

Anna threw back her head and laughed. It was a nervous, melodious laugh. She raised her hand and touched the back of his neck. Slowly he let her hand outline his shoulder then, traced the collar bone down finally caressing his breast. Jackson stood transfixed, his arms still outstretched. He lifted his chest waiting for the thrill of her touch on his other breast, but Anna ignored the movement. Placing one hand in front and one hand behind his right shoulder, she skillfully dipped under his armpit and moved in back of him, noting his strong back muscles. Jackson closed his eyes as she worked her way to his left arm. She followed the contours and Jackson could stand it no longer.

With the quickness and ease of a cat, he grabbed Anna and held her close to him.

"You are right, you are not Annabelle, you are Anna. You have made yourself the strong woman you have become. I admire you."

"No, Jackson, you have made me strong. I must confess. I was ready to give up many times before you came to the house that night. I just made up my mind I would not be inferior to a Colored man. Then, you... not me... you gave me faith, in myself and taught me that I could be a better person. You don't know how many times I was afraid you were going to leave me, and I would be left alone again. It is I who admire you."

Jackson drew her closer. His heart pounding, he kissed her tenderly.

"Anna?"

She looked up at him.

"Anna, we are in love."

Jackson pulled up her dress so she could feel his body welling up with anticipation. Anna bent a little back to let her breasts free from the prison of her chemise. Jackson kissed her throat, her shoulders, her nipples making Anna giggle. He was thrilled to hear her laugh. Throwing all caution to the wind, she opened her arms wide as if holding the sky. Jackson slowly twisted her to the ground. They were covered over by the lush leaves they had planted together.

Jackson undressed her under the green boughs. She lay naked waiting for him. He let his eyes feasted on her beautiful body then he slowly mounted her, enjoying her soft murmuring of pleasure.

Their lovemaking disturbed crickets and grasshoppers and caused them to jump towards the orchard.

# XXXIV

Sam held on to one branch while reaching for the apple furthest away from him. He quickly snapped it off and sprang back to the fork in the tree which held him. This was the end of the day and he was not feeling ambitious. Leaning back, he looked through an opening in the tree and marveled at the sky. Jackson had taught him so many things. For instance, if he learned to speak English and French 'real good' he... Sam... could become an ambassador. Maybe even President of the United States.

Sam let his eyes wander over the beautiful countryside. For a moment he envisioned himself grown up, owning his own land, and taking care of his mother. She would be dressed the way Anna dressed. She would be healthy and strong. Mamma would brag about him to everyone she met. His father would come home to them. But that was not to be.

Then, what was to be? Mr. Freeman told him stories about the success of Colored people in Baltimore and Stanton. They were teachers, architects, doctors, nurses...Mr. Freeman's particular inspiration was Fredrick Douglass, who became a Recorder of Deeds of Santa Domingo and later, Minister to Haiti. Mr. Freeman said, "You can become anything you want to be!"

Sam made up his mind. He did not want to be an ambassador or President of the United States even though Mister Freeman said it was possible.

He would be the best farmer in the whole state.

He would be just like his *new* father.

Printed in the United States
By Bookmasters